TRULY MADLY
AWKWARD

BETH GARROD

SCHOLASTIC

For Chris – and the wonderful staff of the
NHS who helped keep my world together.

Scholastic Children's Books
An imprint of Scholastic Ltd
Euston House, 24 Eversholt Street, London, NW1 1DB, UK
Registered office: Westfield Road, Southam, Warwickshire, CV47 0RA
SCHOLASTIC and associated logos are trademarks and/or
registered trademarks of Scholastic Inc.

First published in the UK by Scholastic Ltd, 2017

Text copyright © Beth Garrod, 2017

Emoji by Madebyoliver and Freepik at flaticon.com

The right of Beth Garrod to be identified as the
author of this work has been asserted by her.

ISBN 978 1407 16641 4

Printed by CPI Group (UK) Ltd, Croydon, CR0 4YY
Papers used by Scholastic Children's Books are made
from wood grown in sustainable forests.

1 3 5 7 9 10 8 6 4 2

www.scholastic.co.uk

CHAPTER

ONE

"GET OFF ME, WEIRDO!!!"

These four words, yelled so hard a bit of spit hit my nose, were not *exactly* how I hoped my in-a-dream-world-one-day-potential-boyfriend was going to greet me. Especially when screamed with such panic an entire playing field stopped in its tracks.

The last time I'd seen anyone that shocked was when Mum opened the door to the postman forgetting she was having a no-trousers day (he shouldn't have looked *that* surprised – it was the fourth time it'd happened. That month).

Sure, it must be a BIT startling to be doing keepie-uppies and have someone run up behind you and laugh-breathe, "Well, helloooo there, straanger?!!" in your ear. (No idea why I'd done a cowboy voice either.) A two-handed prod tickle – *prickle* – in the ribs wasn't exactly un-alarming either.

But the prodee's shock was nowhere near as big as mine, because another player was staring at me with even more confusion than the one backing speedily away from me.

And that player – rooted to the spot, mouth hanging open – was Adam Douglas. Aka Fit Adam. Aka Fadam.

Adam, the guy I'd had on thought-loop for thirteen-and-a-half months solid.

Adam, the boy that one night I'd googled so intensely, I'd had to unplug our entire home internet in case I'd triggered some sort of security alert.

Adam, the boy I try to accidentally-on-purpose run into so much, that last Wednesday evening I did my 10,000 daily steps walking circles of the same playing field (my poor boxer dog, Mumbles, with her shorter legs, must have done at least 40,000).

Adam, the boy that, in my wildest imagination (and I once imagined that school is just a conspiracy theory for adults to get us out of the way while they go to Alton Towers) I hope might one day want me to be his actual girlfriend.

But, no. Instead of saying a hello to this ultimate

specimen of boy, I, Bella Fisher – in front of his entire football team (and an equally-confused away side) – had just made full mouth-to-ear contact with his teammate (which technically is only 12.6 centimetres from being a one-way unwanted snog).

Was there *any way* to style this out? I looked around the gaping football pitch. And at the gapers on the football pitch.

Nope.

So I did the next best thing (which as I could only think of one option, was also joint worst).

"DON'T MIND ME!" I two-handed waved like I was polishing a life-sized window. Face, don't show panic that Adam doesn't look any less less-impressed. Or should that be more less-unimpressed? ARGH. BELLA STOP THINKING ABOUT THE COMPLEXITIES OF THE ENGLISH LANGUAGE AND MAKE THIS LESS TERRIBLE.

"Sorry! I thought this person ..." I pointed at the real Adam (still not smiling), "... was that person." I pointed at not-Adam. Nadam (smiling even less). "Cos from behind, in football kit, you all look the same." I was still shouting. "Although obviously now you are all staring at me, I see you are all totally different, and I really respect you as individuals." Still no one moved, except Nadam, who was now almost sprinting backwards. Not an *excellent* sign. "So I, er, won't forget my glasses again."

I turned and pelted to the safety of the bench. The bench with my friends on. Friends who knew I didn't wear glasses. Amazing how much humiliation can happen so quickly (that was approx thirty h/s – humils per second).

I splodged down into the space between Tegan and Rachel, my peripheral vision pretending to my dignity that it couldn't see Mikey struggling to hold in a laugh.

I dropped my head into my hands.

"C'mon, Bells, it could have happened to *anyone*." Tegan always looked for the positive.

"Straw poll. Has it?"

Rachel absently pulled a strand of her hair across her top lip like a moustache. (The fact that she did things like this in public and was still the most-fancied girl in our village said a lot about how unbelievably beautiful – tache or not – she was). She was humming – which meant she was thinking. She's like a car. If she's in action, you can hear it.

"Well, last Christmas I had a twenty-minute phone call with Granddad until he asked to speak to Aunty Sharon, and I told him I didn't have one. And then I realized he wasn't *my* granddad, he was just *a* granddad, who'd dialled the wrong number."

Mikey snorted, then stopped as he remembered solidarity meant he wasn't supposed to be finding anything funny right now. I mean, it wasn't *exactly* the same (as I assumed/hoped Rach hadn't spent months lusting after this random granddad), but I appreciated the effort, so I opened my fingers just wide enough to give her a grateful look. But instead I suffered another major stomach lurch (MSL) as I caught a glimpse of Adam sprinting about. Like muscle coordination was NBD (when I can't even blink around him properly).

Tegan squeezed my knee.

"Bells, seriously. No one will remember this. Everyone's focused on the game that's about to kick off." She paused. "Right, Mikey?"

Mikey had been our friend for yonks, and he totally adored Tegan, but not even unswerving loyalty to his girlfriend could make him suddenly turn into a convincing liar.

"Er, yeah. Sure?"

His question mark was almost as loud as the shouts on the pitch.

But maybe Teeg was right? She normally was. My malfunction *might* be totally forgettable to anyone who had an actual life. And I could explain myself to Adam later.

YES, BELLA. That was more like it.

As I lifted my head, a football rolled against my foot. Using the chance to test Tegan's theory I looked up at the rando boy chasing after it. Yup, he looked normal. Like he wasn't freaking out. He probably hadn't even *seen* me manhandle his teammate, let alone remembered it. See, freaking-out-bit-of-brain? *Nothing to worry about.*

"Oi, Grabby Hands, kick us the ball?"

Or not.

I scrubbed through "They might forget about it" on my positive thoughts list. And added "Is it possible to be fifteen and have someone else's face tattooed over my face?" to my must-check-when-I'm-alone list, and kicked the ball back. But I was suffering such intense mortification that I only managed to roll it about four metres. To save me from actually shame-melting (shmelting), Tegan leapt up and kicked it back, landing the ball perfectly at his feet.

Please could today call it quits?

I slumped back on the bench, wishing I could disappear. If humans can invent popping candy why can't they hurry up and figure out invisibility hoodies? Priorities, please.

My wallowing was interrupted by a tinny version of "Let It Go" wafting across the playing field. Rachel sat bolt upright like a meerkat and started swaying along.

"Wow! I didn't know they had music. That's *so* cool."

Tegan loud-breathed through her nose – her more polite version of an ordinary person's eye-roll.

"*So* cool – it's actually an ice-cream van. . ."

Mikey looked up from his phone. "Did someone say ice cream?"

He smiled at Tegan the kind of way I dreamt Adam would some day look at me (sort of how I look at the person in the burrito place when they hand over my foil-wrapped parcel of dreams).

Tegan and Mikey were at either end of the bench, Rachel and I sitting between them, like a third and fourth wheel (which technically would actually make a more balanced vehicle). But it didn't feel awkward. We'd all been friends before they got together and from day one they'd made it clear that when we were hanging out we were four friends, not two of them, and two of us. Tegan gave Mikey a big grin back.

"Yeah, I did – and now I'm saying, 'Let's go get one.' Who's with me?"

Even though it was the height of British summer (aka cold and about to rain), ice cream, and getting my mega-blush face further from Adam's view, was win-win. We all leapt up, including Mumbles (who had been napping after tiring herself out chasing a long bit of grass that she hadn't realized was stuck to her head). In an attempt at normality, I waved a casual goodbye in the pitch's general direction, but Adam was too busy having a team talk to see me. Or was he now pretending not to know me? ARGH. Be gone, vile thought.

I didn't have time to dwell on which one it was, as within seconds Rach had cried, "Snacktivation activation," and our walk became a fast walk, which became a jog, and by the time we reached the edge of the field, was a big-laughing, full-on run to be front of the queue.

Tegan got there first. She runs like a gazelle. I run like a baby learning to walk.

"Right, what does everyone want?" She wasn't even vaguely out of breath. I was panting so hard I could feasibly have inhaled a passing bird (pigeon-sized or below). I diverted attention by rummaging in my pocket. My empty pocket. Eurgh. Was fluff legal tender?

"You know what, I think I'm kind of full actually."

Never have my two closest friends given me more of a disbelieving look, and I once told them I'd signed up for a triathlon with my sister (admittedly I forgot to mention it was as a supporter).

"Bells, these are my shout." Rach smiled. "NO ARGUMENTS." Seconds later she shoved a cone into my hand. "Can't go wrong with a ninety-nine. Extra pink sauce, obvs."

I murmured thanks and got stuck in. Rachel was always so generous with getting us stuff – with everything really. Although maybe it was easier when your parents were set to automatic "yes" reply?

I stuck my tongue out to catch a falling sauce blob, but a gust of wind meant I also got a clump of Rachel's long hair. FACT: hairy pink sauce deffo isn't as tasty as the non-hairy kind.

"Argh, sorry." I tried to unpick it, but just smeared sauce all over my face. "I really thought I had some coinage, but forgot Mum has scaled back on the whole pocket-money thing. In a MAJOR way." It sucked. "There should be a minimum wage for being her daughter. It's basically a job."

But I shut up, cos the others had heard me moan enough already about my brokest summer ever. Mum had splurged my "savings account" – aka a shelf of loose-change jars – on a UK cruise with friends she'd met at a fortune-telling class. But they'd all got food poisoning and had to come home early, so obvs hadn't learnt that much.

The four of us stood and slurped, watching the game, which had now kicked off, Mumbles darting underneath us with her mouth open for any drips like a four-legged baby bird.

A tiny invisible animal squeaked. Mikey looked around as Rachel reached into her pocket.

"Chill out. It's just Hillary. My new alert." Hillary was her guinea pig.

But in the time it took Mikey to say "obvs", Rachel had started making an "mmmmmmmmm" noise and jiggling on the spot.

"UPDATE?!" I demanded. Rach stuffed her remaining cone into her mouth so she could use her other hand to scroll. "And also chew. And *breathe*."

"Unooodedahelycnns."

Tegan and I looked at each other, eyes narrowed, trying to interpret. Tegan's friend-lepathy got there first. "The Helicans?"

Rach nodded so fast a bit of cone came out of her nose.

The Helicans were our second-fave band of all time (on group average, they were Rachel's first fave, but mine and Tegan's third). The lead singer, Lis (Alisha to those not in the know), was a life idol – even her dog, Pastry, seemed to have been born extra cool. And the drummer,

Amil, was so funny that new vids on his YouTube channel called for emergency group viewing.

"They've made an ann-n-n. . ."

Tegan finished off the "ouncement" as Rach did a bit more choking, and I did a bit of back-thwacking.

But we knew exactly what she was talking about – and why it was leading to a semi-choke situation.

This month had been the month of Rach doing everything she could – that we could – to get our local radio station, Radio Shire, into the final of a national competition. The prize was epic: an exclusive Helicans gig for the radio station. And as if having them share the same postcode air wasn't enough, Radio Shire had then announced that if they won, they'd arrange their own competition for the gig to be at a local school. YUP. The amazing, world-famous Helicans, possibly playing in one of our weirdo school halls.

It was TOO. MUCH. The whole thing had melted Rach's mind – and along with it, burnt through all our free time and phone credit – as we'd embarked on a thumb-exhausting regime of voting.

Judging by Rach looking like she'd just knelt on a plug, there must be news. But was it good or bad?

Tegan looked at me in a "Ready for me to carry on?" way. Grateful for her perma-calm I gave her a silent "yup" back. She put a hand on Rach's arm.

"Rach, now – don't talk unless there's no more cone left, OK?" Rachel nodded sheepishly (although I've never seen a sheep nod). "What. *Is*. Going. On?"

Rach safety swallowed, and took a deep breath.

"Apaz-the-band-are-about-to-announce-which-radio-station's-won."

She blurted it out so quickly it was one long mega-word.

Mikey wrinkled his face. "You mean the *finalists*?"

Rach gulped. "NO. As in, the ONE with most votes. Winning. Single. Only. Radio station."

Woah. This was unexpected.

"And any second they're going to post who it is, like it's not the biggest news of the decade?!" She shook her phone again as if it would refresh quicker. "How could they do this to meeeee?! What about my feeeeelings?!"

What about ALL our feelings?! We bunched round to look at the screen, but we didn't need to – because Rach let out a squeak that put Hillary to shame, and confirmed to us (and any dogs in a hundred-mile radius) the outcome. Even the football game ground to a halt, the players thinking it was a whistle.

I couldn't believe what was happening.

Radio Shire had done it. *WE'D* DONE IT!

The Helicans – the amazing band who sold out world tours in seconds – were officially coming to our little town?! Where no bands ever played?!

"Yeeee-hhaaaaw!" I yelled (then stopped, shocked that I seem to be reverting to cowboy impressions in all moments of high emotion).

But who cares, y'all? This was BEYOND incredible. The four of us flung our arms round each other and bounced around in a happy, hopping, hooray-ing circle (with Mumbles sitting in the middle like she was above such things – must remind her, she's the one who chews her own burps).

All the time we'd spent voting and asking friends and calling in favours from our parents had paid off.

The Helicans were coming to Worcester.

And a local school was going to win the gig.

And we'd helped make it happen.

I felt invincible!

"All OK?" A voice I recognized interrupted our whooping.

ARGH?! Adam. What was he doing over here?

I suddenly felt totally vincible.

He was holding a football on his hip (was it weird to be jealous of a football?), and smiling like impromptu group-cuddle-leaping was totally normal behaviour.

C'mon, Bella. Just make polite conversation. Maybe apologize for earlier?

"You're holding a football."

NO, mouth. NOT what I was after. Just further proof that, despite eight-and-a-half close encounters of the speaking kind with him, my brain still gets so nervous-excited it goes into auto-pilot. And the kind of auto-pilot that would definitely crash any plane (after doing some really unnecessary loop-the-loops).

But Adam the Ever Chill just laughed. "Sure am. So I guess it's technically a handball."

How dare he smile so effortlessly?! All I could manage was a panic stare like he was an extinct species.

I tried to think of a reply, but my brain was stuck on repeat pondering "How does sweaty-you look even better than normal-you?" and that was *not* the convo gold I was after.

He looked back over his shoulder at the rest of the players who were standing still, waiting. "Anyway, just came to get this, so er. . ."

Tegan stepped next to me. "Sorry, we're just a bit all over the place cos we just found out that Radio Shire won that Helicans comp."

Adam's whole face lit up. "That's *so* cool! I must have

voted at least ten" – he grinned at Rach – "no, sorry, one *hundred* times for you guys." He dropped the ball at his feet. "I'm made up for you."

My jaw dropped in Rach's direction. All the times I'd replayed every syllable I'd exchanged with him and she'd failed to mention she'd roped him in to voting?! She threw me an, "Oops, but it all seems OK, so don't be cross with me," guilty look. I eye-tutted back, but she knew I was over it already.

And so was the convo.

Adam turned back to the pitch, where shouts had started for him to get a move on.

Great. Another chance to not be a total weirdo around him, and I'd blown it. I *had* to get it together. Next time I HAD to be normal. Be in control.

But next time came quicker than I wanted. Because at the exact moment Adam hoofed the ball back to the goalkeeper, Mumbles spontaneously found all her energy and pelted straight after it. And with her lead wrapped around my wrist, she jolted me along with her.

I would like to say nowhere near Adam.

I would like to say, at the worst, lightly *into* Adam's back.

But, oh no. My dog ran with such force, I positively flew *up* and *on to* Adam's back.

15

Oh. My. Holy. Whatballs.

I, Bella Fisher, was mounting the man of my dreams.

SOMEONE CTRL-Z THE WORLD RIGHT NOW.

The force of the impact – grim-pact – was so brutal he fell forward.

With no idea what'd hit him, he spun round, startled, only to discover me bent double, trying to regain my breath after that full body blow. Was I repeating the word "no" in my head – or out loud?

"You all right, Bella?"

Correct answer: OBVS NO COS I JUST SEMI-RUGBY TACKLED THE MAN OF MY DREAMS, AKA YOU.

Luckily all I could manage was a "Sorryyes" and a point at Mumbles who was now panting so hard she had a dribble of spit going all the way down to the floor.

But Adam just laughed, ruffled Mumbles on the head, and ran back to his friends, as if he hadn't just been the unwitting victim of a drive-by piggybacking.

Well, THAT was a disaster. Again.

Tegan gave me a supportive smile. "At least you don't need to stress about what to do if he tries to instigate a hand hold any more – you skipped that base entirely."

She was being too nice for me to point out that hand

holding wasn't a base, unless bases came in quarters to help absolute novices like me.

Rach nudged my arm. "Exactly. A unique-yet-effective approach. And anyway, Bells, life *is* going to be OK! Remember – the Helicans."

I raised an eyebrow, seemingly the only bodily muscle I could rely on. "Yes, Rachel Waters – maybe *Adam's* votes swung it?"

"Ahhhh... I meant to say I'd mentioned the competition when we bumped into him in the shop the other day, but I, er..." Rach chewed her lip. "I, errrr... Anyway, look, SORRY. I'm an idiot. But every vote counted... And he didn't seem to mind."

I raised my other eyebrow. "He also didn't seem to mind me doing a rucksack impersonation on him."

Rach nodded firmly. "And THAT is why he puts the F in Fadam."

She had me. I couldn't help but smile. My friends were the best.

Rach clapped her hands. "Anyway ... mooooving on. Radio Shire have just posted that the first round of the competition to win the gig for the school is gonna be..." She dramatic–paused, ignoring the sound of Mumbles trying to lick up her own slobber. "Tonight! Eight o'clock, to be precise." Rach looked at her wrist

17

even though there was no watch on it. "That's TWO hours' time."

I gulped. Mikey OTT-gasped. But Tegan muttered an, "Oh, sssshhh..." – as close as she ever came to swearing. She swung her kit bag up over her shoulder and gave Mikey the quickest kiss on the cheek, like they were impersonating parents. Weird.

"Guys, sorry, but I *have* to go. If it's six I'm already late for gymnastics." Tegan was never late for anything, let alone training. That's what having a choking, leaping best friend does to someone's punctuality. "Bells, you wanna walk with me?"

Obvs. The first bit of the journey to Tegan's sports hall was also the way to my house, so I'd get company *and* not break my promise to Mum to be back for tea. With Rach saying she'd message our group with full deets for tonight, I scurried after Teeg.

We chatted about the comp the entire way. Things like this *never* happened here. Tegan calculated there must be about a hundred and thirty-five schools in the area, which meant ... some sort of percentage that St Mary's, our one, could win the gig. Which was the biggest percentage we'd probably ever have of seeing the Helicans – especially if I had to exist on a lifetime allowance of 10p a week.

Now that it was just the two of us, Tegan admitted that she probably wasn't going to be able to help us take part tonight because training was going to be one of her mega-long sessions. But I got it – and Rach would too. Tegan's try-out for a place on this gymnastics training camp was only four weeks away. It was the gateway to the national team, aka her life dream, and she'd been putting in more hours than ever.

She was so talented she'd definitely get a place, but in all the time I'd known her (since my memory began) I'd never seen her so stressed. Or even stressed at all. I used the walk to try and hint again that I was worried she was doing too much. But as usual she subject changed like a pro and headed off to do some stretches that sounded like a form of torture.

I messaged Rach to give her the heads-up that it would just be us doing the competition tonight. In her usual positive Rach way, she replied with a stream of motivational gifs of power women. She was fired up.

And she was right – winning the gig for St Mary's would be a TOTAL dream. But with Tegan out of the picture, that's probably all it would stay.

CHAPTER

TWO

Thanks to my double-speed walk home I made it back on time. Annoyingly, that also meant Mum roped me into vegetable peeling. It got less annoying when I beat my previous best-ever single potato-peel length by four centimetres. (Mum offered to pin it on the noticeboard next to Jo, my wonder-sis's certificate for "Outstanding Citizenship", but I declined.) I'd got more practice than ever now Jo was staying at uni for the summer. She'd probably done it just to avoid peeling things.

After a surprisingly filling dinner of "Carrot-sserole" (Mum's casserole that consists only of carrot), I headed up to my room to tune into the competition.

JO: Tell me I didn't spot Mum in that photo of the Naked Swimming protest????

Her message popped up on my laptop.

ME: I totally COULD tell you that.

I pressed send then waited for just a second too long before following up.

ME: But I'd be lying.

I felt Jo recoil, even though she was a hundred and thirty miles away. Her response took a while.

JO: Just wiping vom off my keyboard.

ME: As if?! I'm the one stuck here with people recognizing her. You're freeeeeeeeee!

JO: If by free you mean spending summer working in a garden centre where my boss hates me and makes me hand-pick slugs off manky plants? Yeah! Freeeeeee's GREAT.

ME: Sludder (Slug-Shudder). Do the managers
pay extra $$$ for crustacean trauma?

JO: They're molluscs.

ME: That's no way to talk about your bosses.

JO: Ha. Very ha.

She paused.

JO: Sorry, Peahead. I sound like a right moan.

I couldn't help but admire her effective apology/
insult combo.
"..." appeared and disappeared as she typed and
deleted what to say next.

JO: Just uni stuff isn't so good at the mo.

Woah, role reversal. It was never Jo who came to ME
with problems. How could I cheer up her up?

ME: But ... you get to eat Dairy Milk
sandwiches as an actual meal?

It had been the one thing Jo had told me about uni life that had made me think further education was the right choice for me.

JO: Plus I have zero time for running training.

This also sounded like a positive.

But hearing her worry was weird. Through all her exams, athletics meets, and family drama (even that time Mumbles put the neighbours' tortoise in her bag and we didn't discover it till we were midway through a film in the cinema) I'd never seen my big sister even the tiniest bit flustered. This *had* to be a blip.

As I went to reply, my door banged, and then flew open. Mum doesn't understand knock and wait. It's a knock-and-walk single fluid motion with her. Instinctively I pulled my laptop in tighter and sat upright on my bed. Mum's eyes lit up with excitement that I might have something to hide.

"Oooh, chatting with *friends*?" Mum thought that anyone below the age of twenty only used the internet to talk to mysterious hot strangers around the world. She didn't understand I mainly used it to chat to the two people who I spent most of the rest of the day chatting to. Or looking at slow-mo dog videos.

"Messaging Jo, actually."

She mouthed an overly large, "HOW IS SHE?" as if Jo could hear. I glanced down.

> JO: I seriously hate my life RN. Might jack it all
> in and live on a commune.

I gave an overly enthusiastic "GREAT!" back at Mum and tried to waft her out of my room. She mouthed, "SEND HER MY LOVE," and walked out backwards, sort of weirdly bowing while blowing kisses. It's such a worry that we're related.

As a deterrent to her coming back in, I flicked my speakers up a couple of notches.

> ME: Mum says hi. And is being weird.

> JO: It would be more weird if she wasn't.

Ouch. I shifted around on the mattress, as I'd developed a weird bum twitch.

> ME: She also said (with her eyes)(probably) tell
> Jo not to run off to a commune cos then I can't
> 24/7 brag about my favourite child.

Jo sent back a cry-laugh face, but I could *tell* she didn't mean it.

I must have *something* that could help? Anything?

ME: Look, Josephine.

That wasn't her name, but it was harder for her to interrupt me when I could type faster than her.

ME: What would you say if it was the other way round?

Excellent question from me – her big-sis ego loved nothing more than dishing out words of wisdom, whether I wanted them or not. (I never did.)

JO: I'd say – woah! You actually managed to hold down a job?

ME: And I'd stab you with a pencil.

ME: But then what would you say?

JO: Stop stabbing me?

ME: Y'know what I mean.

JO: I'd say. . .

Yesssss. Actual thinking. I *knew* she wouldn't be able to resist being wise and knowing.

JO: Hang in there. . . Life's always up and down. Getting qualifications and getting paid both take effort, 'specially at the same time. But you get out what you put in.

Man, my sis was fluent in Mum-Speak. I highlighted the text.

ME: OK, Jo. So now I've had a think, I know what I want to say.

I pasted and sent her advice right back at her.

JO: OHWOWLIKEURSOFUNNY.

ME: Finally, something we agree on!

My bum twitched again. At least I had a muscle in there somewhere.

JO: Gotta go. House viewing of University Challenge.

ME: Forget the degree. THAT'S what you need to stay for.

JO: Good point. Sis done good. Seeya xxx

Being reminded of all those fam evenings in front of the TV (Jo shouting right answers, me shouting abuse at how the words in the questions didn't even make sense) made me want to flick *University Challenge* on too. Not that I missed her or anything.

Although. . . WAIT. EIGHT P.M.?!

AM I OFFICIALLY THE WORLD'S BIGGEST IDIOT?!

If it was almost eight, that meant. . .

I ran to my radio, and scrolled up to Radio Shire. How did I almost miss this?? WHAT IS WRONG WITH MY BRAIN?!

"So, after the MAH-OO-SIVE news that it's US, Radio Shire, who've won the Helicans gig. . ." A loud whoop went up from the studio. Jaz, the presenter, giggled. "Kind of amazing, huh? Big thanks to all you guys who voted..."

Rach had probably sent half of them. Thank goodness her parents aren't into phone-bill tracking. "It's now time to follow up on what we promised." Dramatic pause. "One of YOU GUYS winning the gig for your school."

This was met with general whistling and cheering.

"So ... here's how it's going to work."

Positive thoughts it was going to be something Rach and I could be good at. Jumbled-up lyrics, or a crisp-eating contest.

"As you know, the band's new album – and lemme tell you, I've heard it and it's EH-PICK – is called *Take Our Advice (Don't Listen to a Word We Say)*. Soooo, we're going to get you lot to battle it out with our very own ... advice showdown."

An "oooooh" went up. But my heart went down.

Advice was NOT my forte.

"Tonight we'll kick things off with our first question to choose which ten schools will be in the running. Then there'll be two more rounds to whittle it down for a head-to-head final!"

Another "wooooo" went up in the studio. I wish

paying people to react well to everything you say was a service they offered IRL.

"And, not to give any spoilers . . ." (One of the studio team hollered "Spoiler!" but it was met with a silence that sounded like a full on Jaz glare) – "the band themselves might even be joining us to help along the way!"

The studio cheering hit new levels, like it was news they were hearing for the first time, not written on a script in front of them. I was too nervous to feel anything except stomach cramps.

Could it *really* only be four questions that stood between us and the best thing that could ever happen to us?

"So – are you ready for round one?"

I shouted "NOPE" back at the radio, but Jaz cared not for my woes.

"If YOU want to be in with a chance of getting YOUR school into the final ten, all you need to do is help us out with this dilemma. Emails to the usual address."

Oh phew, email. Tegan could send over some ideas after training, and we could make it decent together. Maybe Jo could even help?

"And you'll have until the end of the next song to send it in. . ."

Or not. I leapt back on to my bed and grabbed my

laptop, only to see the gazillion messages from Rach on my phone (that I'd been sitting on, thinking it was a bum twitch). I messaged back, "Sorry," and, "On it," (literal) and listened back in. Jaz was fake-chuckling.

"OK, guys – confession time. When I said we *might* have the band to help us along the way, it was a tiiiny bit of a lie. Cos it's a DEFINITE. Aaaaand we have Lis on the line right now, all the way from their hotel in Tokyo. Lis, are you there?"

"Sure am – hi, Jaz; hi, everyone at Radio Shire."

The studio shouted "Hi" back. Lis laughed awkwardly. Yes, she was a lead singer, but she was always shy doing interviews.

A message from Rach pinged up – every single variation of heart emoji.

"Can I just say congrats to everyone listening for winning the national competition? We had SO many stations enter, but you guys blew them all out of the water. We cannot WAIT to come to Worcester."

From Japan to my hometown – I *bet* she couldn't wait. Still, reality didn't stop my heart flipping a bit at her just saying the name of where I lived, like now we officially had something in common because we'd shared a word.

"And we can't wait to have you." Jaz put on her

serious voice. "So – are you ready with round one?"

"Yeah – apparently you guys are going to be giving us some advice?"

I spluttered at the ridiculousness of Lis even saying that – she was the one on a world tour right now, and I was the one wearing novelty horse slippers panicking about writing an email, but hey-ho.

"So, the question is. . ."

Suddenly, there was a loud snuffle into the mic. Lis laughed. "Sorry, that was Pastry. You *might* have caught me FaceTiming her in the background?! We always have her on it on tour!"

There was a sound of licking. Hopefully also Pastry.

"Anyway, the question is . . . when we first started the Helicans we were at college, playing to crowds of three people – one being my dad! – and we really, nearly quit."

Jaz made a way OTT "Noooooo". Lis replied with a polite "Yes", which clearly meant, "As we just discussed in rehearsals."

"Soooo, the question is: what advice would you give to someone in that position now?"

Great. Life advice for successful people. Something I'm doubly unqualified in.

The only advice I could legitimately give to people would be to never take advice from me. I waved a mental bye to my dream of helping St Mary's win as it sped away – and tripped down a manhole.

But terrible or not, I needed to send *something*. Rach wouldn't forgive me if I just gave up. And I needed to do it fast, cos Jaz had started playing the song and we had to email before the end of it.

I really hoped Rach, along with every single other person at our school – teachers included – was currently in the process of sending something dazzling in.

"Annnnd – sixty seconds left. Tick tock – the clock's ticking."

Thanks for the reminder on how time passes, Jaz. JUST WHAT I NEEDED.

What could I write?!

RACH: Done!!!

Phew. At least St Mary's had one entry.

To try and kick-start my brain I opened a blank email and went to copy in Radio Shire's address. But when I pasted it, it didn't copy at all. Instead an actual miracle did. The last thing on my clipboard – aka the advice I'd copied from Jo. AKA THE EXACT THING I NEEDED FOR THIS SITUATION RIGHT NOW.

Yes, sister dearest!!!

Jaz started counting down from ten.

My fingers were wobbling all over the keys.

FIVE SECONDS.

I grabbed the email address.

THREE.

Pasted.

TWO.

Wrote name.

ONE.

And sent!

Just before Jaz hit zero.

YEEEHAAAA! I'd officially achieved sending an email!

One small step for man, one giant leap for me-kind.

I looked at my handiwork. Well, fing-iwork. If entering was a competition (it was) I'd win (I probably haven't).

But after a few songs, instead of putting us out of our misery, Jaz dropped the bombshell that as there were so many entries, we'd have to wait three whole days to find out who was through. Seventy-two unbearable hours of tension. But it was because the band wanted to read them all themselves. Which was ridic. The Helicans reading something I/Jo had written? SQUEE. This was like being 0.000000001% friends with them.

And the high of this new-found 0.000000001% friendship Rach and I now had with them, is probably why, by the time Tegan finished training, she had over a hundred unread messages in our group about it. Luckily, ninety-nine of them were the same thing – imagine if we won?! (The other one was me wondering if we'd get excused from lessons if we did.) As much as I knew chances were small, I couldn't help but cling on to the thought of something, anything, un-ordinary happening to my very ordinary life.

CHAPTER

THREE

A lot can happen in three days.

Is what I've heard people say.

However, in three days as me, a surprising un-lot can happen – mainly because my friends are way better at life than me, so I was flying solo. Tegan had two all-day training sessions (two more than I've had in MY WHOLE LIFE) and Rachel's mum took her and HOB (Hot Older Brother, technically christened Dan) to get a late-summer mid-season wardrobe refresh at some posh shops in Birmingham. There wasn't even any football on so I could accidentally-on-purpose bump (not physically this time) into Adam. Even Mikey seemed to be busy with a hectic schedule of falling into pavements (he calls it skateboarding, but I've seen it IRL and have to disagree).

I'd had to resort to plan E: lying on my bed and thinking about Adam. Luckily I had the stamina to do this for days.

Ignoring our last encounter, this summer had really notched things up a gear between us. Even if it had just gone from "Reverse" to "Parked".

It had kicked off last term with us commenting on each other's posts, not realizing who we were, and ended with him turning up on my doorstep when I was in my pyjamas with teddy bears on them (as much as I wanted to forget this detail, Jo enjoyed reminding me on the reg).

Since then we'd had:

- 1 × solo hanging out, aka maybe a date (I had no idea). (We were meant to go bowling, but I'm so embarrassingly bad at it I talked him into milkshake drinking instead, which I'm naturally gifted at.)
- 2 × group hangs aka just being in the same place at the same time. This was mainly playlist wars on the playing field, while Rach and Tegan stood in formations that facilitated my full-on secret-staring at him. (Inventor of reflective sunglasses – I owe you one.)

- 2 × casual runnings-into (that may have involved a less-casual three-and-a-half hours of walking Mumbles to increase the likelihood of this happening. One day it rained so hard I'd had to fashion a dog-umbrella for her out of a crisp packet and twigs).
- 2.5 × us watching him play football. Tegan's amazing at football – well, all sports, really – so we pretended we went because of her love of the beautiful game (nothing to do with my love of the beautiful man playing the beautiful game).
- 1 × actual accidental runnings-into (I realized afterwards I'd had a piece of hair caught upright in my sunglasses, like an antenna).

But despite these 8.5 being-near-hims, I had no idea how he felt about me, all made worse by two things.

- Every second I spent with him, I liked him more and more.
- Every second I spent with him, I got weirder and weirder.

Yup, as I seemed to be devolving from human back into gibbering blob, Adam had carried on looking more and more like he could be in the Helicans and still be The Fit One. *And* The Funny One.

EURGH.

I didn't have a *clue* if he liked me, or just liked me as one of the gazillion friends he already had? It wasn't a great sign that he hadn't suggested any plans since not-bowling (nowling). And not hearing from him at all since Mounting Day meant checking my phone every 0.1 seconds, which made time drag extra hard. BLEURGH.

Maybe thinking about him wasn't so fun after all?

I drifted into picturing his eyebrows that were so cute they made me want to stroke them like baby hamsters.

Nope, scrap that. Thinking about him was all kinds of fun.

But Thursday six p.m. finally ticked round. Tegan, Rach and my meet time to find out if St Mary's had made it through. Right on cue, the doorbell rang and in they walked, not even breaking their convo. Instinctively I joined in without knowing what it was about. I herded them straight into the kitchen as Mum had taken out a tub of fancy-looking ice cream, and I thought we should eat it all to avoid the potential sadness of it melting. She was busy chatting on the phone in the lounge anyway.

Rach plonked her bag on the table, spilling out an entire Superdrug's worth of nail varnishes.

"Say hello to *Plan: Distraction.*" She stood her iPad up on the table, and opened a gallery of all of the Helicans' singles and albums. "Thought we could try and recreate these," she nodded at the artwork, "on these." She waggled her fingers, nails forward.

Only in Rach's world could paying minute, intense detail to the Helicans, as you add them to your own body, be a distraction from thinking about them. But it's not a friend's job to point these sorts of things out – that's what teachers get paid for. It's a friend's job to go along regardless. At least she hadn't asked us to join in with her good-luck ritual of drawing the band's "H" logo on her ankle, which she'd done every day since the competition was announced. Her white trainer had developed a bluey tint to it.

Teeg began lining the bottles up in rainbow colour order.

"Sounds like a plan to me. Even though I'm gonna to have to take it all off tomorrow. It's non team regulation *apparently.*"

Rach and I glanced at each other. What fun *did* they allow her to have at training?

"Well, something that deffo IS team regulation – in fact, requirement for qualifying for the national team, I've heard – is ice cream. Right, Rach?"

Tegan laughed as Rach gave a very firm "YES". I handed out spoons, served up some bowls, and we got stuck in. But, as with everything in this house, it didn't taste as expected. And by the looks on the others' faces, it wasn't my paranoia – it really *was* an acquired taste. The proof really was in the pudding. And the proof was . . . oaty.

Nobody rushed back in for seconds. Except me, as I eat things I don't like, just because I enjoy eating so much.

"Knock knock!"

Mum breezed in from the hallway, verbally knocking on an imaginary door. Ironic since she can't master the concept with real ones.

"Girls! How lovely to see you?!" She gave Rach and Teeg each a hug/body press even though they had their arms out wide to avoid getting her jumper fluff in their wet nail varnish. But they were used to her.

She stood back and looked at them both like a proud mother (of two children who aren't hers). "Soooooo, what's the news?"

I hate it when she tries to get gossip via unfair-friend-pressure routes. I jumped in before they could buckle.

"The thing on every night on BBC One."

Ignoring me, she pulled up a chair. "Tegan Allen. I must say – you get more beautiful every day." Mum brushed her cheek gently. Tegan didn't flinch but I knew she was crying inside tears at this personal boundary overstep. "Or is that what luuurve does to you?" Rach snorted. I inhaled a glob of ice cream (still eating it, still not enjoying it).

DOES MY MOTHER HAVE NO SHAME?!

(Although I've seen the pics of her nude yoga retreat, so I know the answer to this already.)

BUT SERIOUSLY, AS IF PEOPLE SAY THIS?

Tegan tried to mask her squirm by putting her hand up to her face.

"Erm, I wouldn't exactly say that, Ms Fisher."

I *wish* I'd never told my fam about Mikey and Tegan, but Jo *had* kind of played a big part in making it all happen.

But Mum had stopped listening. She'd spotted the semi-eaten ice cream. Annoying. I'd risked a parent rant – pa-rant – on something that wasn't even that delicious.

"Bella No-Middle-Name Fisher. *Tell me* you haven't eaten that ice cream?"

"I can honestly tell you I wish I hadn't?"

The other two shot me mini-evils. *Mevils*. I *may* have forgotten to mention I hadn't explicitly got the eating of it agreed by all interested parties, i.e. my mother.

"And *how* was it?"

Tegan and Rachel murmured a combo of "cold", "creamy" and "icy" – all factually true. It was down to me to be honest.

"Well, if there was nice ice cream – nice-cream – and not-nice ice cream … it would definitely be nearer the 'not' end."

"And do you have *any* idea why that might be?"

I shrugged.

"Well … it's actually part one of my news."

Mum had news?! This was news to me.

She walked over to the freezer and flung the door open. Had she finally thrown away that weird leg of lamb she'd bought before I was born? I got my phone out to message Jo, but stopped as I noticed all that was in the freezer were more pots of the ice cream. Had my prayers finally been answered? (Obvs world peace was first, but I'd take what I could get.)

"TA-DAAAAAA!"

Too many seconds passed of us all smiling in a *we-support-you-but-have-no-idea-why-you're-standing-*

42

proudly-by-a-freezer way and her standing proudly by a freezer.

"It's the stock for my new business. It arrived!"

WAIT. What in the blessed name of Sir Ben and Lord Jerry was happening?

"Erm, explain???"

She pointed to the pot on the table.

"It's an idea that came to me while I was relaxing on the cruise. Where I met Paula, my new vet friend? Since then I've been working with her, and my supplier ... and it's finally all here." She pointed at the half-eaten pot again as if any of this made sense. "Yes, girls. You are now looking at the proud producer of..." She closed her eyes and breathed in like she was winning an Oscar. "Doggie ice cream."

Thank. Goodness. I. Was. Sitting. Down.

Why hadn't she shared any of these details before?!

She mistook my shock for confusion. "Ice cream – for dogs, Bella! So they can have a summer treat too." She said it like it was the most obvious statement. But summer treats?! Was this just the tip of the ice(cream) berg?! What was next? Dog bikinis? Bark-inis.

"Paula's helped me make a dog-friendly non-dairy recipe with all natural ingredients!"

Still no words.

Mum pointed at the circular logo I'd not bothered to look at before. "I'm *sure* I told you about it."

I shook my head. "I'm sure you haven't."

"Didn't you wonder where I'd been disappearing to for all those meetings?"

I decided "blank face" was a better response than, "No, cos I was just happy I could have control of the TV remote."

"Aaaaand, news two. I'm going to sell it in a shop on the edge of town. I've rented a shop!! Can you imagine? It's called... Wait for it, I'm really proud of this... Give A Dog A Cone!"

Actual. State. Of. Shock.

Mum held my hand, looking me right in the eye.

"This could be it, Bella – our ticket to financial stability. I really think this could work for us."

So many thoughts rushed through my mind, I wasn't sure which one to deal with first. Top were:

Mum had a new business.

Mum had a business at all?

Mum's business involved dogs AND ice cream?!

Mum's business had a really good name, but could dogs hold cones? Unless they were sitting upright using their paws as hands, which seems quite poised for a pooch.

Had Mum thrown that lamb out after all?

And a late entry:

44

OH MY WHATBALLS? I'd just fed my friends animal food.

"MUM?! TELL ME IT'S SAFE FOR HUMANS!"

I ran my tongue over my teeth, trying to remove all traces but just causing an extra-oaty blast. She looked reassuringly at us. Phew. As unhinged as my mother is, even *she* wouldn't put non-human food in a freezer. That's parenting rule number two. Behind "Don't leave things on the stairs" (despite them basically being shelves you can walk up).

She smiled. "I . . . I don't really know at this stage . . . but you guys seem fine?"

Not the words I was hoping for. She picked up the tub we'd (mainly me) just eaten.

"Ooooh – *Cookie Spaniel*. Doggie biscuit with dog choc chips. Nice. You *could* have picked up *Live A Little* – bone marrow with liver chunks."

I gave Tegan a look that said, "Don't worry, you'll be fine and I *probably* haven't jeopardized your entire gymnastics career with a potential bout of food poisoning." I think she interpreted it as, "I might be sick on the table." Also correct. Rach, however, was taking the whole thing in her stride. Maybe it's cos her legs were so much longer.

"Congrats, Ms Fisher. That's amazing news. And as a

non-dog, I still thought it tasted pretty good. When does the shop open?"

"Well, the launch party's the week you go back to school. You *must* come along!"

"Try and stop us!" Tegan sounded like she actually meant it.

"Totally. Bells, let us know all the deets." Rach gave me a genuinely excited nod.

Mum beamed at them before remembering something else. "Oh – and I totally forgot to mention. Each tub sold will support the charity we got Mumbles from. The Bark Shelter. Cool, huh?" Mum ruffled Mumbles' ears.

CONFUSION.

Was the twinge I felt pride, or a reaction to eating dog biscuit? It *was* kind of a cool (/frozen) idea. I had NO idea her dream of a business had come so far. Her own shop?! That *was* kind of bad-ass. Especially when she'd never done anything like it before.

I grinned at Mum, then noticed my friends were one step ahead and smiling already. Trust them to twig on to the brilliantness of this before I did.

"Thanks, girls. That means a lot." Mum gave my knee an affectionate squeeze under the table. "Now, seeing as you've taken that so well, how about part three of my news?"

My stomach sank (again, maybe eating-animal-food related). If parts one and two were anything to go by, was I ready for another instalment?

I attempted a guess. "You're launching Deep Pan Purrza – a pizza chain for cats?" Only a *half*-joke.

Rach laughed. "With Paw-purr-oni toppings?"

Overexcited, I threw another one in.

"And Miaow-garita?" OK, that didn't work as well as I thought it would.

Mum shook her head. "Sadly not. It is something that's going to affect the family . . . through hopefully in a great way."

She smiled at the three of us. Had she forgotten only *one* of us had come out of her vagina?

Tegan raised an eyebrow at me. Did she have insider info?

OH. MY. DOG. ICE CREAM.

Was she eyebrow-reminding me of when her mum and dad made their "family announcement"?

IF MUM'S HAVING A BABY I AM LEAVING RIGHT NOW AND MOVING TO JO'S COMMUNE.

Although then Mum wouldn't feel guilty about converting my room into a nursery.

IF MUM'S HAVING A BABY I'M DEFINITELY STAYING IN THIS HOUSE IN PROTEST. FOR EVER.

Mum's grin got bigger. "We're going to have a new addition."

Rach clapped her hands together. I slammed mine down on the table. We sounded like the world's worst percussion band.

HOW HAD I GOT THE DEFINITION OF MENOPAUSE SO WRONG?!

Mum leaned back in her chair. "I'm so happy you're pleased!"

Pleased? This conversation was the kind of emotional rollercoaster I didn't have the height requirement to be on. Undeterred by my hyperventilating, Mum carried on.

"I really *hoped* you'd be into the idea of a lodger."

WAIT. A lodger! No one was pregnant!

I relief-exhaled so hard I blew over one of Rach's nearly empty nail varnishes.

"MOTHER???? I THOUGHT YOU WERE TELLING ME YOU WERE HAVING A BABY?!"

Mum chuckled, but even my pancreas was sighing with relief (and I don't know where it is). A lodger? I could maybe get my head around a lodger. (Although I guess a baby's a lodger, just one with really bad table manners.)

We'd just need to be really careful who we chose.

"Jeeez, Mum. You had me worried. When did you even make this decision?"

"Well, you know things have been a bit tight since the old people's home closed down." It was where she'd worked part-time for years. "And the costs of setting up the business means we're not going to have a lot of money coming in for a while. I thought it could be fun!"

As much as I didn't want a stranger in the house, the only contribution I made to our finances was making sure biscuits never got wasted, so I couldn't really argue. I tried to channel my inner Jo. Be rational.

"OK. Guess we just need to figure some stuff out. Like how will we choose someone? And what if we don't like them? And where will Jo stay when she's back?" Mum blinked blankly at me. "And how can we make sure they like Mumbles? And will it be too much when you're trying to launch the shop? And have you definitely thought this through?"

Her extra blink meant both, "Don't question me, I'm your mother," and, "Of course I haven't; I never think things through, so don't ask again."

"And how soon are you thinking of finding this *person*? And where?"

"Well, that's an easy one."

Finally. Some answers.

"She's in the lounge."

CHAPTER

FOUR

Was this a joke?

Even Rach and Tegan looked completely freaked out, and they don't live here?! Mum leaned across the table and whispered. "She's my friend Brenda's friend's neighbour's hairdresser's niece, and she couldn't find any flats that would do short-term rents, so I thought this would be perfect."

Oh, well, that's OK then?!

Rach untucked her hair from behind her ears to prep for new person meet-age. But I couldn't stop my mouth from hanging open like a fish.

Rach's first impression = the dream. Mine = a bream.

Mum walked to the door, hissing a quick, "Be. Nice."

This really wasn't a joke.

"Shay . . . meet the girls."

Oh.

Wow.

A really beautiful, tall lady, wearing some sort of ultra on-trend jumpsuit with a statement necklace and lipstick that was so bright even Mumbles did a double-take, shimmied in. She looked like a magazine cut-out.

"Hi." Shay stuck her hand out towards me. Did she have pastel-ombre nails? And did an actual beam of sunlight just glisten off her perfect bob?

"I'm, er, Bella. Bells for short."

"And I'm Shay. Short for . . . well, everything when I take off my ridiculous shoes." She winked and laughed, and everyone else did too, in the same giggly way we do when we get served by the really fit man in Tesco, who looks like Matt Healy when you squint (aka the cunningly named Tesco Matt Healy – TMH).

"Sooo great to meet you. Your mum's been telling me aaaaaalll about you." Shay had a way of looking at me that made me feel important. "Don't you have a big thing on tonight?"

I nodded, my brain working overtime to try and take this all in. As usual, Tegan stepped up to do the proper adulting. She waved across the table.

"I'm Tegan. And yeah – we're in a comp to win a gig. It's with a band called the Helicans. We find out tonight if our school's through."

I was about to try and explain that this was kind of a big deal, but Shay cut me off.

"Wow – that's HUGE. Their last album was killer!"

Sorry, what? Did Model Lodger (Modger) also have excellent taste in music? Jo was going to *love* that Mum had traded her in for a cooler model (who also *paid* for the privilege of being in Casa Fisher).

"TOTALLY! I've had it on repeat alllll summer." Rach legit blushed at her outburst. "Sorry. Hi. I'm Rach."

Shay smiled knowingly. "Ah, Rachel. Such a symbolic name. Purity and love, right?" Rach went even redder. "I think names are *so* important. Shay means majesty and strength. That's a lot to live up to!"

I think I heard Mum swoon. If Shay started talking about lunar cycles she was going to apply for adult adoption on the spot. Modger spotted Rachel's fingers.

"Wait. Is that the cover of *Don't Waste a Second of Me* on your actual nails?!"

I stepped behind Rach in case she fainted with delight. Mum did a little wiggle of excitement. "See, isn't this lovely? I *knew* it would be! And I *promised* Brenda that while Shay's here, she won't just be a lodger – she'll be a proper part of the family."

Shay smiled back, not knowing the full horror of what being in Fam Fisher entailed, and we all made general "yes/good" noises.

But Tegan was looking at the cuckoo clock on our wall (it wasn't a real cuckoo clock, it was just shaped like a cuckoo and we couldn't think of a better way of describing it).

"Sounds great, Ms Fisher – although, and I don't mean to sound rude, but we kind of need to go..."

Argh, yes. Only ten minutes to get upstairs, tune in and freak out. We waved bye to Modger – me promising to chat properly later, Rach asking for her Insta name – and pegged it upstairs.

We tuned in just in time to hear Jaz getting the band back on the line to make the announcement. HELLO, MOMENT OF TRUTH.

We held our breath. And each other's hands.

It felt like the whole summer had been building to this moment.

Or not.

As Lis and Rosie, the bass guitarist, started nattering about when Amil accidentally knocked out a tooth while they were doing a way-too enthusiastic Little Mix cover.

It was quite a long story so eventually we had to resume breathing.

"Sorry to cut you off, girls," Jaz clearly wasn't a dental-anecdote fan, "but we've got loads of messages coming through from people *desperate* to know which schools are in the running. You ready to do the honours?"

Lis cleared her throat. We re-stopped breathing.

"I know people always say this, but we *genuinely* had such a hard time choosing. You guys were great!" A big "uh-huh, yes" came from her bandmates. The three of us squeezed our hands even tighter.

"Sorry it took us so long to get through all the entries. They were SO good." Trust Rosie to be extra supportive of the fandom.

"All five thousand of 'em!" Amil heckled from the background.

EURGH. Ten entries was more what we wanted to hear. The odds were for ever not in our favour. Amil cleared his throat. Rach had started muttering "pleasepleasepleasepleaseplease" on repeat. But I felt the same – please let someone, *anyone*, have got St Mary's through.

"I'll keep it quick, and tell you which schools are through. You can head to the Radio Shire Facebook to see what their winning advice was and who sent it in. If you're a finalist – stay tuned for an email direct from us too." He took a deep breath sounding nervous himself. "So, let's get on with it. In no particular order ... the schools in the final are ... St Mary's."

WHAT?!

"... of The Prior."

Oh. Not us: the super-exclusive school out of town. My stomach plunged like it was on a bouncy castle. And as Amil reeled off more and more names, it dropped so far it felt like it had taken up permanent residency in my big toe.

Oh well. That was that.

Rach did a stuttery sniff like she might be about to cry.

But what had we really expected?

"I'm so sorry, Rach." I felt crap for me, but even worse for her.

"Fat lot of good this did." She pulled her sock up over the biro "H" on her ankle.

But Amil's Welsh voice cut back through. "Oops, sorry, guys. Missed one off!"

What? There was one more chance? SOMEONE HAD SEEN OUR DEAD DREAM AND GIVEN IT CPR.

We resumed the tense hand-grabbing position.

"Drumroll, please – the last school isssss . . . St Mary's."

Wait. What?!

OUR St Mary's?!

WE WERE IN THE FINAL?!

This. Was. EVERYTHING!

I stared at the other two checking I hadn't halluci-heard. But Tegan nodded. It. Was. Real. And after a split second of being too shocked to move, we exploded into the loudest cheers, leaping around on my bed, hands, legs, everything in the air. Mum guessed the result from the commotion and shouted up a big, "Well done," (and something about it sounding like a herd of elephants upstairs).

We were celebrating like our school had already won the whole thing.

"I wonder," Tegan panted as we collapsed in a heap, "who," (breath) "made it through for us?" She refreshed the Radio Shire page again but nothing had gone up. Rach and I had even checked our emails but we'd had nothing, so it wasn't us.

"Whoever it is," Rach wheezed, "is going to be," (pant) "an instant heeeroooo." (Gasp) "Lifelong celeb status guaranteed."

"You know what this means?" Tegan shook her head like she couldn't quite believe it herself – and it took a lot to blow her mind. "Only three questions are between us and having the actual Helicans. At. Our. School."

Rach wheeze-squealed. "We HAVE to do WHATEVER it takes to make sure St Mary's wins, agreed?" But before I could check whether I should be worried about the crazed look in her eye she put her finger to her lips. Jaz had more details.

"The next round we'll be cutting ten to five, and this time the question is going to be all about exes."

Generic studio "Oooooh."

"So, as it's back to a public vote, make sure YOU tune in to vote for your favourite!"

Rach snorted. She was doing the full farmyard of noises tonight.

"Thank goodness it's not about one of our exes — imagine *that* being shared with the Helicans?"

Involuntary Nostril Flare.

"Well, I'm the one who went out with a boy who tried to make a whole school call me Blobfish." Yup, going out with Luke had been a total mistake.

Teeg laughed. "Fair point. And I don't have one, so that's me out."

Rach scrunched up her nose. "Do you think we'll know the person who got us through? Cos soz to say it, but they might officially have to be my new best mate."

"Oi!" I dug her in the ribs. But I knew she was

messing – the whole school was probably thinking the same. I knew I was. All of our hopes of a single exciting thing happening were totally pinned on this mystery wise person. They'd better have nerves of steel. Rach had started writing down ideas of how we could befriend them. She looked up from her list (which currently only said "buy all the cake for them").

"Imagine if they really mess it up?! They'll have to switch schools." She jotted down *"invite skiing"*. "Or at least invest in some serious disguise."

"Uh-huh." I nodded slowly at the thought. "People have no mercy. They cut you off just for taking the last plate of Friday chips."

But Tegan didn't laugh. In fact she looked kind of freaked out.

"Bells. You might want to look into fake moustaches..." She pointed at the Radio Shire page. "It was you."

CHAPTER

FIVE

If I thought the tidal wave of messages I got straight after Radio Shire posted my entry (followed by Jaz going the whole hog and announcing my name on air) might be a blip, I was wrong.

My anonymous life had started trending.

And four days afterwards, it hadn't stopped. That one email had catapulted my life into a mix of school faces I hardly recognized chatting to me in the street (and laughing way too much at my non-jokes), a deluge of good-luck messages from numbers I didn't know, and ten times more likes on everything I posted.

Suddenly everyone who'd never bothered to say hi wanted to be my best mate.

All the pressure to win was on me.

Despite Rach and Tegan telling me at least fifty times a day it would be OK, I was freaking out.

Freaking out about the next round.

Freaking out about going back to school.

And freaking out-out that these two freak-outs were only twelve hours apart.

This could only end one of two ways:

Hero Bella.

Being-Chased-Out-Of-Town-With-Pitchforks Bella.

And that's both scary AND a real mouthful. The only positive I'd come up with was that I didn't think anyone sold pitchforks any more, so it might be downgraded to rakes (but they still seem quite pointy).

It hadn't helped that the Helicans comp was also the hottest topic of convo at home too. Mum was enjoying the novelty of boasting about *two* daughters, and Modger was relieved her new home wasn't as uncool as she'd assumed. There was NO escape.

EURGH. Why had I ever thought this was a good idea?

I slumped forward over Mum's supermarket trolley. Yup, I was so desperate to distract myself from obsessing about it, I'd agreed to my third supermarket trip of the week with her. Living the school holiday dream (everyone else's summer involved

Tenerife – mine involved Tesco). The only plus side was that Mum was so pumped about Give A Dog A Cone launching next week she'd agreed I could buy some brand-name ice creams as "research".

Remembering this deal, I marched towards the freezer section.

THWACK.

There is something beyond painful about a supermarket trolley wheel catching the back of your heel. And I'd just inflicted it full speed on an unsuspecting human.

As my victim turned round, I contemplated leaping into the fridge unit and hiding under a pile of butter.

The victim was Tesco Matt Healy. TMH.

And to make matters worse, he'd been totally stationary, stacking Stilton.

"OHMYGAWDI'MSOSORRY."

He crouched down to rub at the injury, putting him eye level with the current contents of my trolley – loo roll (pack of twenty-four, no less), dog-worming tablets and extra-strength toilet cleaner. If a trolley could anti-flirt, mine was achieving it.

"No worries. It's a hazard of the job."

No. It *was* a hazard of looking so dreamy people forgot appropriate stopping distances. For the sake of his health, I should warn him to stay away from pelican crossings.

Going redder than the Edam next to him I muttered another five "sorrys" before we both did the eyebrow-raise-smile combo signifying "this conversation has ended, but as it never really began there aren't words we can use to politely acknowledge this, so let's both be on our way".

"Oooh, Bells, is *this* 'The Cheese Man'?"

Please no. Why did my mum have to find me at that exact second? And why did she still manage to do air quotes with her fingers, despite clutching what looked like a bumper tube of athlete's foot cream?

"Idon'tknowwhatyou'retalkingabout." I couldn't be speaking any faster. "Other than yes, he is a man. I think. I mean, I hadn't noticed."

"Errr, I am, yes," TMH clarified quietly.

"And yes – he clearly *is* involved with cheese in some way." I pointed at the mozzarella. "I mean, not romantically, but in a working relationship kind of way."

TMH awkwardly got back to opening up a new box of cheese, as if dealing with dysfunctional families was a normal part of his job.

"Aaanyway, we must bid you adieu." I grabbed Mum's hand. "Don't want to get in the way of your balls." BELLA, WHAT ARE YOU *SAYING*!? I *swear* my brain doesn't function at the speed needed for normal conversation skills. I panic-shouted. "AS IN, MOZZARELLA BALLS." Silence. "But you knew that."

My work here was done.

I dragged us away as quickly as I could. When we got to the safety of the battery display at the end of the aisle, Mum leaned over and whispered.

"Well, he seemed lovely."

I rolled my eyes and messaged the others to tell them we were going to have to give hanging out in the cold section a break till Ball-gate blew over. Farewell, only silver lining of being held chore-hostage. As I traipsed behind Mum in a mood, sporadically throwing in essential purchases (Wotsits, Pot Noodles, Daim Dairy Milk), my phone buzzed. It was something even more unexpected than my TMH assault.

Hiyyyerrrrrr. Free Friday evening? I've got a cinema ticket with your name on it.

It buzzed again.

I haven't, that would be weird. But you get what I mean.

Tannoy announcement: *LIFE EVENT IN AISLE THREE.*

THE FADAM HAD LANDED.

Adam had got in contact?! Yessssssss! And despite my teammate-attack/accidental-mount combo, he wanted to see me again?!

Hallelujah!

I shook a pack of breath freshener mints like they were celebration maracas.

THIS WAS BIG.

Adam – offa being total amazing – wanted to go on a second solo-hang/maybe date. With me?!

My face = officially grinning like a gibbon. That's what reading a message from him does to me. How lame is that? But it wasn't *my* fault he made my major organs go all giddy. I've seriously never liked ANYONE how I like him.

He was like a Yorkshire pudding: his ingredients were all excellent, but combined they achieved a previously unimaginable extra level of perfection.

And this Yorkshire pudding wanted to see me again.

I dropped some kitchen foil in the trolley, smiling way too hard for the baking aisle, as I drifted into my pre-prepared "Why Adam is so Fadam" list.

- He's dead funny (but in a quiet way where

he doesn't make a big deal out of his jokes).
- He's clumsy in a cute way (like when he caught my hair in his hoodie zip and apologized for two weeks).
- He plays the drums (fit).
- And football (fit).
- He has an entertaining obsession with *The One Show* (meaning he is more likely to be OK with my *DIY SOS* obsession).

I threw in some plastic food bags (Wow! I love plastic bags! I love life!) and carried on.

- He remembers things I say (he even did further research on my hermaphroditic fish chat).
- He wears T-shirts that are just the perfect amount too big (something extra swoon about boys in baggy stuff).
- He has the best taste in music (we had ten matches on our "recently played" lists).
- Plus the nicest hair (especially that one bit that always curls up at the front).
- And *those* forearms (UFOs. Unexplainable Fit Objects).

- And he has such a beautiful. . .

"Spotted dick?"

Sorry, what? I blinked five times and discovered Mum holding up two tins.

"Or good old rice pudding?"

I pointed at the rice pudding and tried not to give away I'd been lost in full-on AdamPervlandia. Thankfully, Mum scurried straight off to get some scented candles, leaving me alone with a way more difficult decision: how to reply.

It had to be perfect. Getting things on track with Adam was as big to me as winning the Helicans gig. Maybe even bigger. I SO wanted him to like me as much as I liked him. Or even a tenth (still a pretty daunting prospect when I counted empty-crisp-packet origami as one of my major hobbies/skills).

I took a deep breath.

I could do this.

OR COULD I?!

Because there – in the frozen vegetables section – he was.

Adam. IRL. Just casually joking around and buying a bag of peas with his mate Marcus, as if this was perfectly acceptable behaviour. As if people like him did normal things like eat or buy chilled legumes.

Fact: supermarkets should NOT allow boys this hot to be in their freezer aisles. He was one hair flick away from causing a defrosting disaster.

I dived into the cleaning aisle, my heart thundering so loud I couldn't even think straight.

SUBLIMINAL NOTE TO ADAM'S BRAIN: turning up unannounced like this In Real Life is *NOT* OK.

Quick, Bella. Think. What to do?!

There was a clear winner – I HAD to make sure my mum and me did not, in any way, shape or form, have an encounter with him.

I scurried – as fast as you can in a supermarket without getting chased by a security guard – to find her. Darting around like a ninja, I ushered her to the hopefully boy-safe haven of sanitary products. I kept her chatting there for twenty minutes until I calculated the coast would be clear. Never have I used the words "heavy flow" so much in my entire life. I will *never* be able to forget Mum's story about the first time she used a menstrual cup.

But the mental scarring was worth it, as I managed to get us back to the car without another sighting. And as we headed home, I relaxed into buzzing so much about my potential date I found myself singing along to Mum's Christmas pan-pipe album (the tape had got stuck – our car is so old it brings a whole new meaning to *Antiques Roadshow*).

"Successful trip, huh?" Mum gave me a double thumbs-up leaving zero hands on the wheel. But unlike her, it wasn't the excellent yellow discount label on a butternut squash that had me so happy. I replied with a non-committal "uh-huh".

"What a week it's been. I can't wait for you to see the shop! It's really beginning to look quite something."

She did an excited teeth-together nervous grin. I hadn't seen her giddy like this over anything before (except that one yoga teacher whose wife had run off).

"I can't wait to see it either." I meant it, but she didn't want me there till it was nearer being finished. "How long till the big day?"

"Only nine days now?! You'll be there, won't you? Official launch-party photographer?"

"Try and stop me." Although if things didn't go well with the Helicans comp, I *may* have emigrated/been brutally murdered by then. But she didn't need those kinds of details.

For the rest of the journey she nattered away about freezer units, the signs and boxes that had filled up our house, and how her friends were all doing positive energy rituals to help her "little radio star". Turns out Mum being proud of you is actually quite exhausting – that's probably why I've left it to Jo all these years.

When we pulled up outside our house, I was relieved to see Shay's car on the driveway (it was basically the great-granddaughter of ours. Yes, they were both Minis, but ours was old, brown, and contained over thirty-two million types of bacteria from all the crumbs we'd dropped in it over the years. Hers was red, shiny and looked like it was only ever used to get to VIP parking at festivals).

I was even happier when I headed in and discovered Shay was busy baking, an excellent playlist blaring out. And she paid *us* to live here.

She gave us a welcome-home shimmy. "Hey, rockstar." Shay'd called me that ever since the comp. No big deal. She nodded at the tray of green-ish biscuits on the side. "Want one?"

I gave a "hell, yes" and took a pic of them to send Jo, alongside the caption "Better come back from uni with some serious skills, or Shay will be replacing you on a permanent basis".

Jo replied with a potato emoji – her way of telling me to get lost (without the effort of typing it). I didn't bother then telling her the biscuits were rank – and Shay's special ingredient was courgette.

When Shay and her perfect red lipstick (who bakes wearing lipstick?! Is she a vlogger?) joined me at the kitchen table, I turned my phone so she couldn't see my fan-girling.

"Is this playlist one of yours?"

She nodded, pleased. "Sure is. You want? It's called. . ." She scrolled through. "Oh, yeah. *Bands I Have Met*."

Sorry, what?! Was I seriously sharing a table with someone who had shared personal space with these bands?

Shay laughed. "Oi, pick that mouth up. They're just people with jobs, like the rest of us."

She clearly hadn't seen Zayn Malik recently. He was not made of human.

But this revelation was the perfect opportunity to do some proper Shay digging. She'd dropped clues about her London life, and Rach, Tegan and I had spent hours wondering just how glam it really was.

"Soooo, er. . ." I tried to use my best "this isn't a question I've been wanting to ask for ages" voice. "What *is* it that you actually do?" All I knew was it had something to do with TV and she was here for a couple of months.

"TV production. Head office sent me up here to try

and help out on something at Midlands TV. Bring some of my creative know-how to the project."

Oooh. She must be a pretty big cheese. I bet TMH would love her/try and stack her. "What kind of TV do you make?"

"Oh y'know."

I didn't. "I don't."

She blinked, taken aback at my lack of conversation skills.

"Music, mainly. Some of the live ents shows." She noticed my confused face. "Sorry, *entertainment*."

WOAH.

"Isn't that an *amazing* job?"

She took an incredibly large sip of wine. "I lucked out, yeah."

"And have you, er . . ." I didn't want to sound like a massive loser, but then remembered she'd seen me in my pyjamas that made me look like a life-sized burger, so had clearly passed that point ". . . met the Helicans?"

"As in" – she flicked about on her phone – "*these* Helicans?"

WHAT THE HELL-ICAN?!

It was a pic of her and Lis lying on a floor.

Yes. Thanks to Shay I was officially one selfie-degree of separation from Lis. Any chill I had instantly melted.

"That's SO awesome. Can you send it to me?"

She nodded. "Course." This was going STRAIGHT to Rach. And Jo.

"What were they like?!"

She swirled the wine round her glass. "Exactly what you'd imagine. Total babes. In fact, good point. Let me know how you get on with this radio thing, cos I could always drop them a line. . ."

The room went dizzy without my chair moving. "What. You . . . you'd do that for me?"

Shay laughed. "Course. Just like family, right? Isn't that what your mum said?"

"Said what?" Mum walked into the kitchen as if on cue, but lessened the smoothness by tripping over Shay's shoes.

Shay winced. "Sorry, I meant to shift them. Just didn't want to ruin your floor. It's solid oak, isn't it?"

Mum positively beamed. How amazing *was* this woman? Chatting to me about bands I love, and complimenting Mum on something weird like floors – which for normal people are really only there to be stepped on (bet ceilings are annoyed they get all the glory).

"Oak, indeed. Couldn't afford it for the shop though – had to go for lino."

Shay managed to look like this wasn't the most boring sentence uttered this millennium and took another bite of her biscuit. She really was incredible. She should be a class in school.

"How's everything for the launch going? Not long now, right?"

Mum pulled up a chair. "I know. Where does the time go! But it's all coming together. Just need some more bits and bobs designed and printed, and it'll almost be there."

Shay picked her phone back up and opened up a browser. "I can REALLY recommend these guys. They do all our stuff, and it's always on point."

Mum's eyes widened. "Wow. They look *so* professional."

I peered over and totally agreed. The pics were amazing. From huge billboards, to super-cool lanyards, everything looked like one of those design Instagram accounts that only posted in threes. They'd even done a Helicans launch party. "Bet they're London prices, though."

"Totally worth every penny. Here, let me put you in touch." Shay winked. "They might be able to do you a deal."

And just like that, she sent an email and fixed another problem.

The three of us spent the rest of the evening chilling on the sofas and watching a documentary on the rise of crowdfunded filmmaking (Shay's choice). I had to prod Mum whenever she snored too loudly over it (even though every single time she woke up, she'd immediately say "fascinating", as if it covered up she'd just been fast asleep). In fairness, I also zoned out and used the time to construct a reply to Adam. And then a reply to his reply. By the end of the evening we'd confirmed all the details for Friday's date (which worryingly was going to be like composing 7,500 messages back-to-back, but out loud).

Waving night to the others (Mum woke up with a start and said, "Fascinatinggoodnightyes!"), I headed up to bed. But instead of sleeping, in a date-induced panic, I ended up revising Adam's favourite show, as emergency conversation back-up. Annoyingly it was *Game of Thrones*, which turned out to be more complex than real-life history. I had to go full exam highlighters and coloured pens to make adequate notes. Which took ages to scrub off my face in the morning, when I woke up with them stuck to my head.

If I couldn't even sleep without getting it wrong, how on earth was I ever going to get through Friday?

CHAPTER

SIX

I wasted 3,036 of precious getting-ready seconds recording a variety of "Hi, how are you"s to see what sounded casual-yet-excited enough to use for my *actual* Adam greeting. I wasted another twenty-nine seconds working out how many seconds I'd wasted doing it.

And I was standing next to the Elgar statue, still practising silent hellos, doing tooth-checks in the reflection of my phone, when I felt a jab in the ribs.

ARGH?! I span round.

"You see, the difference between you and me is I make sure I actually *know* the person I'm prodding." It was Adam.

And he was teasing me.

And he'd just made human-to-human contact with me.

And he smelt amazing.

I laughed (a fake one, as even though it *was* funny, I was too nervous for my real reactions to work) and shuffled awkwardly, as if standing was a new concept my feet were getting used to.

I opened my mouth to say something but no words came out. So I shut it. But it sprang back open again as the tall fitness of Adam hit my eyes (had to hope the number-one quality he wanted in a girl was badly timed goldfish impressions). But I couldn't blame mouth. Adam was all music-vid in white T-shirt, black jeans and scruffed-up Converse (I see you, forearms, peeping out like the sexy limbs you are).

Luckily, he filled the silence. "A person of few words today?"

I tried to say "yes" but had one too few words to manage it.

Adam looked nervous, like he thought something might be up with me.

It was – being this close to him had mouth-frozen me (but I couldn't explain due to the mouth-freeze).

He put his hands in his pockets and swung his shoulders. "Sorry ... is it my fault? Do I smell weird or something?" He scruffed his hands through his hair.

PLEASE STOP. This is seriously not helping my brain get its act together.

"Football went into extra time and I had to have the world's quickest shower."

BRAIN, DO NOT PICTURE THIS.

"I sprinted all the way here. It's over a mile and a half?"

OMG he physically exerted himself for me.

"And this is the best I could do."

And it was tremendous.

BUT I STILL HADN'T SAID ANYTHING.

I took a deep breath and composed myself mentally, like my brain was about to do a gymnastic floor routine (but without the leotard).

"No! Sorry. You don't smell. Well, you do, but with your nose."

He laughed (even though I hadn't meant it to be a joke). Still, at least I had convo lift-off. I sneaked a glance at my phone, where I'd set a screengrab of Tegan and Rach's You Can Do This WhatsApp group as my home screen.

Just read, Bella. Just read. You *know* you've got this. By being friends with Tegan, who has always got this.

"Where does he want to get food?" Nooooo. THIS IS

WHY I NEED TO STICK TO FEW WORDS. "I mean, *we*. Where does *WE*. *Do* we. Where do we want to get food? If we do? DO we?"

Adam's strokeable brow scrunched. Was he trying to figure out why he'd actively suggested spending an evening with me?

"We do. *Definitely* do. If you do? Pizza? I know a good place..."

Annoyingly all my normal reactions came back to life at that exact moment and I let out an overly loud "YAS", which I tried to cover up by quickly saying Italian food was my fave, but got "fave" and "dream" mixed up and ended up saying, "Yes, it's my Dave."

But Adam, who has a knack of making me feel both wildly out of control, and simultaneously like everything was the most fine it had ever been, didn't even mention it (maybe he didn't hear?).

"Pasta La Vista it is then. Wanna head straight there?"

I nodded and together we started to stroll down the high street at half speed, kicking a stone back and forth between us, chatting about what had happened since we last properly saw each other. (Technically I'd properly seen him purchasing peas, but he didn't need to know this.)

I was glad I had the stone to stare at, to hide my face which kept being invaded by unauthorized mega-smiles. It felt so amazing for it to be the two of us. Me, Bella Fisher, and Fadam. Aka a couple of people – which is only two words away from "a couple".

Sure, we did have a *slight* blip when I spotted Angela, a girl from school who had sent me over fifty DMs about her extreme love for the Helicans. In a panic to hide, I said, "Ooh, look," and turned to intensely study the nearest shop window. Annoyingly it was a Greggs, so I just looked like I'd never seen a pasty before. But Adam joined in my staring and made the excellent point about what an amazing idea putting marshmallow in an ice-cream cone was, and soon we were ambling along again.

"Sooo, what happened with the Helicans?" He said it gently, like he was apprehensive in case I didn't have good news. I felt kind of shy admitting it had gone well.

"We . . . we got through to the second round."

"Woah – that's awesome!" He gave me his biggest smile yet, making his braces look extra cute. "You must have nailed it!"

Joy shudder! *Judder.* Was this Hottest Man Human seriously complimenting *me* about being good at life? The ridiculousness of this caused me to trip over my own foot and almost face-plant. "I wouldn't say that."

"Well, I would! When's the next round? I'll listen in."

"NO," I snapped back, way more aggressively than I meant. As chuffed as I was that he offered, the last thing I needed was more pressure. "Please don't... Thanks though."

Embarrassed by my outburst, I moved the conversation on by launching into a chat about Mum's new business. I was careful to keep details vague (I *may* have called it a "pet friendly café") as unleashing the full Fisher weird was definitely not on my list of "how not to make him run away" conversation topics. He said it sounded mega and we'd have to go one day. He then asked if Mumbles had recovered from eating that bee (he remembers details about my life/dog's swollen face! Swoooon!!!), and I discovered he'd once made a pact with himself to pat every dog that walked past (which explained why we'd already made four stroke stops).

I asked him how the drumming was going, and he told me he was still practising in his shed, but was now also teaching himself guitar. (Like, FOR REAL, what's next? He's a volunteer hedgehog-rescuer in his spare time?) I then tried to think of something equally as impressive, but the best I could do was talk about breaking my longest ever potato-peeling record.

I showed him the pic of it and he said it was a "remarkable photo", but I wasn't sure if he meant in a good way, or remarkable that someone would take a photo of it. I replied, "It's very a-peel-ing." And then neither of knew what to say for approximately forty seconds. Thankfully we then arrived at Pasta La Vista, and a waitress rushed straight over and broke the silence.

Adam reverted to his serious voice and asked for a "table for two" as if it wasn't the most romantic thing that has ever happened to me. I'd never had a sit-down meal out with a boy before (or even a stand-up one), but Adam seemed totally at home anywhere. I wondered what he was like in his *actual* home? Did he morph into a sofa? He was only four months older than me, but those sixteen weeks must be *crucial* for picking up some serious adulting skills (note to self: find out where he learnt them and enrol Mum on a course).

"So, what are you getting?" He put his menu down on the table and did whatever he did when his hands weren't holding something – little mini-drummings with his fingers on any available surface. Before today I never knew "tapping things" could be so alluring.

I picked my menu up to try and look like I had very strong opinions about food. However, I only had twelve pounds for the whole evening so knew within one second what I was getting.

"The spaghetti, I think."

He nodded, with a smile. "Gotta get your Dave."

I thought he hadn't heard?! I managed to keep a straight face. "And what's your *Dave*?"

He did a dramatic finger-based drum roll. "Dave is totally Four Seasons pizza – can't go wrong." He rocked back in his chair, but panicked as it went too far back and had to grab the table.

"Nice. Although I'm not really sure how 'mushroom' is a season, but who am I to argue with the inventor of pizza?"

Adam smiled. "Who I really hope is called Peter."

I laughed so hard thinking about this that I think I felt my first ab forming.

All too soon, our plates arrived. I thought I'd been an amazing budget-menu-item chooser, but it quickly became clear I was more of a terrible-public-eating planner. Despite trying my hardest, I kept flicking meat flecks everywhere. Adam politely ignored it (darn you and your easy-to-cut-and-chew season of ham), even when one flew into his water and bobbed about like a tiny brown meat beach ball (he didn't say anything, but I couldn't help but notice he never drank from it again).

Forget calorie info, menus should really come with an "ease of eating in front of a fit significant other" rating instead.

Give or take the constant panic about what I was saying/doing/chewing/flicking, I was having the kind of evening I'd only ever had with my friends. One where you laugh so much the waiter has to come back two times to ask if you want dessert. Except I was having it with a boy. Who I really, really liked.

But despite us being able to chat so easily, I still had no idea what was going on inside his head – other than that he really enjoyed pizza. It was so hard to tell with him – he was the same warm, friendly guy with everyone, the disgustingly nice human he was. I definitely couldn't spot him doing any of those signs that magazines tell you to look out for (although if he did mirror my body language he'd be wrestling invisible spaghetti on to a fork).

ARGH.

It was all SO confusing. Was I just someone he saw as a friend? Someone to talk about GoT with (he did *really* like my Jon Snow impression)? Or could he possibly, maybe, ever think of me as something more?! If only people held up scorecards like in *Strictly Come Dancing*, so you didn't think that you'd been funny in an endearing way, only to discover you'd been funny in a "they double-checked the location of the emergency exit" way.

I figured it *must* be a good sign that we were so caught up eating that neither of us realized we'd missed the start of the film. (I chose to ignore the alternative that it was just a sign we're both as equally disorganized/obsessed with pudding.)

We headed to the cinema regardless. Adam bought some popcorn (he agreed with my "separate stomachs for foods you like" theory) for us to eat outside. Three times we went for the popcorn at the same time, resulting in full-on hand clashing (the snacking version of hand holding?!).

Adam held up a piece of popcorn like he was about to say something very profound.

"You know the best bit of any film?"

Eating a family-sized bag of Revels in the dark, so no one could judge me on nibbling the chocolate off the raisins (eurgh raisins!), or ask to share?

Or not. I went for something safer.

"When people in the audience say 'shush' like it's a real word?" Always a highlight for me and Tegan."

"Nope. The trailers."

"SHUSH YOURSELF." In NO WORLD were

trailers better than toffee Revels. Not even if they were a trailer *for* toffee Revels.

"SHUSH *YOU*. Like who are these people that do the voice-overs? Is that how they order a chip butty?" He cleared his throat even though it didn't need clearing, and looked around till he spotted something.

"One woman."

YES. HE WENT THERE. HE WAS MOVIE-VOICING. I shook my head as if embarrassed (but actually was shaking my brain to keep its calm at yet another Adam-sexy thing being unleashed on us).

"One absurdly loud wheelie suitcase. One small cup of coffee. She's ready to take on the world. But first... Her biggest obstacle yet..." Dramatic pause. *"A revolving door?!"*

I laughed. Then laughed even more as the lady's suitcase got fully stuck and the whole thing squeaked to a halt. Then quickly stopped as she turned round and shot us evils.

My turn. I cleared my throat, looked around for inspo, and took a deep breath. All eyes on me.

"Thuuurghs." OH MY GOD MY THROAT CLEARING HAD GIVEN ME A WEIRD THROAT AIR BUBBLE AND I SOUNDED LIKE AN ALIEN IN A BATH. Quick. All eyes OFF me. I pointed back

at the woman still stuck in the door, tried to fashion my gurgle into an extra-late-incoming laugh, and emergency swallowed.

"Er, yes. *THIS Autumn. A nightmare is coming to town. Everyone must face it. But only a few will come out alive. Meet ... DRAMATIC PAUSE ... the new dentist.*"

Adam nose-laughed.

"*Some* people might say it's more dramatic when you *leave* a dramatic pause, rather than say it?"

Fake outrage (foutrage) face. "*Obviously* I'm not one of them."

I unleashed the full force of my party trick (not saying the alphabet backwards, as I didn't think backwards alphabeticalizing/gnizilacitebahpla was approps right now) – on-demand raising and wiggling of any eyebrow (well, any of the two I have, not anyone else's).

Adam held up his hands as if he was witnessing a miracle (EYES/BRAIN, don't get distracted by the revelation his forearms look even nicer vertical). "Woah, you never told me your eyebrows had been trained by Ashley Banjo?"

I gave a big double-eyebrow wiggle. "That was them bowing, FYI."

He laughed. Was it becoming a regular thing? I liked it. Maybe I was better at this "normal interaction" business than I thought? I suddenly felt all warm and glowy.

"So, where shall we go next? We could walk down to the river?" I sneaked a look at my watch. "Last bus isn't for an hour and a half – I could show you the swan that looks like Clare Balding?" His laugh gave me an extra bravery spurt. Maybe I could suss out if a potential date three was on the cards. "Or ... we could save that for the next date? Go full-on animals-who-look-like-celebs spotting at that creepy farm place with the mini steam train that always breaks down?"

OH.

As soon as I said it, I wished I hadn't. It wasn't my imagination – Adam's smile had totally vanished.

"I'm..." He was stuttering, looking all kinds of awkward. "I can't, actually. And I, er, I'm going to have to head."

Well, hello, exact opposite of what I hoped would happen.

Was it cos I'd used the word "date"? Oh man – what if he hadn't even thought *this* was a date?!

My insides chucked out warm and glowy and replaced them with cold and anxious. How could I have been so stupid?

I tried to muster the most upbeat "sure" I could.

How could a couple of words make you feel the same

queasy that eating dog ice cream did? We headed to the bus station, both trying to avoid talking about what I'd just said. Annoyingly we arrived at the exact same time as our bus, meaning another twenty minutes of potential Adam time got snatched away.

Not letting him see how gutted I was, I sat down first. I felt a little bit better when he chose to sit beside me. And even better-er when just as the doors closed, his massive smile returned.

"All right, mate!"

Oh. Be gone, better feeling. It wasn't anything to do with me. Someone I didn't know, who didn't seem to understand the importance of these final seconds of 73% of my side body being in contact with Adam's side body, sat down in front of us. Adam leaned forward to do that one-arm boy-hug-pat.

"Mate!"

"Maaate," the Adam-stealer replied.

They smiled at each other as if they'd now covered all important convo.

Adam gestured at his friend. "I haven't seen Nate in ages. He's been away for the whole summer!"

Nate looked towards me with a knowing smile. "And *who's* this?"

I waved. "I'm Bella."

Nate looked back at Adam. "Aaaaand?"

And what?

But from the way Nate was grinning, I knew *he* was asking what significance I had to Adam.

PLEASE, NO.

Nate, why would you do this to me?! We go way back! (Eight whole seconds.) Plus, if anyone needs the answer to this question, it's ME!

"Annnd..." Oh man, Adam was going to give an actual answer! "She's the one I told you about ... in the Helicans competition." Yes! Adam had batted Nate away. And, even bigger yes! He'd been talking about me?! "... and probably the only friend I'd be happy adding to our *Game of Thrones* group."

Bam. Right between the ears.

FRIEND.

There it was. It had happened. Now Nate knew. Now I knew.

Friend. I was Adam's friend.

All hopes I had of today being the proper start of Adam and Bella = officially crushed like a bag of Chipsticks at the bottom of my school bag.

No wonder he'd freaked out at my "date" question. He was probably embarrassed for me. Maybe that's why now he was all back happy again, chatting with Nate – grateful to be able to clear up my misunderstanding. I tried to muster a semi-smile for Nate, who was now attempting to high-five me about something to do with the winter coming. I swear they shot each other a look at my bad mood. C'mon, Bells. Channel Taylor Swift. Shake it off. Well, at least until you're off the bus (although I'd never heard that particular lyric).

"So, this is me." I rang the bell and forced my best I'm-Not-Totally-Heartbroken-Face.

"I'll get off too, walk you home."

Adam said GET OFF. Involuntary nostril flare. Nate totally clocked it. Who *was* this man?! Hope destroyer AND nostril police? But I didn't want my last impression to be all downbeat and lame.

"Nah, you stay on with Nate. Catch up on your catching up."

"Well. . ." Adam half-stood up. "Message me when you're in?"

My shattered heart broke into even tinier pieces. A tiny bit of me had hoped he was going to come anyway. What is it with mouths and brains playing opposites?

I walked to the front of the bus, gave them both a big friendly wave, and stepped off. As I watched it pull away, Adam moved to sit beside Nate. Side body contact with a person is obvs NBD to him.

I splatted the flat of my hand into my forehead and let out a spontaneous, "Bleugh". What *was* my problem? Why couldn't I have not messed this up? Not misread the signs. At *least* I should have said what a nice time I'd had – checked if he wanted to do anything again as a non-date? Or at least read it off my home screen, where Tegan had typed it out ready for me? WHAT A GRADE-A IDIOT.

"Talking to yourself?"

I looked around for the voice (and stopped hitting myself on the head).

I knew it all too well.

It belonged to the only boy in the entire world I'd sort-of gone out with. A boy who'd only done it for a dare, and, when I began to suspect that was the case, and suggested we take a break, had dedicated his time to making my life a misery.

My friends and I called him Puke. Everyone else called him Luke. And to make matters worse he had his arm around what looked like an off-duty Victoria's Secret model. Well, one in a coat, anyway.

But if fifteen years of having a big sister had taught me one thing, it was "if you don't want drama, pretend you can't hear your sibling".

I applied this logic to Puke, and carried on walking.

"Making out you can't hear me? Mature."

What was even more mature was pretending to want to have a convo with me, just to entertain him and his new girlf. But I wasn't Siri. I had a choice about whether to reply. I carried on.

"Keep walking, Blobfish. Maybe you'll find some friends on the way."

He laughed. I knew he'd be nodding to the girl like he'd scored the winning point. EURGH.

What reason on *earth* would I have for wanting to stop and be a part of this?

Although. . .

I stopped.

And became a part of it.

Deep breath. Game face. Big smile. Great British Fake Off.

"Sorry, did you say something?" Luke's smile vanished. I waved at the girl beside him. "I'm Bella. Nice to meet-slash-wave at you from afar."

Without returning my smile, she lifted her left hand and dropped it back down. So *that's* how moody girls wave.

"I'm Ska."

Ah yes. The disinterest. The superiority. The slightly

confusing nickname. The overall annoyingness. She was perfect for Luke.

He pulled her into him. "She's a model."

I looked at Ska. "Do you model boyfriends who think you can't speak for yourself?"

I laughed like it was a playful joke. Luke did not. "She models beachwear, *actually*. And watches."

"And DEFINITELY boys who still think she can't speak for herself."

I flashed a smile on-and-off. Luke clearly wanted to launch off on one at me, but didn't want to risk his chill around this hottie.

"Sorry, er, Ska." I always felt uncomfortable calling people I hardly knew by names meant for people who knew them much better. "He makes it too easy. What *do* you watch?"

Her annoyed glare thawed into indifference. Progress.

"Luke means I model watches. Not I watch models." Ah, that *did* make more sense. She leaned a tiny bit away from Luke. "What was your name again?"

"Bella," I replied, at the exact moment Luke said, "Blobfish."

She ignored him. "Nice to meet you, Bella."

Luke dropped his arm from around her. She didn't

even acknowledge it. He really had met his match.

"And you!" My eyebrows accidentally shot up in surprise at how believable my lie sounded. "But I shall leave you guys to it. . . Seeya!"

I smiled and started to walk home, feeling surprisingly happy: yup, even though my ex's new girlf was a model, I'd been a model citizen. Which was way more important. And that however I felt about Luke, I hadn't lived up to his guaranteed negative hype in front of her.

But best of all he'd helped me. Because the next Radio Shire dilemma was going to be about exes, and his attempt to humiliate me had backfired. So with a tiny bit more confidence than I'd had before, I cranked up my headphones, tried to forget what had happened with Adam, and model-strutted to the Helicans (complete with sassy wrist-model wave) all the way home.

CHAPTER

SEVEN

The end of the summer holidays is meant to feel like a wind down. But this final Sunday/pre-Monday felt like the biggest day of the last seven weeks.

After two nights of replaying my evening with Adam, and the double whammy of the competition tonight/ going back to school tomorrow now imminent, I'd come to some big decisions.

1) I had to do everything I could to win this gig (or I'd be a social outcast for ever).
2) I had to do everything I could to see Adam again just to check he did only see me as a friend (or I'd socially outcast myself for ever).
3) I had to reinvent myself for the return to

school (because I already am a social outcast there).

I'd been trying to keep calm about tonight's Radio Shire competition, but right now social media was a terrifying place. EVERYONE was talking about what was going to happen. Could someone turn the internet off? Just for a bit?

Tomorrow it would be the same but IRL. The only way I was going to cope with the attention was as Shay suggested – by looking "total fire". She'd said I needed a "high impact, on-trend" look (clearly forgetting the limitations of a brown uniform and no make-up rule). Together we'd looked through magazines and found the perfect shorter, ombre bob. YAS. I could DO this!

Or not.

Cos Mum immediately said she wasn't paying for a haircut when we had scissors at home (and I still remembered how Jo skipped college for a week when Mum trimmed her fringe).

On a more positive note, after popping to Tegan's last night to run through Adam's Friday weirdness she'd given me back a flicker of hope. Despite having her feet touching her head she managed to remind me that if Mikey had given up at the first friend-word hurdle (wordle) they'd never have got together. She said that if I really liked Adam, I had to hang in there till I knew how he really felt. Cos what if he meant friend *for now*? I owed it to myself to find out. She'd then played her trump card – saying I owed it to *her*, cos she didn't want to have spent all summer listening to every minute detail about him for nothing. She wasn't complaining – she never did – she was just being extra wise knowing I'd be more likely to do something for her than I would for myself. So I'd promised her I'd suggest one more hanging-out to him (I'd banned the word "date" from all communications. We'd even had to rebrand the fruit to "mutant raisin").

But right now I had to defocus on boy/inanimate foodstuff stress, and get back to life stress. The second round of the competition was less than an hour away, and nerves were making me do weird things; for the first time in my life I was running early. Even after Shay had French-plaited my hair, I still had twenty minutes before I needed to set off to Rachel's. I messaged Jo to see if she was online. Truly desperate times. She'd just got home from work, and was good to go.

I climbed under my duvet. Everything always felt better in bed.

Now Jo's friends were heading back for term, she was

loving uni life again. And in between winning her last running meet (she was vibed it meant she'd got a place on some tour) and slug-relocating, she'd spent her time sending me vids of dogs heavy breathing, and generally lifting my spirits. It was weird how much better we got on when we didn't have to live together (and she wasn't around to know that I *may* have accidentally finished her glitter nail varnish).

ME: What news?

JO: I officially just attended and survived the greatest house party ever thrown.

ME: What was that bang?? OH, JUST THE CLANG OF YOUR HUMBLEBRAG.

JO: Loser.

ME: OK. Enough pleasantries.

JO: You haven't even said hello?!

ME: Hello.

JO: Goodbye.

ME: Shut up.

JO: . . .

ME: I NEED ADVICE.

Yup, my decision to deprioritize Adam over-analysis had officially lasted less than two minutes. I really needed to prioritize getting better at prioritizing.

JO: Has your head finally got stuck up Shay's 🍑

ME: Not funny.

JO: Wasn't joking.

ME: JEALOUS.

JO: That she has to live with you? Yeah. Much.

JO: 🥔

ME: Stop sending vegetables and HELP ME.

JO:

ME: Oi. It's BOT STUFF.

JO: DO NOT WANT BUM RASH PICS. NOT AGAIN.

ME: BOY. BOY STUFF.

JO: Oh.

ME: I need to ask someone out.

JO: WHAT?

ME: Not *out* out. (It was so much easier to lie over typing) Just out to DO something with me.

JO: Like what?

ME: Dunno. Definitely not a Phoenix Dactylifera though.

There was a pause as Jo googled. It wasn't my fault she didn't know the Latin name for the mutant raisin.

JO: Good to know you're still weird. So if it's not a DATE what are you going to do?

ME: Oi! Do not use that word?!

JO: It could be a DATE to build a Shay shrine?

ME: Still not laughing.

JO: So what's the prob?

ME: What do I say?

JO: Will you go out with me?

ME: BUT THEN IT SOUNDS LIKE I WANT TO GO OUT OUT WITH HIM.

JO: You do.

ME: ...

JO: It's MIAGTM right?

Jo had lived through the years of me only knowing

Adam as Man I Am Going To Marry. I was more optimistic about our chances in those days. Probs cos he hadn't met me.

> ME: Yeah. But I don't think he likes me in THAT way. And I kinda asked once. And he kinda already said no.

> JO: Kinda isn't definitely. So don't be a loser. JUST ASK!

I think I knew that she was going to say that. I think that's why I asked her.

> JO: I'M GIVING YOU FIVE MINS TO DO IT OR I POST THAT PIC OF YOU WHEN YOU GOT THAT RICE KRISPIE CAKE STUCK ROUND YOUR MOUTH AND PRETENDED YOU WERE A VICTORIAN PAUPER WITH MOUTH SYPHILIS.

> JO: AND YES, I DO STILL KNOW YOUR INSTA LOGIN.

No – she only knew my parent-friendly account

login, but that was bad enough.

ME: YOU WOULDN'T

JO: Try me.

JO: Evil cackle.

JO: And screenshot or it didn't happen.

Was she SERIOUSLY serious?

JO: 270 seconds.

OH MY DISEASED HISTORICAL MOUTH. She was.

I grabbed my phone and opened Notes.

Oh hai! Want to hang out Saturday?

WHAT WAS I?! The annoying star of an American teen drama?

Saturday. Free? You and me? Some fun?

DELETE!!! It sounded like a dodgy webcam ad.

JO: 155 seconds.

JO: Oh – and good luck tonight.

Unexpected nicety.

JO: Mum tells me the entire town is going berserk over the competition, and if you don't get St Mary's through she's going to rent your room out too.

Ah. The comfort of the familiar had returned.

ME: Stop trying to distract me. I know your game.

JO: 122 seconds.

I returned grimly to my phone.

Hi Adam. Hope you're guuuuud. You free on Saturday?

The pic of my fake mouth pustules popped up on my laptop screen. Jo had already tracked it down. She was the Usain Bolt of the embarrassing photo finding world.

JO: 80 seconds.

ME: SSSSSSSSSSSSSSSSSSSSSSSHHHHHHHHH

I had another attempt.

I had a lot of fun not seeing a film with you.
Wanna not see another one with me on
Saturday?

No. Anything that sounded like it should end with a winky face was not good enough for this sitch. I needed more casual. More not-datey.

JO: What've you got?

ME: A dictator of a sister?

JO: 👄

I stared at my screen. None of the words seemed

right. None of them seemed to say, "Don't freak out, but I really like you. And would like to see you more, just in case you like me in any sort of more-than-friends way, although no pressure if you don't, but I owe it to Tegan to be doubly sure." Which was a good thing, as he'd sue me for crimes against lame-ness. (I'd deleted my fourth attempt which just said "LOOOVVVVEEEEEEEE MEEEEEEEEEEEEEEEEEEEEEEEEEEEEEE" just in case my phone ever fell into the wrong hands. Or just my own hands, which had an equally risky track record).

JO: ⏱

JO: 40 seconds.

I wasted ten more seconds finding a reply.

ME: 🌳

Jo sent me an even more zoomed-in photo of my mouth. DAMN HER AND HER REIGN OF VIRTUAL TERROR.

I *had* to send something. I chose option three.

THIS WAS TERRIFYING.

Shaking, I pressed send.

And immediately realized the only thing scarier than sending a question like this was the horror of waiting for a reply. And who knew *when* this was going to end? Damn my sister and her "just ask him" ways.

My fingers were trembling so much it took three attempts to get the screenshot. But when I did, Jo replied with ten hand claps and disappeared offline.

I was still a bit leg wobbly by the time I dashed out to Rachel's, not helped by having to sprint-walk the whole way as I'd managed to make myself late. By the time I got to her front door, I was sweating like when Mum makes me do hot yoga in the lounge (she doesn't like wasting money turning up the heating, so forces me to wear woollen accessories instead – though scarves are banned after I almost garrotted myself during warrior pose). I rang Rach's doorbell, wiped off as much face-sweat as I could, and willed it to be her who answered (or anyone other than Hot Older Brother).

The door opened.

It was HOB.

Yelling hello so he didn't have time to fully survey the disaster that was my face, I scurried into Rach's bedroom (no knocking needed) and leapt beside her on to her mega beanbag, causing her to drop her battered copy of *The Goblet of Fire* she was reading.

I loved being in her room. It was the size of the whole of the upstairs of our house and had a range of seating (not just bed or floor). And where there weren't shelves of books on the walls, there was actual art.

But we weren't staying inside. It was one of those weirdly warm, late-summer evenings, and she'd already set up a massive cushion camp in her garden. We hurried out and I carefully positioned myself to get an excellent line of sight of HOB and his boyf who were in the hammocks at the far end of the garden.

As Rach shuffled on her beanbag (this was an outdoor AND indoor beanbag kind of house) I spotted her nails. She'd had them done pastel.

"Nice. . . And totally coincidentally just the same as Modger's?"

She waggled her fingers at me. "Tooootally coincidental."

Yeah, right – Rach and Shay had been sub-posting each other all week, all up in each other's comments. It probs helped that Rach was just as effortlessly stylish, and even more beautiful. But right now she looked sad.

"You know it's just us tonight?" I didn't. "Teeg got a last-minute all-day training session booked in."

"Way to spend your last night of freedom."

"I know." Rach scrunched her mouth up like she was chewing on a bad thought. "She's *really* freaking out about this try-out. She's convinced that she won't get a place – and that'll be her only chance for the national team gone. Mikey had a day of fun planned for them and everything – all cancelled last minute."

"Lucky he's Patron Saint of Understanding Boyfs." I was joking, but it was met with silence. Maybe Rach was thinking the same as me – that Tegan just wasn't herself these days. It really wasn't like her to cancel on her friends. Again.

But we understood. We'd known her for long enough to know how much she wanted to get a place on the training camp. So if Rach wasn't going to bring up Tegan's recent personality transplant, I certainly wasn't either.

"Shay says hi, btw."

Rach fluttered her eyes like she was being slightly electrocuted.

"Tell her hi back. And that new silver top she Snapchatted last night is," she kissed her fingers, "ICONIC." Weird that Rach knew more about the person who lived on the other side of a wall from me than I did.

"I'm sure the same one will end up in your wardrobe soon."

She threw a cushion at me, deliberately missing.

"Anyway. . ." I gave up on trying not to talk about my woes. Rach was my best friend. Unfiltered convo was our duty. "News. I'm only running at 10% thinkingness cos. . . OH GUESS WHAT – DESPITE WHAT HAPPENED ON FRIDAY I MESSAGED ADAM TO SORT OF ASK HIM BACK OUT AND HE HASN'T REPLIED AND I'M GOING TO BE SICK."

Rachel's already massive blue eyes doubled in size. Her face was a permanent meme waiting to happen.

"YEAH LIKE NO BIG DEAL EXCEPT MY LIFE IS JUST BUFFERING UNTIL HE REPLIES."

She fake-fainted, and then unfainted to see what I'd written. And was still zooming in and out of the screengrab of it saying "waaaaaah" when Jaz's ever-enthusiastic voice chimed over the radio.

It was time.

"So if everyone's set for round two?"

I couldn't help but "pah". If by "all set" she meant "so stressed I might have to go and have a quiet lie down for the next two-and-a-half years" then, yeah, sure.

"It's time to whittle ten down to five."

Rach held her phone out. "Bella, I don't know if this helps, but look. EVERYONE at school is totally fired up to start voting."

I looked at the stream of comments popping up on

every network – and wished I hadn't.

"It helps me want to bury myself in your extensive garden and spend my life living entirely in burrows."

Rach looked hurt. But it was Tegan who liked to rise to challenges. I liked to run from them. Still, I didn't want to upset Rach, so pulled my game face back on just in time for Jaz to hit us with the question.

"So here's today's big dilemma. Remember, these quessies are all to do with the band – and it's up to YOU at home to decide which top five answers make it through to the semi."

I was so nervous I didn't even vaguely snigger at the use of "semi".

My phone lit up. Tegan.

GOOD LUCK. MESSAGE ME AS SOON AS
YOU KNOW ANYTHING!!

Jaz started playing a thumping tension track – but it wasn't half as loud as the one running through my own body.

"So tonight's question is all about . . . Lis."

Rach held her fingers up in a heart shape and mouthed, "K-ween."

"As you know, she had a *much* publicized break-up

with the lead singer of Smashed Avocados." How she could ever have gone out with anyone who thought that was a good band name was the biggest horror to me.

"And we ALL saw what he said in the press." Rach snapped her hand-heart in two. "But these last weeks it's taken an EVEN MORE dramatic turn, as his new girlfriend's claimed he only ever went out with Lis to get his band noticed."

Jaz's studio crew group "oooh"-ed. I'd half-seen the stories, but had glossed over them, not wanting to give them the time of day. Tbh, I was kind of surprised Jaz had gone there, considering this whole comp was for fans of the band – and we were more into their music than slagging off their exes.

"So, in the next minute we want our finalists to answer this question: in one sentence only... If YOU were the Helicans' manager, what would YOU tell Lis to do? GO, GO, GO!"

Rach full-on huffed. "Eurgh. How dare they bring up Lis's love life – I bet she'd never agreed to it."

I was equally as annoyed. "And how dare they have made me speak to Luke for such a rubbish question?"

But regardless of our feelings about the question, we still wanted to win. Or more specifically, if I wanted to survive tomorrow/the rest of my life – I *needed* to win. I began to type.

"Hi, Jaz!!!"

(Rach: Three exclamation marks is too keeno.)

"Our."

(Rach: MY!!)

"... advice is IGNORE, IGNORE, IGNORE. In
fact ignore SO MUCH that you don't even listen
to this advice, cos you've already moved on ...
and have got back to making the next album."

(Rach: Nod of approval.)

It wasn't great, but it was the best I could do. So we
sent, and immediately began nerve-chomping our way
through an entire bag of Percy Pigs until Jaz read out
the entries. They were all kind of similar except the one
from James Owen Girls' School (JOGS) who said Lis
should *"dish the dirt on her ex and get more publicity than
he could have ever hoped for, cos it worked for me and
made my itsyergirlletty blog go viral."*

Totally gross answer – and weird that as a fan of the

band, she didn't get that Lis hated talking about her personal life. But the vote wasn't up to us (other than the eighty-three we sent between the two of us and Mikey). Ten minutes later, once the lines were closed, all we could do was wait. And eat crisps. Till the ever-perky Jaz was back to happily ruin someone's dream.

"So, guys, it's time to say bye to five of our finalists. Are you ready?"

Rach was holding my hand so tightly I could no longer feel fingers three or four.

"Let's count down from ten..."

But before Jaz started my phone buzzed. A sweaty Tegan popped up on screen, leaning against a bus stop.

"I MANAGED TO DUCK OUT EARLY." She was mega panting. "WHAT'S HAPPENED???"

"Putting you on speaker. About to find out."

I pressed speaker just as Jaz got to "seven".

Seven seconds can pass by at two speeds. The speed of your morning alarm clock (which makes you time-travel forward, it's so quick) or the speed of a YouTube ad (aka two days). This seven seconds felt so slow it was like every YouTube ad ever made in one continuous loop. But Jaz *finally* got to zero.

"So, without further ado," said Jaz, the QUEEN of a-doing, "today we're saying goodbye to ... St Mark's,

Worcester City, Blossom Park, St Christopher's, and one more . . ."

You could have heard a pin drop, if anyone carried pins, and we weren't on a lawn.

". . . Glyn Wood."

I couldn't tell who whooped more. Rach, me – or the phone. We were in the final five!

My phone pic went all blurry as despite being on a street, Tegan was waving her arms around in celebration, yelling, "You diiiiiiid it!!!!"

Rach was chanting, "We love Bella! We love Bella!"

HOB was chanting back, "We love peace and quiet."

I went horizontal, wibbling all of my limbs in the air. But I didn't care. We'd done it! We were through!

I could survive school tomorrow after all!

A message popped up over Tegan's face. Rach saw my Adam-radar beep.

"It's Mikey," she said, trying to soften my disappointment (I said a mental sorry to Mikey), before reading it out in her best Welsh accent.

I OWE YOU A PINT! (OF CHIPS). CONGRATS XX

A video message then came through of Mum singing,

"Simply The Best" by Tina Turner. She was doing an alarming sort of sexy-chicken-strut at the camera, while blowing kisses and saying, "So proud of my darling daughter! Living the dreams!"

When we switched back to Tegan she was squinting at the screen. "OK, I spy a foot. Are you doing your upturned ladybird, Bells?"

Rach tilted the camera towards me.

"You know me toooo weeelllll." There really weren't any flies on Tegan (which makes no sense, as people who aren't clever don't exactly coat themselves in honey, or pollen, or whatever it is flies like. Sexy other flies maybe?)

"*Sure* you two are OK?" A male voice interrupted. HOB. He looked at Rach doing her one-person Mexican wave, and at me, who looked like a sloth dangling from an imaginary branch, and shook his head and went inside, without waiting for an answer.

Normal abnormal behaviour resumed.

"Soz, just my brother being annoying." Rach handed me back my phone.

"No worries." Tegan looked behind her to check for the bus.

Woah. As she moved Rach and I spotted a Jaden Smith-alike behind her, leaning against the tree, looking all moody-filter. She got the best bus stop strangers. I only ever got old women.

Although – wait. Was he waving – in Tegan's direction?!

But as Tegan moved her phone, he disappeared from view.

"Better go anyway." Was it my imagination or did she suddenly sound shifty? "So see you tomorrow, at..."

Together we all wailed: "Schooooooool." And with the same gag-face we waved bye.

As soon as I put my phone down, it started vibrating like when I use my broken charger. Messages from randoms and notifications were coming in faster than I could read them. Eurgh. Tomorrow was going to be overwhelming.

"Turn off alerts." Rach pressed the power button making my screen black. "And listen!? Jaz is talking about the semi-final..."

"This next round is going to be from the fandom. That's right, Amil himself is going to pick one of YOUR dilemmas for the final five to answer... So if you've got a question, head to the thread on the thehelicans.com forum, and you could get your quessie on air! Maybe even bag some merch?!" The people in the studio whooped more than they should do about a message board.

"OK, Rach." I sat back up. "Here's a dilemma. Reckon *I* could send in a question asking for the best advice to help me survive this competition?"

She looked baffled. "Mind. Blown... Talking of which, did you finish up that maths homework?"

I shook my head. All the homework we'd been set roughly equalled the same amount as all the homework I hadn't done. Which equalled me now having to head home to ruin my own life.

But when I was back in my room, scribbling away, resenting that numbers had ever been invented (there's only ten of them, so how much can there *really* be to know?) something happened that rocketed straight into the Worst Thing To Happen Today hotspot.

Something so bad that I had to give up on finishing any of my homework, immediately crawl into bed (bra on, teeth unbrushed) and resign myself to getting a future yelling-at instead. Something so bad, I wasn't sure even the greatest minds in the world (aka Tegan, Rach and the internet) were ever going to be able to fix it.

It was Adam.

He'd replied. And he'd turned me down.

EiGHT

Monday morning went like this.

- LOUD NOISE!
- House fire! House fire!
- BRAIN THUD. The realization it's *my* alarm.
- But what ungodly hour is this?! There *must* be an error.
- Pillow on head. SOMEONE MAKE THAT NOISE STOP.
- Ewwww. Why does my mouth taste of dog breath?
- BRAIN THUD. The realization no one is going to make that noise stop for me.
- Put my hand out to hit phone. Phone falls

on floor. I now have to move entire body and open one eye.

- INTENSE SELF-LOATHING.
- Worst day ever and it's only one minute in.
- 6.55 a.m. 6.55 A.M.?!
- Tell me it's NOT the start of term?! Holidays have only just begun. Haven't they?!
- BRAIN THUD. The realization I set my alarm early to try and look decent for today (esp. critical as last night I'd discovered my skirt in my bag from when we'd had a sleepover at Teeg's on the last day of term. It smelt of swimming-pool changing room).
- Thinkofsomethinggood. Thinkofsomethinggood.
- Adam.
- THUD. The realization of last night's message.
- HE HATES ME.
- Pillow back on head.
- Searing light burning through my eyelids.
- "Bells, you're going to be late for schooooool."
- Prise one eye open to communicate to Mum that I blame her for this nightmare.
- "It's 8.30, and we need to leave in ten minutes."

- She lies! She lies! I pick up my phone. SHE TRUTHS!!
- Shouts of "WHY DID YOU LET ME SLEEP IN?"
- The world's quickest shower (not helped by losing three mins waiting for Shay to finish perfecting her eyeliner). (It did look increds, though.)
- As much dog-breath removing as possible.
- Spraying my crumpled uniform in body spray.
- Running to school with wet hair.
- Being the last to arrive in form room, making my entrance way more dramatic than I wanted.
- Everyone turning round to suss what dramatic appearance changes I'd achieved over the holidays. Only to realize I was the only person who'd managed a downgrade. And I smelt of changing rooms.

As soon as the register was done, the entire class rushed over to ask a million questions about the Helicans competition. Cue sitting on my desk while Tegan rubbed my back saying soothing things about it being lunchtime soon.

It didn't get any less full on as the day continued. Actual crowds gathered around me when I walked down the corridor. A group of Year Sevens did a Mexican wave when I walked by. Sean K – aka Boxer Boy – high-fived me (then checked his mate Luke hadn't seen. Luckily, Luke was too busy elbowing a small blond boy into the bin, loudly declaring that anyone who liked the Helicans should get a life.)

Like the amazing best friends/bouncers they are, Rachel and Tegan did their best to try and put themselves between me and all the questions.

It was a sign of the worrying times (we gotta get away from here) that the best parts of my day were lessons, cos at least when a teacher was talking, it meant no one else could be.

Still, at least there were small sections of the school who hadn't heard about my new-found fame. And places we could hide. So, at lunchtime, in a bid to finally get some peace, Rachel, Tegan, Mikey and I ditched our usual lunch spot, and went to eat in one of the language classrooms that were always empty. Except today it wasn't – Ava was there – which figured, as she seemed to hate every single person at school. Today had kicked off with rumours of her getting caught smoking in the disabled loos before first bell. Yawn. But she had headphones in and barely looked up from under her long hair.

I smiled anyway, in "I also want to be alone" solidarity. She blanked me and looked back at her magazine.

I plonked my tray down on a desk, and stabbed at my jacket potato like it was responsible for this sorry state of affairs.

"C'mon, Bells, it's not that bad." I was staring at my food so hard it took me a second to realize it wasn't the potato talking, it was Rach. But it was easy for her to say. She had a #lifegoals existence, and I currently had an elastic band in my hair a random postman had lent me.

Tegan reached out for my phone. "What did it say again?"

I slid it across the table – Mikey stopping it just before it flopped off.

"'Aloha, Dave.' *Dave?!?*" Mikey read out, repeating "Dave" for good measure. I shrugged as I couldn't be bothered to explain, and mouthed along dejectedly with the rest of it (seven words, zero hope).

"Sorry, can't do this weekend. Long story. . ."

But the misery hadn't stopped there. He'd followed up.

"Molly and I are heading to HillFest on Friday if you want to join?"

My heart had sunk so much it'd plummeted straight through the middle of the Earth and plopped out in Australia, probably on someone's BBQ.

He might as well have messaged, *"THIS IS ANOTHER HINT BECAUSE I AM A NICE PERSON. WE ARE JUST FRIENDS."*

"Plus side." Tegan held up a finger as if going to count all the ways this wasn't rubbish. "He replied."

"Teeg, even our dentist surgery replies to texts." She ignored me, not humouring my fun-sponging.

But Tegan was on a mission, and my protests were no obstacle.

"Two – there's a 'long story'. It wasn't a flat-out no." If Tegan was having a hard time positively spinning this, I really *was* in trouble. I huffed.

"Is the long story that he's having a commitment ceremony with Molly, who's probably his mega-hot girlfriend that he's had all along, but they're one of those couples that are so in love they hang out with friends all the time and so he assumed I knew?"

Mikey coughed, reminding us he was here. And was *that* person.

"Sorry, Mikey." I stabbed my potato again.

I'd spent all night racking my brains. I *had* heard Adam mention Molly before, but it was in a story about a terrible car journey, and I was too distracted thinking about how he even made stories about traffic seem interesting (I assumed, as wasn't listening to the actual details). Why was I such an idiot? He'd been trying to tell me all along.

"So *are* you going to HillFest?" Mikey asked innocently as if it was a reasonable thing to ask in the circumstances.

"Er, NO?! I took the hint. With grace and dignity." Well technically I'd replied to say, "Thanks, but no thanks," then spent thirty minutes yelling "Whhhhhhhyyyyyyy" into my pillow. And googling Adam and Molly like I was going to find a Wiki on their relationship to date.

I flopped my head on to the table, hitting it way harder than I meant to. May have to add potential loss of brain function to "Reasons today is terrible". "It's fine, guys, it's fine. I GET it. The only guy I've ever really liked is into someone else. And I'm destined to a life of single beds and getting stuck in dresses cos there's no one there to undo the zip, but at least I can legit have Pot Noodles for dinner every night of my adult life."

Tegan put her hands on my shoulders and pulled me back up. Mikey was staring at me with genuine concern.

"Bells, c'mon. It might not be as bad as you think."

"Please tell me what on earth could be worse?" I took a dramatic sip of my Ribena, which made a satisfying gurgle.

Mikey thought. "His long story is that he's also dating your sister?"

Rach nodded, impressed. "Or that he's dying to go out with your mum? Or just dying?"

"Orrrrr," Tegan interrupted, "how about . . . instead of listing really terrible things to cheer Bella up, we talk about something happy. . ." She pushed an open packet of Skips my way. I *so* wanted to eat them, but didn't want to look as if I'd moved on.

I accidentally stuffed two in my mouth.

"Don't think I'm over this. I just like crisps."

But Tegan was determined to cheer me up.

"So – what GOOD stuff *have* we got?" She held a finger out. "We're already half a school day down this term which leaves," she looked up as her brain calculator whirred, "ninety-nine and a half days until Christmas."

"I thought we were meant to be cheering her up?!" Mikey laughed.

Rach lifted up another of Tegan's fingers. "OK. What about the fact that Tesco Matt Healy exists?" She *hhmmmmmed* – the official noise of barrel scraping. "Orrrr, the fact that everyone here thinks Bella is AMAZING, and cos of her, the actual Helicans might be playing in this actual school vicinity?! For our real-life eyes?!"

Fair play. Maybe this one was a tiny bit OK. In the safety of my friend bubble (frubble) I let my mind wander to what *could* happen if we won.

Where would they play? Outside on the football pitch? Or in the canteen? Everyone leaping about as Lis rocked out on the tables (must warn her the squashed baked beans that never got cleaned up were a serious slip-hazard).

And *what* would they play?

Would we get a half-day? Be able to wear non-uniform?

Oh man. Would I have to go up and say something?!

My heart sped up just thinking about it.

But I mustn't get carried away. The worlds of the Helicans and St Mary's were so polar opposite it surely wasn't physically possible for them to coexist?

The most dramatic thing that had ever happened here was last term when Sean K was trying to stop a fight Luke was involved in – Sean kicked out, somehow dislodging a pair of old boxer shorts that must have been stuck down one of the legs of his trousers, and they flew across the canteen, landing on a tray of macaroni cheese. He's been known as Boxer Boy ever since.

And the Helicans were deffo better than that. Lis's eyeliner alone was going to contravene at least four school rules.

"Bumface. Serious BUMFACE." Tegan's almost-swear snapped me out of my something-going-right-for-a-change daydream. She was glaring at her phone. "They've put in *another* gymnastics session." She shoved it back in her bag, muttering, "As if ALL evening on Friday wasn't enough."

Mikey put his arm gently round her and lowered his voice to talk privately. But Rach and I could still hear (maybe because we instinctively leaned nearer to listen in. Teeg would only tell us later, so technically it was just time saving).

"Please don't push yourself too hard, T. You've worked so hard already. You're amazing as you are."

I totally agreed – and was so glad he was looking out for her too. The try-out was still two weekends away, and she was already exhausted.

But Tegan shook her head stubbornly, her mind already made up. "No, no, I HAVE to. Whatever it takes. You haven't seen my valdez. If I even want to *think* about getting a place, it needs *serious* work."

Mikey gave her another squeeze. "I'm sure if any of us had a *clue* what that meant, we would tell you it's already excellent."

Tegan looked up at me and Rachel eavesdropping, which I figured was the green-light to joining in.

"I'd also say, 'be careful' cos it sounds all sorts of painful." I was joking. But inside I wasn't laughing, cos I wanted to say more. I was worried about her. But underachieving me wasn't exactly the life guru anyone needed, let alone someone as on it as Tegan. I had to choose my words carefully. "Seriously, Teeg, like Mikey said, you've done soooo much already. And not just these last months, *all* the years. So, er, please don't overdo it now?"

"*Overdo it?*" Tegan's eyes narrowed like she couldn't believe what had come out of my mouth. "When it's what I've worked my whole life for?! Yeah, *course*."

WOAH. Well, that backfired.

But as quickly as Tegan's anger flared up, it disappeared. She put her hand on my arm. "Sorry, Bells, I just. . ." She looked down at the desk. "I know what I'm doing, OK?"

I nodded, and said, "Sure," although I didn't think I was.

Checking she was OK was cut short by an unexpected person. Ava.

"Yeah. So. I thought you should know that Luke's telling everyone it was basically him that got this dive through last night's round."

Well that was one way to start a conversation.

"Er, hello to you too?"

I was more surprised she was speaking to us, or even speaking at all, than I was about Luke being an idiot. I was even-even more surprised when I spotted a Helicans T-shirt under Ava's regulation school shirt. Who knew she was a fan?!

"He says you're still not over him, and based your answer on him blanking you."

I *think* Ava expected me to be shocked. But instead I laughed. At Luke's total patheticness. One minute I'm too lame to be associated with, next he's trying to get some glory through being my ex.

"He's such a douche."

Ava nodded. "Agreed ... just thought you should know."

"Well, thanks – I guess?"

But I had a good idea why Ava was suddenly on Team Bella (considering she'd never even returned an "er, hi" before).

She side-eyed me.

"I'm not being one of those people that's only speaking to you cos of the Radio Shire thing. . . If that's what you're thinking."

I said "noooooooo" with hopefully enough enthusiasm to cover that I'd been thinking "yesssssss".

She grimaced. I think. It might have been an attempt at a smile.

"I've just had a summer of Luke trolling every post I've done about the competition. So I'm not exactly his biggest fan." She swung her bag over her shoulder. "Anyway, see ya – and good luck, I guess."

I didn't know if she meant with Luke or the comp. Mikey then remembered he was meant to be meeting up with his best mate Jay and dashed out in the same direction.

Rach was first to acknowledge what'd just happened. "Intense."

"Kinda. Still – good to know we've got someone on our side." Tegan snapped her lunchbox closed. Her trainer had put her on a weird protein diet thing so she was off the school's beige-food options for the next ten days.

"How you feeling about Puke, Bells?"

We'd been through this before. It was old ground.

"After last term? Not wasting a single second on him." It felt good knowing I meant it. "And if I DO get knocked out at the next round... I'll just find a way of making him get the credit for that too!"

We set off to take our plates back to the canteen, laughing, which soon stopped as the gawping started again. I felt like a human goldfish. If my bowl was the school. And I had legs.

"Can someone change the subject?! Pleeease?" I hissed.

Rach's eyes lit up. "I've got a good one." She prodded Teeg. "Whoooo was that dude at the bus stop yesterday? Don't *think* we didn't see him?!"

But Tegan looked blank. "Who d'ya mean?"

"Who do I mean? Who do I meaaaan? The grey-tracksuit loiterer, that's who."

But Tegan wasn't even 1% smiling. Was she confused? Or ... annoyed?

Rach pushed the canteen door open for us. "C'mon, Teeg. Do I have to spell it out? The really fit guy. Dreads and shaved side. Six foot something. More brooding than Brooklyn Beckham?"

Tegan walked through, not making eye contact. "Oh, *him*? He's no one."

Rach snorted. "Errrr, a no one who could be on the cover of *Vogue*?!"

But Tegan still wasn't getting on board. "I told you. He's not important. And definitely not on *Vogue*?!"

At that exact awkward moment Mikey crashed back into our convo. "Oooh – who's gone rogue!?"

No one attempted an answer and Tegan swerved the convo with a detour to the water cooler. A totally oblivious Mikey then launched into a full story about how Jay had just asked him to be in a music video for his band. And he was all hyped until he realized his role was "background guy who can't skateboard".

I was happy to let him talk, cos I was trying to get my head around instalment two of Tegan's bad mood. And by the way Rach was so quiet, I guessed she was doing the same.

But by the time we'd all finished scraping our plates – and trying not to gag at the squashed up mound of mashed potato and custard heaped up over the top of the bin – I was ready to put the weirdness behind us.

"Soooo, you guys still free Wednesday night?"

"Give a Dog a Cone launch?" Tegan nodded. "Try and stop me."

Phew – the stand-off was over.

"And me." Mikey successfully threw his empty can into the bin that was two metres away, and celebrated like he'd scored a winning World Cup goal.

Rach blinked all innocently. "Me too – will Modger be there?"

I fake humphed. *Fumphed*.

"Probs, yeah. And *I will be too*. NOT THAT YOU CHECKED."

Rach blew me a shower of mini-kisses. "Maybe she'll give us more inside Helicans deets?!" A huge smile spread across her face. "Maaaaybe she's been messaging Lis about us?!"

"Errr, maybe." I didn't want to tell her that yesterday Shay had ranted about how tragic it was when people tried to chat to her about the famous people she worked with.

"In fact, I wanted to show her my potential outfit for the launch. I've been thinking of buying these AMAZING shoes. I've been lusting after them for MONTHS."

Tegan raised her eyebrows at Rach. "You say that like you haven't been SHARING your lust of these AMAZING shoes for MONTHS too. Do our opinions not count any more?!"

But she was teasing. Tegan mainly bought shoes that helped you leap around, and I went for anything that lessened the chances of me tripping over my own feet. Plus Shay was fluent in designer speak.

BANG.

The classroom door flew open and Mrs Hitchman, our headmistress, stormed in. Conversations came to a halt. Except for ours, as Mikey muttered, "What fresh hell is this?"

She'd missed assembly this morning, and it was reassuring to see the holiday hadn't altered even one hair on her head. She was still rocking the daily tweed two-piece (she had the same one in five colours. Probs in matching pyjamas too). (Although, brain – why are you using your free time to think about our headmistress in bed, you weirdo?)

"Good afternoon, everybody," she chirped. "I won't keep you." Lie – she is literally the one who keeps us here every day of our lives. "At three-thirty please make your way to the hall." She paused. "Understood?"

It would be a pretty bleak school if we didn't. It wasn't like she'd said it in French. Although *je ne sais pas* what the French is for "understood".

Despite zero answer, she gave a satisfied nod, and strode out to spread the bad news elsewhere. EURGH. Emergency assemblies were never a good thing – unless you enjoyed watching detentions getting dished out. I always felt nervous about them even though I didn't think I had anything to feel guilty for (except wishing the school would burn down for the last four years... Oh, and discovering/utilizing Jo's blackhead squeezer, but that would be a weird thing for a school to intervene with).

I felt on edge right through PE. We'd ended up staying late, as much to mine and Rach's regret, we persuaded Tegan to show us what a valdez was. Forget my limbs – even the stitches in my pants couldn't cope with one. By the time we dashed to the hall I was a sweaty mess. Of course the first person to spot me was Luke. I gave him my best evil. He gave me a one-handed wave. I gave him a fake big smile. He turned his hand wave into one finger up. I fake grinned even more. Which evolved into a real one as he looked around to check a teacher hadn't caught him. Such a bad boy. Bet Ska would be *really* impressed.

I dabbed a fresh layer of head sweat on to my sleeve as Mrs Hitchman took her place on the stage. She'd even had her lectern moved to the centre of it. This. Was. Serious.

"Some of you might know why I've gathered you together." The way everyone turned to look at Ava suggested they had an idea. Smokers *always* got called out in front of the whole school. But Ava didn't move a single muscle – icy cool. "I'm not going to pretend it's good news."

Please, no – a school couldn't extend its opening hours, could it?!

Mrs Hitchman inhaled for the big moment. "It's EXCELLENT news!"

Hold up. What? Was she pointing a finger in my direction?!

"Our very own BELLA FISHER..."

WAS I MELTING OR IS THIS WHAT IT FEELS LIKE FOR 672 EYES TO BE ON YOU?

"Has got St Mary's ..."

Why hadn't I brushed my hair after PE?! Or maybe even all day?

"... through to the Radio Shire competition to win the 'mighty'..."

Yes, as if this couldn't get any more cringe she did air quotes.

"... Helicans to come and play right here – maybe in this very room!"

Forget having periods in sync; Tegan, Rach and I simul-gulped.

All tiny hopes of having anywhere to hide, or any students not know about the comp, about *me*, had just been annihilated.

Thanks a lot, Mrs Hitchman.

Bursts of cheering broke out around the room. Did

no one realize I hadn't won yet?!

MEMO TO ALL TEACHERS: the phrase "manage expectations" can be quite useful.

Mrs Hitchman was now doing weird double-handed fist pumps, like she was trying to contain them, but they kept popping out. "So let's all give Bella, our STAR PUPIL, the huge round of applause she deserves!"

Everyone – except Luke who looked like he was chewing on egg-flavoured bubble gum – roared like the Helicans were arriving in ten minutes and we never had to do lessons again.

Rach, Tegan and I looked at each other. None of us needed to say what we were thinking. We wouldn't have been able to hear over the hysteria anyway.

It was only day one of term and already I was totally out of my depth.

And if I didn't get this school through the next round, I might sink entirely.

CHAPTER

NINE

Making a discreet exit from school was somewhat harder when people kept yelling, "Look, there's that Helicans girl," wherever I went. The pointing didn't help either. I had to physically hide behind a hedge while Rach did up her shoe.

Was this how life was going to be until the semi-final on Sunday? Was there a five-day illness I could contract?

But right in the middle of one particularly alarming heckle ("Don't mess this up, cos we know what you look like", to which I was so startled I replied, "Thank you"), like some sort of guardian angel with wheels, a car beeped. The driver wound down the window and leaned over. Only one person could look that good sideways. Shay.

"Need a lift?"

Without having to be asked twice, we piled in, me getting automatic front-seat privileges. So *this* is what new car smells like?!

Rach was all bouncy and excited like when a dog goes for a car ride. "Thanks so much for the lift, Mod—" I turned and shot her a look. "Shay."

Shay winked at her via the rear-view mirror. "No probs – you wanna choose the music?" Rach nodded double speed. She was one tongue muscle away from panting.

Tegan and I exchanged a secret smile at seeing her happy again, because in amongst everything today, at first break we'd caught Rach book-drowning her sorrows in the pages of Harry Potter. Mr Tucker had just set us a mega assignment on "What Makes A True Hero In A Classic Book?" which was hard enough already, but then had grabbed Rach after to tell her he was "disappointed with her standard" last term – and that if she didn't nail this essay he might put her down a set. And for someone whose bedroom was basically a library, it had hit her hard.

But the car had already made it feel like lesson drama was a million miles (as opposed to the actual 134 metres) away as Rach hooked her phone up to the network "Sounds of Shay", cranked up the Helicans and we began our escape home. Shay even put on the heated front seat (I only realized when I thought I'd weed myself).

When we hit a red at the traffic lights, Rach thrust her phone in front of Modger.

"Shay – can I ask for an opinion, please?" She didn't wait for a reply. "What do you think about these? I might get them for the Give a Dog A Cone launch?"

Shay looked down at the pic of the Wonder Shoes™.

"I maaaaay have already reserved the last pair in store?!"

But Shay just shrugged. "Yeah. Nice, I guess. Like, coral is a great colour for summer, but we're coming into autumn/winter now, y'know." She took another quick look at the shoes before the lights changed. "And they're kind of . . . I dunno . . . basic."

Rach snatched her phone back, mortified. "Oh yeah, yeah. Totally. That's why I wanted a second opinion." She looked out of the window. "I wasn't sure about them anyway."

Tegan and I caught each other's eye. Poor Rach.

"Well I think they'd look amazing on you," Tegan said loudly, giving me the impression she was making the point more to Shay than to Rach. But Shay had zero idea how much her opinion mattered to our friend.

Despite going the long way back (everyone understood we couldn't go the normal way in case we drove past Adam, or even worse Adam and Molly), Rach was still quiet when we pulled up outside her house. Ten minutes later it was Tegan's turn to head to training, leaving me alone with Shay.

Shay hadn't noticed Rach's change of mood, and as we set off towards our house she was nothing but smiles. "So, rockstar, I didn't see you properly to say congrats last night."

"Awww, thanks." It was a bit embarrassing that this was as near as I could ever get to being as cool as her.

"I maaay have voted at least twenty times . . . on the landline." She bit her lip. "Don't tell your mum!"

As if. But had Shay brought the comp up for a reason? She *had* said she'd get in touch with the band, put in a good word for us if we got through. And that would *deffo* bring back Rach's good mood.

I waited.

This *could* be the Best News Ever.

Shay did the longest breath in. Moment of truth?!

"Really MUST get the air-con cleaned in here."

Or not. Cringed out by my optimism, I moved the convo on.

"Soooo, how's life Chez Fisher?"

Shay shrugged. "Good. Good. You guys are great."

I *would* bask in the compliment, but I could tell there was a "but" coming.

"But, I really want to have a word with your mum about downstairs – it's so. . . I dunno? Cluttered." I pictured the scene. I guess it was a *bit* crowded, but Mum was the kind of person that could watch a show about extreme hoarders and consider them lightweights. "I mean, does she even know the words 'interior' and 'design'?"

Now was not the time to share that when Mum first saw Rach's top-of-the-range, all metal and white designer kitchen she said it looked like a morgue.

"Stick with it. With us. It'll be way better once all the Give a Dog A Cone boxes empty out." Shay "Ummm"-ed unconvincingly. "Don't suppose Mum's told you much about what's happening with the launch party?"

"Only what she said at dinner last night."

I made an of-course "ahhhhh". Yes, I'd technically been there in body, but my mind had been occupied staring at my phone, waiting for Adam to reply. And there wasn't an "ahhhh" for that.

"So happy she went with my design guys." Shay looked pleased with herself. "Seriously – the new signs and labels look SO cool."

143

"They should be if they're for ice cream."

Shay laughed. I MADE SHAY LAUGH. Must let the WhatsApp group know this development. But looking at my phone meant thinking about Adam's messages again.

"Don't suppose I could pick your brains for boy advice?" The words left my mouth before I even knew they were there. "Asking for a friend."

Shay did a throaty laugh. "You are looking at the Queen of boy drams."

Technically not true – I was looking in the mirror to see if I had any leftover Skips stuck in my teeth.

"What's up? For your *friend*?"

But I didn't really know why I'd asked. Cos no advice could make him magically start liking me – or go back to the start of the summer when I thought we had a chance.

"AhhhIdunno. Nothing really." I paused. "Or everything." I humphed. "Oh who knows?"

"Well, you can always talk to me. My lips are sealed." I smiled, happy that Modger was Team Me. She didn't even do that Jo-thing of asking a million questions I didn't want to answer either. Shay puckered her mouth. "And they are also *rocking* my new burnt orange lipstick, if I do say so myself."

Suddenly, she swore at a little blue car blocking her normal spot on the driveway.

I knew EXACTLY who it was.

With a garbled, "Thanks for the lift," I jumped out and ran towards the house. I got to the door just as she opened it.

"Fancy seeing you here." The visitor leaned on the doorframe, still in her coat. She must have only just arrived too. She looked me up and down. "As I suspected, your tiny peahead hasn't got any more normal and less peahead in size since I've been away."

I swung my bag into her leg. But we were both grinning. My sister was home. This warranted a hug.

Just a quick one.

After stepping back, Jo waved at Shay, shouting a loud, "Hiya," before whispering at me, "So *this* is who all the fuss is about."

I hissed back. "You WAIT till you see that burnt orange lippy up close."

"Isn't burnt orange technically just black?" She snapped back almost without moving her mouth. Was ventriloquism one of her uni modules?

Shay walked up the drive, and put her hand out. I raised my eyebrows at Jo. If they could talk they'd be saying, "Told you so," as my sister did a double take at the metallic gold nails that were in front of her. Yup, she was finally understanding this human was next level.

"Shay." Modger straightened up, flashing a smile so wide you could almost hear a "ding". In heels she was nearly the same height as Jo on the step. "It symbolizes majesty."

"I see." Jo shook her hand firmly back, her clipped nails looking like the before to Shay's after. "I'm Jo." I really hoped she wasn't going to pull the genetics>rent power play ". . . and *I* symbolize the better half of the two Fisher offspring."

Shay laughed.

I couldn't help but say, "Oi." This wasn't how it was meant to work? I thought Jo was going to hate Shay after all of her virtual eye-rolls whenever I mentioned her. Which meant I could guilt-free trade Shay in for Jo, not be the victim in their double gang up.

Still, Jo wouldn't be so pally when she saw Shay's stuff in her room – and throughout the whole house. I flung my bag down and headed for the living room – only to discover it was even more full of Give A Dog A Cone (GADAC) boxes. The only visible bit of floor space was full of Mum, who in her green hippy dress, bits of wire, Sellotape and thread handing off every inch, looked like a human Christmas tree. Suddenly its branches lunged towards me, as she exploited the 0.003 seconds of me standing in shock to seize an unauthorized cuddle. (This affection outburst had happened multiple times since I'd got through to the semi-final. This morning she'd sent me four messages saying how proud she was – and one saying, "I had another one of THOSE Harrison Ford dreams last night," but I think that was meant for Brenda. Shudder.)

Jo whistled as she followed me into the room.

"Mum – this looks terrific." Who says *terrific*?! "Even better than the photos." Yup, I'd been keeping Jo updated.

"You think?" Mum sounded kind of shy.

"I KNOW. Who knew you were the next Karren Brady? Can't WAIT to see it all in action."

"Well, it's all for my girls." "Girls" was normally what Mum called her boobs, but as she put her arms round me and Jo, I had to hope this time it was a daughter reference. "The start of the Fisher empire."

I put my hand on hers. "I'm down for ANY empire that is built on ice cream. Oh, and did I tell you Rach, Tegan AND Mikey will be at the launch too?"

Mum replied with a "great" but her body language tensed.

"Everything OK?" Jo had noticed too.

"Always OK." But Mum paused longer that she should if she wanted us to believe her. "But . . . it will be even more OK once it's all gone smoothly. Did I tell you the local newspaper is coming? AND Shay's signed up ten of her 'industry' people – whatever that means? And an influential!"

As Mum still truly called Instagram "Instagran", I wasn't even going to begin to explain influencers.

I caught Jo flinching at Mum's Shay-compliment. So it *was* still getting to her? But as my big sister was a master of parental dark arts, Mum didn't clock it, and just caught Jo's sweet smile at the end. "Well just let me know what I can do to help. I'm all yours."

"Oh, thank you, love. So happy to have you back." Mum kissed Jo's cheek confirming the instant dethroning of me from my temporary – and only – time in the Number One Daughter spot. Well played, big sister, well played.

The three of us then spent the rest of the evening opening boxes of cardboard, sticking the new labels on the tubs (the new GADAC font *did* look sick) and loading up crates. Mum flipped between nervous singing and outbursts of, "I can't believe this is really happening!"

Shay stayed in the safety of the kitchen, rustling us up a meal. Jo was less than impressed when it turned out to be squashed-up juice pulp made into sausage shapes, with a side of bone broth. Shay was less than less impressed when Jo then rang for a Domino's.

But this was only the start of the hard work. And the following morning AND evening it was still all hands on deck. Shamefully, it was actually a relief to have something, anything, to distract me from the horror of being so popular at school. After Mrs Hitchman's official announcement everyone was acting like the comp was no big deal. They were acting like it was a bigger deal than the invention of the brick. As I stuck on labels, and folded boxes, I couldn't work out if I was in a massive hurry for Sunday's round to be over, or too scared for it to ever begin. I couldn't even chat to Tegan about it, as she was training again, and Rach was making a start on that essay. BLEURGH.

Still, chin up, Bella. At least all this helping was earning serious Mum points. I'd even let Jo do my daily Mumbles walk this evening. In reality this wasn't me trying to give Mum more of my time. It was because I'd entered a new stage of dealing with Adam's rejection: avoiding him at all costs. I was going to such detailed lengths I was technically an anti-stalker. I'd even had to duck behind a car at one point. On the plus side Rach, Tegan and I had all drawn internet blanks on who

Molly was, so at least I couldn't waste my spare time staring moist-eyed at every picture of her ever posted. Instead I was focusing on working hard for Mum. And it was exhausting. So when all the final prep was done, I headed straight to bed. Jo came up not long after. Having her home meant sharing my bed. She walked in and surveyed the piles of clothes.

"Nice floordrobe."

I smiled lovingly.

"Nice nightie." I pulled it out from under the pillow and threw it in her direction. Shay hadn't been able to remember where she'd packed away Jo's pyjamas, so she was begrudgingly borrowing mine. She normally wore stylish check ones, so I'd taken great pleasure lending her my nightie with a giant pug face on.

After what felt like hours in the bathroom, Jo finally climbed into bed, adopting the universally agreed sleep position – back to back with the obligatory minimum twenty-five centimetre gap. I flicked the light off. Lying next to someone in the dark there were two options. Wait to relax until you heard the other person start heavy sleep-breathing. Or chat.

Jo went for option two.

"Do you think the launch tomorrow's going to be OK?"

"It *has* to be."

"Fair point... Are ... are you picking your toenail?"

"Maybe."

"So gross."

"Go share with Shay then."

"Too dangerous. She probably sleeps in heels."

Jo's Modger enthusiasm had dwindled over the last twenty-four hours. I was quite enjoying having someone wind her up almost as much as I did.

"Why'd you come back, anyway?" That sounded like I was annoyed she had, which wasn't what I meant. "Although obvs it's *always* a total delight to see your face."

"Wanted to support Mum. And check up on my favourite sister."

"*Only* sister."

"Semantics. Plus I need the shop to go well for Mum so she'll be more up for paying for my athletics tour."

"Can't you pay for it yourself?" I didn't mean to snap. But I knew despite all the scrimping we'd been doing at this end, Mum would probably still say yes. That's how it worked with Jo.

"Like you pay for your crisp habit?! A packet a day is like..." Jo muttered a calculation. "Sixty pence times three sixty-five is like ... two, hundred and ... two hundred and nineteen pounds a year!"

WOAH.

I never thought my love of Wotsits could push our family to the brink of financial ruin. I changed the subject quickly, and chatted about other important stuff, like the Helicans comp (and whether 3D printing was advanced enough to make a fake me I could send to school), Tegan's gymnastics try-out (Jo was always quite interested cos of her own love of competitive exercise), and whether flies call humans "walks". Jo then strayed from approved-convo and brought up Adam. I decided to be brave and pour my heart out in an attempt to feel better. But as I got stuck in, Jo started half-snoring. So instead of getting enough sleep, I ended up lying awake wondering how I always got everything so wrong.

Thanks a lot, Jo.

CHAPTER

TEN

As soon as I opened my eyes three thoughts hit me.

1) OMG. It's Give A Dog A Cone launch day.
2) OMG. I really hope I haven't overslept cos I was meant to be helping out before school.
3) OMG. Please don't let that be a new cheek spot I can feel.

I picked up my phone, my reflection in the screen confirming I didn't have a spot. I had two. And I'd overslept by half an hour. I jumped in the shower and pulled on the nearest bits of uniform I could find (while shouting at Jo that this is why floordrobes saved time).

By the time I got downstairs, prep for the evening

was fully underway. The final decorations were being loaded into the cars and Mum was ironing her dress at double speed, getting her full-on fret on. Apparently the sculptor of today's big centrepiece – a huge dog ice sculpture that Shay had said would be perfect for press to write about – had got stuck in traffic.

I made a joke about ice dogs dying in hot cars.

Jo shook her head to tell me this was unwise.

Mum looked like she might cry.

So I did the most reassuring thing I could think of, and made everyone toast and Marmite. I then realized the next best thing would probably be to offer some help, and carried out the last few boxes, before heading to school.

Although it was still terrifying being there (and I'd developed the nickname Helican Bellican) the excitement for Mum's big day got me through. I'd only told Tegan, Rach and Mikey about GADAC, but that didn't mean I wasn't proud. It just meant I wasn't necessarily ready for the world to join the dots between me, my mother, and innovation in dog puddings.

Right on time, Jo picked me up from school (with special guest, Mumbles, on the backseat). We had to have the windows down, it was such a scorching September day – excellent for ice cream demand. Thanks, sun. Jo let me jump out with Mumbles while she found a parking spot. And when I stepped round the corner and saw the shop for the first time, I couldn't help but gasp. It was suddenly SO REAL. All big and official – a freshly painted GIVE A DOG A CONE sign above the door. Sparkling clean windows and upright freezers stacked with shelves and shelves of stock.

I'd never had butterflies from a building before. Mum had done an amazing job.

I set foot inside as slowly as I could, trying to etch this first time in my memory. I was tempted to think it was a seminal moment, but I always worry I get the definition of that word wrong, and it's actually something to do with man fluid.

Mumbles trotted in behind me. I tugged her lead, trying to encourage her to symbolically strut, and mark the historical moment from a dog/consumer perspective. Sadly she totally missed the point and did a last-minute dive for some rubbish, walking in sideways, chewing on a plastic bag which then blew over her head.

Mum's face lit up when she saw us. She walked over and gave my hand a squeeze – neither of us needing words to say how cool this was. She looked around, smiling to herself. It was only a little room, but it was such a big dream for her.

It was a beautiful moment.

Which lasted 0.2 seconds until Jo burst in, and along with her came one-and-a-half hours of the most frantic:

- Lifting
- Unpacking
- Sweating
- Heaving
- Thinking there was a gas leak
- Realizing there was – and it came from our dog
- Almost crying at what was left to be done
- Actually crying when Shay's stiletto heel landed on my foot
- Making way too many jokes about feeling paw-ly
- Making even more about fetch-ing boxes
- And throwing in a final flurry of ones about being hounded by the press.

But it was worth it, as an hour before the grand opening, give or take final tweaks, it looked exactly as Mum had described it way back when she was planning the whole thing. And this was no mean feat (or "meatfeast" as Rach always said) as Mum had been aiming for "the world's biggest gold and glittery tribute to all things dog and ice cream". It was fit for the Queen's corgis (if they liked hanging out in eighties discos). The pièce de résistance was the box mounted in the middle. The sculpture. It had arrived in the nick of time. It may have cost a zillion pounds and caused Mum a mini heart attack but it was increds. The ice-dog looked totally lifelike (if dogs were see-through) and was so ginormous it made a Great Dane look like a Moderately Small-Sized Dane. It stood in a special freezer display box Mum had hired and was happily licking at a giant cone (with real GADAC ice cream, and dog choc flake in it!). It even had a leather collar around its neck in GADAC-logo green, and frozen flowers around its feet. It was paw-fect. So paw-fect people were already trying to take pics through the window. To keep the reveal for the big unveiling, Mum closed up the gold curtains she'd made, hiding it away. Shay was right: the press pics were going to look great.

I gave Mum a big double thumbs up. "Feeling good?"

She was deffo nervous as she kept doing blinks that were too big for her face and calling both Jo and I *Jella* (her combo daughter name she uses when she's distracted).

"How could I not be? You guys have been

WONDERFUL. And Brenda just sent me a video of her lighting a success candle for us. What more could I want?"

She pointed at my camera around my neck. "You still OK to be official photographer?"

I nodded. "And official social-media producer? Sure am."

Although my phone battery was *dangerously* low. With a shout of, "One sec," I dived behind the counter to charge both my camera and phone. Couldn't take any chances today. But Shay and her hair straighteners and iPads seemed to have taken every socket. I gestured to the problem. Shay was on her mobile, but pointed at her laptop plug. She looked kind of cross I had to switch it out, but I had a job to do.

When I turned back, Mum was still shaking her head, trying to take it all in.

"It's going to be *barking* mad having actual press down here..." She nudged Shay. "All thanks to this one." But Shay brushed her away, annoyed at being disturbed as she was talking. So it wasn't just me she was being mardy with. Must be important; the only words I could catch were, "red carpet" and "designer look". But it didn't matter cos Mum had started to get a hazy look in her eye.

"Imagine... Mary Fisher... My name in lights?!"

Now wasn't the time to point out newspapers tended to go with ink, rather than torches—

Oh.

My.

Frozen dog.

S.T.R.

SUDDEN. TERRIFYING. REALIZATION.

Press meant thousands of people reading about the business. Which was great. But it also meant thousands of people reading about my mum. Who was currently wearing dog-ears on her head. And was related to me.

"And er, just to check. Will you be using your real name?"

She gave me a weirded out look. And a "Yessssss" that went surprisingly high at the end.

"And your real, er, face?"

She slapped my bum for the second time in a minute.

"I'm going to pretend you didn't ask that, daughter who I fed from my actual breast for eight months."

Inward spew.

"Bells, move the conversation on before she starts talking about how her waters broke in a shoe shop," Jo shouted from behind the counter, where she was stretching to pin up some bone bunting.

This time it was Jo's turn to get a Shay glare, as an

annoyed Shay stepped outside to protect the poor ears of whoever she was speaking to.

"Sobacktotoday." The quicker I spoke, the more likely I could herd Mum on to a new topic. "Which flavour do you think's gonna be the top seller?"

I picked a tub up. It was colder than I thought (I clearly don't understand the concept of ice).

But before Mum could answer the room filled with "oooh"s (Rachel), "ahhh"s (Tegan), a "pretty dope" (Mikey) and some low-level growling (hopefully Mikey's sausage dog, Hamster). Like knights in shining armour/ battered trainers my friends had arrived to help. I grinned as they told Mum how amazing it all looked (Tegan, Rach and Mikey) and licking Mumbles' face (Hamster). I was pretty proud this was the kind of event that had a separate guest list just for dogs.

With only forty minutes left till the opening, they quickly joined in helping with the finishing touches, Jo leading the charge. Rach was assigned the role of chatting to anyone who stopped to look in, giving out bone-shaped flyers, and telling them what GADAC was all about. As she'd arrived with her outfit already on – tiny A-line skirt and tucked in baggy Helicans T-shirt – she headed straight outside to start.

The rest of us took turns to get changed in the tiny

loo. Jo had chosen a black shift dress and Doc Martens shoes, as she "didn't want to take any attention away from Mum". Shay obvs hadn't got that memo and had gone for a sequinned catsuit. Her selfie of it already had over three-hundred likes. Tegan looked her normal super-stylish self, wearing a yellowy-orange shirt dress I could never pull off, but that looked totally designer on her (as much as she complained throughout, Mikey took at least seven pics of just her cos she looked so great). On the flipside, Mikey had borrowed his dad's suit jacket so just looked like he'd shrunk.

Annoyingly, I'd forgotten to pack anything, so put on the dungarees Tegan had arrived in and brushed my hair a lot. I didn't even have time for make-up as I spent the final minutes trying to pick out a blob of bubblegum from Mumbles' teeth that she'd accidentally chomped on when chewing her way through a bin bag. It was a three-man job as whenever she huffed, she'd make tiny bubbles that freaked her out so much she fled across the floor. When Mikey got together with Tegan, I really don't think this was how he pictured spending their evenings. But the same could be said about when Tegan became friends with me. Thank goodness toddler Tegan didn't have better judgment.

When seven p.m. – the official opening time – ticked

round, Jo beckoned us all together. Pep-talk time. A silence filled the shop as we huddled together, arm over shoulder, like a weirdly dressed rugby team.

My sister cleared her throat. "Before we officially open, I just wanted to say – on behalf of Fam Fisher – a big thank you to all of you." Mum nodded, but also looked a bit like she might cry. I prodded Jo to hurry it along. "And may this evening be a HUGE success!" We all whooped. "So here's to Give a Dog a Cone..." (More yee-haw-ing), "and an amazing laugh night..." (more hell-yeah-ing), "and most importantly, MY MUM." Pardon, Jo? I coughed. "OUR MUM!"

With shouts and high-fives and hugs, my friends, Shay, my sister and I bundled Mum into the middle, and in a mess of arms and squashed faces, had a seven-person hug.

And with that, it was time for Give A Dog A Cone to open. We spread out across the shop, put our game faces on, and watched nervously as Mum opened the doors up to the public for the very first time.

162

CHAPTER

ELEVEN

I knew the launch was going to be busy, but I didn't know just *how* busy. And by the massive grin on Mum's face, neither did she. The crowd was so big people were having to mingle on the street. #Blessed. There were loads of dogs too, most of them from the Bark Shelter – the dog charity Mum was putting some of the profits towards. #Woof. The volunteers kept describing Mum as a legend, but it was hard to chat when at their feet were some of the cutest fluffballs on four legs I'd ever seen.

An hour later, when the time for Mum's speech arrived, the room was buzzing. Rach and I handed out samples of ice cream to all the dogs, and Shay and Jo handed out glasses of Champagne to all the non-dogs. The press pushed forward ready to capture the grand unveiling.

Mum looked relatively collected on the outside (well, as collected as someone can who is wearing dog ears and a bone necklace) but I knew she hated public speaking, so gave her the BSL for G and L, which was our fam thing for good luck.

She didn't need it. She was amazing. Telling the story of how the idea came about, Paula the vet's advice, her big dreams for the business, why she was supporting the Bark Shelter, and how grateful she was to her daughters for all the support (me! I got a shout out!). When I spotted Jo wiping away a tear, I zoomed in as hard as I could to capture this beautiful moment (/get any blackmail material for later). The entire speech went without a hiccup (give or take two from Mumbles). As I clicked away taking pics of all the important people looking impressed and Mum looking like she was in complete control, I was convinced that anyone who hadn't been sure that dogs needed ice cream before definitely had a new opinion now. And a new respect for the woman who had made it all happen.

Mum got the biggest round of applause and, looking relaxed for the first time in weeks, stepped across to the gold curtains, inviting the local mayor to come up. It was time to use the special ceremonial scissors (aka the ones from our kitchen drawer I'd wiped clean with loo roll) to unveil the ice sculpture, and declare Give A Dog A Cone officially "open".

I pushed myself alongside the professional photographers, who had formed a tight circle at the front.

The mayor clinked her medal against her glass, the loud *ting* stopping the chatter.

Mum cleared her throat.

"Thanks again for all coming down. It means the WORLD." She smiled at the mayor, whose blank expression suggested she could do these things with her eyes closed (but would keep them open, or she would look weird in official photos).

"The pleasure's all mine. Thank YOU for having me!" The mayor engaged auto-smile. Mum gave her a playful nudge on the arm, but as she was over-excited, sort of punched her. The mayor's smile slipped a touch.

"Anyway," the smile programmed itself back into place, "on with the proceedings. With this..." Mum handed her the scissors, "erm, curtain opening, I declare," she bunched the ribbon up in her hand, "Give A Dog A Cone", she cut and yanked the curtain, "OFFICIALLY OPEN!"

Flashes went off. A big "ooooh" went up from the guests. A beaming Mum stepped forward to pose in front of the sculpture in all its glory.

And there it was. Breathtaking.

The clicks of the camera sped up.

Mum's jaw dropped even more than I'd hoped. The mayor looked like she'd never seen anything like it. And so did everyone else.

But my camera had stopped.

Because behind the curtain was Mum's dog sculpture.

Entirely and completely melted.

A glass box full of murky, sludgy water: floppy bits of flowers swirling around, a sinister collar clinging on the side, and small chocolate flake logs bobbing on the surface.

The crowd didn't know whether to laugh or clap, not sure if this was the intended big reveal.

Was Mum going to cry?!

The only two mammals who knew what to do were Mumbles and Hamster, and they started licking at the puddle that was seeping out, tails a-wagging.

The cameras were relentlessly capturing every second. I looked at Shay. She *must* know what to do?! But she was currently sliding in the wet splodge as she sidestepped quickly away.

However, someone else was calmly stepping right into the space Shay had left.

"So, everyone. . ." confidently Jo stopped right in front of the freezer, blocking the hideous sight. "Obviously there's been a bit of technical hitch." How was she acting as cool as a cucumber?! (Which, sadly, was a lot cooler than the melted dog.) "So, carry on having a look round, follow us on social media, and feel free to ask any questions. . . On behalf of our mum, Mary, and everyone at Give A Dog A Cone ... thanks for coming!"

She finished with a huge smile and a clap enthusiastic enough that, slowly, the room joined in, a mixture of entertained and embarrassed.

But it was too late – the atmosphere was ruined and Mum was frozen in horror at the un-frozen blob that was meant to be the centrepiece of the night. People couldn't leave quick enough.

It was like a joy Hoover (Joover) had sucked the good vibes right out of the room.

I was glad people were leaving – even my friends. Mum was heartbroken, and fixing that was a family-only thing.

I put my arm round her. I'd only seen her cry twice, and didn't want to see it ever again.

"Forget the finale. Forget it. It was a *great* evening – everyone was SO into what you've done here. I PROMISE."

She smiled with only the left side of her mouth. "I just don't know how this could have happened. The freezer was working *fine*?!"

To try and cheer her up, I showed her all the good photos from earlier in the evening. But it didn't help. Nor did Jo's equally enthusiastic attempts – and Shay had headed and Shay had headed off with her press mates to do "damage limitation" (even though I swore I heard them say they were going to Pizza Express). Quietly we began to pack up to head home.

But as Mum went to flick off the lights she stopped dead.

Then turned to me, her face like thunder – even though thunder is technically invisible.

She had some wires in her hand.

"What... Is... This?" Her voice was all angry and cracky. This was serious. She pushed the leads nearer to me. "Bella?!"

I shrugged. "My camera charger?"

She dropped it flat on the floor.

What was the big deal?

My brain spun. Before jerking a halt.

It was me. I'd unplugged the freezer to charge my battery.

I'd ruined everything.

CHAPTER

TWELVE

It wasn't just the launch I'd ruined.

I'd also ruined the next morning, when the articles went up online about Give A Dog A Cone and its, to quote, "RUFF START". I was properly in the doghouse. Shay said all press was good press, but I wondered if it still applied when it's pics of people laughing at what looked like a floating chocolate poo, my mum standing proudly beside it?

I ruined the afternoon too, when newspapers came out saying the same thing. And two days after the launch, despite Mum spending every hour there, the shop had only had four customers in total – and three of them had been Mikey, Hamster and Mash.

I felt awful. Like Grim Reaper levels of grimness.

If I was a tennis tournament I'd be Grimbledon. Not helped by the fact Jo had gone back to uni and I'd had to do all the cooking for Shay and myself, meaning the only vegetables we'd consumed since the launch was corn (which was in the Wotsits I'd served up with some toast).

I could have *sworn* Shay had pointed at that plug and told me to use it. But she swore she hadn't. For a change Jo was on my side, but I think that's just cos she was mad at Shay for not doing more to help when it all went wrong. The atmosphere at home was frostier than the non-selling ice cream. The only time I saw Mum smile was when I offered to work Saturdays for free as a way of saying sorry. I didn't tell her it was Jo's idea, and that I was really hoping she'd say no.

At home, everyone hated me.

At school they loved me too much.

And both sucked.

But here I was, back at my desk, trying to survive the last day of the first week of term. Tegan was late again, as with only nine days left before the audition she'd moved on to pre-school gym practice (how she could function pre eighty-thirty a.m., let alone spend it exercising, I would never know), and Rach was in the library, scribbling away on that English coursework.

So, unless I wanted to speak to someone who only wanted to ask whether I'd "hook them up with a meet with the band *when* I won" I was stuck with me, myself and I. And I was rubbish company, because when I wasn't worrying about how to make it up to Mum, I was worrying about what would happen if my brain never stopped thinking about Adam. Wasn't this phase meant to be over? It'd been almost five whole days since I'd said no to Hillfest. We'd never even kissed but he seemed to have permanently taken over an entire lobe of my brain. Maybe it was a good job I'd found out about Molly when I did, in case he'd taken over the other lobes too. Also, lobe is a really weird word.

THUD.

I lifted my head up off my desk to see the scrunched-up bit of paper which had just landed.

GOOD LUCK FOR SUNDAY! YOU ROCK
LIKE JELLY TOTS. LOVE LOZZA XXXXXX
PS. REMEMBER WHO LENT YOU
THEIR MATHS HOMEWORK IN YEAR
8??????

Oh good. I'd file that away with the other twenty-three notes from randomers who all wanted something.

To keep life simple I gave Lozza a half-hearted smile. She returned it with a thumbs up like a deal was done.

But it wasn't just her. The whole school was in a frenzy about Sunday. It was like they'd forgotten not-winning was even a possibility.

Posters had gone up all over school saying "Yes We Heli-CAN!" (creepy), "Belican's Got The X Factor" (think they'd got confused with which competition I was in) and the plain scary "VOTE BELLA OR DIE".

It was the only thing anyone was talking about – terrible for me, but a big relief to Boxer Boy, who had returned from holiday with a henna hand tattoo of a phallus (as our biology teacher described it) that wouldn't budge.

This morning I'd got so distracted by Mrs Hitchman pinning up yet another "Vote for the Helicans!" poster (she'd stuck it over the fire-drill instructions, proving winning was officially more important to her than avoiding multiple deaths) that I tripped into a bunch of "Vote Bella!" balloons tied to a radiator.

Yup, after eleven years of school wilderness wondering what it was like to be popular, I knew. It was *awful*. So awful that I'd secretly wondered about the plus side of not getting through the next round. Going back to being invisible. But . . . but, the Helicans playing here, and making Rach for ever happy, and Mum proud of me and basically being a general total hero, still won through. Just.

As usual, lunchtime couldn't come quickly enough. I swung myself on to a stool next to Rach and opened up my Pokémon lunchbox. It was meant to be ironic, but I did think Jigglypuffs were pretty excellent. Rach's mum had got their family on a new Cavewoman-eating delivery programme – which is why her food was unopened and she was eating three Dairylea Dunkers.

I picked up the container. It seemed to be 90% garden.

"And you're *sure* this is meant to go in a stomach, not a vase?"

"Alledge," Rach replied through a cheesy mouthful. "Not *my* stomach though. It only recognizes things that are at least 40% beige."

Tegan laughed, which said a lot considering she was the healthiest person I knew. "It looks like something my nan would wear in her hat at a wedding."

Yup, even on my worst days, my friends could make me laugh when I didn't think it was possible. It was nice to see both of them a bit happier than they'd been lately. Tegan was exhausted from training, and when she wasn't there she'd taken to going in deep on the national squad's personal Instagrams. Even *I* felt on first-name terms with them (although four of them *were* called Katie). And Rach was putting on the worst-ever brave face about maybe being moved down a set in English. But she was easier to read than a book – a book with really large font. Maybe even an audiobook.

Still, whatever our own stuff was, we always looked out for each other. So if anyone could find a positive for me having zero fun tomorrow, it was them.

"Guyyyyys, it's my first shift at Give A Dog A Cone tomoz." I was dreading it. I'd bartered with Mum that I should have a day off school a week in return, but she made some comment about "Just wait till you're my age".

"Ooh, exciting." Tegan was genuinely enthused. Did she not understand how boring it was going to be?! "Want any visitors?" I considered replying with a "More than anything, I love you, and please bring snacks" but knew she needed all the spare time she could get her hands on.

"Thanks for the offer, but I'll be fine." I slurped some Ribena. "How was training this morning?"

Tegan shrugged. "You know."

I didn't. The only thing I'd ever trained for was a sponsored crisp-eating marathon for Comic Relief. I shrugged back.

"Not really."

Rach waved her cheesestring contraband. "Nor me."

"OK. How do I describe it?" Tegan scrunched up her mouth. "Well, put it this way, I'm trying really hard, but am not sure I'm getting anywhere." She crunched a piece of cucumber. "And I have just over a week to become so good they think I'm worthy of one of the ten places. Or I can basically wave goodbye to any hope of ever making the national squad."

I hated her being so down on herself.

"Oi. Enough of that. You're MORE than worthy." Wow, so that's what my stern voice sounds like. "You're basically an Olympian, but are too nice to bang on about it."

"Hey, guys." Mikey threw himself on to the chair next to me, all out of breath. "Now don't freak out buuuuut Jay just gave me this." He slapped a postcard down on the table. The entire front was just two words: "VOTE LETTY".

Tegan's face hardened. "She's the JOGS finalist in the comp, right?" Rach and I nodded in unison.

"The one who, and I swear I'm not being bitter, has honestly had THE worst entries so far." Woah. This was the most angry I'd ever seen Rach.

"Gross, huh?" Mikey flipped it over. "Look – all the

deets of how to vote for her. Apparently some ffff" – he stopped himself saying fit in front of Tegan – "ffriendly girls. . ." he held his hands up, "Jay's words not mine! Were giving them out in town last night."

"The cowbag?!!" Tegan was almost as cross as Rach. "Is that even legal?"

Mikey shrugged. "Annnnd they were giving out free chocolate with them."

Woah. This was TOO far. "So what?! I'm meant to compete with food bribery?! How can we do *that*?"

Rach looked desperate. "Mum could buy cake? Lots of cake? Everyone loves cake, right?"

But I shook my head. I wasn't ready to stoop to Letty's level. Not yet. Plus, I bet Letty didn't live with an actual friend of the Helicans. Not that I was going to say *that* out loud.

Instead I went with something less dodgy.

"We're just going to have to remind everyone to vote for St Mary's – again."

Tegan nodded firmly. "I'll remind everyone at gymnastics tonight – whatever it takes to beat Letty."

"Aka Queen of Evil," Rach interrupted.

"Aka Queevil," I rounded off.

"Anyone sitting here?" A voice cut through our rally cry. Ava.

I shook my head, trying to not let her see how surprised I was. "All yours."

She was normally in and out the canteen in under a minute. Maybe she felt less weird around us now she knew we'd been lunch loners too.

Her fingernails were all bitten right down and she was struggling to get her Diet Coke open. Should I offer to help?

"Need a hand?" Tegan beat me to it. She reached over and flicked it open. But as she did, the entire can completely exploded. It sprayed evverrrryyywherrrre.

Tegan leapt back but not before getting absolutely soaked. A loud cheer went up, along with a heckle of, "Wet T-shirt!" (obvs from Luke) which made no sense as Tegan was wearing her school jumper, and wool is not notoriously see-through (sheep do not look naked when it rains).

Had Ava done it on purpose? I was NOT going to let her get away with this.

But when I turned to say something, she looked horrified. Woah. The first emotion I'd ever seen her have.

"Oh my God. I'm SO sorry. I did. Not. Know. That was going to happen." She reached in her bag and pulled out the band T-shirt she'd had on the other day. "Here, use this."

It was neatly folded, but she didn't hesitate to use it to mop up the spillage.

Ava wouldn't stop apologizing – it was clear it had been an accident after all. I downgraded my loyalty rage and let the conversation move on to Mikey's discovery about Letty. Ava told us she'd help get more support, and had already roped her friends in from the county's Youth Orchestra to vote for us (online, phone AND text – triple threat), as they'd all already had their schools knocked out. Rach, Tegan and I kept giving each other *what the what?!* looks. Ava spoke? She played the oboe? She had friends? In the two minutes we'd learnt more about her than we'd done in the last three years – which I totally didn't want to admit, but ended up telling her. She laughed (she laughed?!) and said it was the longest she'd spent in the canteen since starting, so no surprise. We carried on chatting till the bell went.

The Ava-speaking revelation was so good, that Tegan, Rach and I talked about it the entire walk home. By the time we were on my driveway it was five p.m., exactly when I said I'd be back. If you can't be on time – choose friends who can.

"Hiya, girls!" Mum flung the door open with a massive wave. She loved my friends almost as much as I did. It was nice seeing her happy. Had today finally been a good day at GADAC?

"You're more than welcome to stay for some chicken-less kievs, you know! We don't mind sharing, do we, Bells?" I shook my head. "I've even made my famous pink potato."

It was famous among my friends for being one of her worst creations – mashed potato with Thousand Island Dressing stirred in. Weirdly, coloured carbs weren't enough to tempt them out of their own plans, and soon it was just Shay, Mum and me sat around the table.

Mum proudly plonked a blob of mash on my plate so large it made the noise I imagined a cowpat would. Dilemma – smile enough to make Mum happy, and risk her thinking it was actual joy at her famous creation, risking more regular appearance of it at mealtimes; or, look as scared as I felt, and save me being served this in the future, but upset Mum even more.

"MMMMM, looks delish." I swallowed down a forkful – and said a mental sorry to future-Bella. Shay went for the other option, but Mum was too distracted trying to wipe up a blob that had splattered right between Mumbles' eyebrows. It must be SO annoying not having hands, although it would be pretty cool not having school and for "lying down napping" to be a legitimate way to spend a day.

"So. . ." I held my breath, and swallowed the second potato globule with zero chewing – a technique I'd perfected over the years. "How's the shop?"

"Looking forward to doing your first shift tomorrow?" Mum flashed a smile. My innards whimpered and said, "What is this pink floof you have bestowed on us?"

"It'll be a blast," Shay said in the weirdest voice, giving away that she was holding her breath too. It really did make anything taste better.

"We have SO many followers on Instagran, you know!" Mum looked dead proud. Oh good – I *was* making redeeming-myself progress. "Twelve now!"

DO NOT MOVE, FACE. KEEP THAT SMILE. THINK SUPPORTIVE THOUGHTS.

"That's *great* news." I hoped I'd sounded convincing. Twelve followers was less than the account Mikey made on behalf of his big toenail, charting it going black and falling off. "I'll put up some more stuff tomoz."

"And how are things with you, Bells?" Mum stroked the back of my hand in that weird way mums do, like you're a human cat. Still, at least she wasn't as mad at me any more. "Anything to tell us about your Pelicans thing?"

I could start with the fact they're called the Helicans.

And end with how being at school was stressing me out more than the actual competition. But I went with a no.

I foraged in my brain for something, anything, to change the convo from "the life and times of Bella". It ended up being a question: did Shay and Mum know that cows had best friends? This was met with even more silence. I dug even deeper for another fact morsel. And hit them with how some turtles breathe through their bums.

Mum said I sometimes spoke through mine – Shay laughed too much for my liking. So I shut up for a bit, which was good timing as Shay was tackling the subject of putting away Mum's life-sized Benny from ABBA cardboard cut-out and replacing it with a Swiss cheese plant (which blew my mind, until Shay pointed out that it doesn't grow cheese, just looked like one. But green). Mum wasn't sure until Shay pointed out how helpful its aura could be to our happiness. I then zoned out even further as Shay started talking about a work meeting, and I only tuned back in when I was looking for a way of asking to leave.

"And that's why I said to them, 'You've just got to spice the branding up. You can't be everything to everyone. Cos then you're nothing to no one.' Know what I mean?"

Mum murmured a noise which Shay took to mean "Deffo, you are so right", but I knew meant, "I have no idea what this woman is on about, and think I'll go make a cup of tea as an excuse to leave."

"Want a cup of tea?"

I nodded at Mum and, after helping wash the dishes, headed upstairs. I sat on my bed looking through my phone – amongst all the messages from school peeps was one from Jo asking if Mum was still mad at me. She said she'd put in a good word for me if I helped soften Mum up about paying for her athletics tour.

But I didn't have time to talk to anyone. With working on Saturday, and the competition on Sunday, I had to use any spare time to relax to the max.

So I spent the next thirty-five minutes having a surprisingly long wee, squeezing three-and-a-half spots, and discovering what I think is a bona fide toe hair (I tried to pull it out with my fingernails, but ended up curling it like a ribbon on a present). I then spent the next hour playing Puppy Dash Saga, taking selfies with a dolphin filter on, and googling "How to get rid of toe hair". I then found a man who got such a long one wrapped around his toe that the blood stopped and the whole thing fell off.

But I knew I should be using my time more wisely,

like looking at the posts on the Helicans forum. Any prep meant more chance of beating Letty – of getting into the final. But after reading page after page of posts I had even less idea what question Amil might pick. So, I did the next best thing: scrolled through Instagram looking at everyone's way better Friday nights till I fell asleep.

CHAPTER

THIRTEEN

Was there an emergency downstairs?

I'd never heard a noise like it.

I pulled my pillow back over my head.

Yes I *was* due to do my first shift at Give A Dog A Cone later BUT it was a SATURDAY.

I needed sleep.

An emergency could wait.

But even two pillows couldn't block it out.

It sounded like an Olympic opening ceremony, played entirely with pieces of metal.

FINE, EMERGENCY. YOU WIN.

I crawled out of bed and stumbled downstairs, shouting as I went. I think I resembled – in both hair and movement – a bear that has just been released from a small box after a five-year sleep.

"EVERYONE ALIVE?"

"Yes, darl!" Mum called back from the kitchen. Phew. One human ticked off. "Didn't think you'd be awake at this time!"

I ran in to see what the crisis was.

And discovered the crisis was Mum putting away the draining board with absolutely no regard to resting warriors who had endured five days of new term and needed serious sleep.

"I THOUGHT SOMEONE HAD DIED?!"

She lunged at me with the utensil in her hand. Like a medieval knight, but with no horse, and wearing a tie-dye romper instead of armour.

"No whisk of death here!" Amused by her own joke she pointed at the kettle. "Tea?"

I nodded but she'd already poured the water. My pink-floof eating had obviously worked – she seemed almost back to normal with me. Well, as normal as she could ever be.

"Where's Shay?"

"At work prepping for her big thing. I said I'd pick up some plant-based snacks."

"Sounds good."

"You can come?"

"I meant the snacks."

"Company would be great. Thanks, joint-favourite daughter."

I obvs hadn't been clear enough.

"I meant the *snacks* sounded good."

"I'm setting off in thirty, so you'd better get a move on. And deep breath. We're going straight to the dentist after your shift." She winked. "Filling time!"

It was like we existed in two parallel universes. One where I said things that made sense. And the other where Mum heard what she wanted and jousted with kitchen utensils. And delivered terrible news with a smile.

In fairness, I was *so* petrified about having fillings (three?!) I'd told her not to tell me when it got booked. I assumed she'd forget for ever and I could just slowly lose my teeth, phase out speaking and communicate by text, which seemed less hassle.

But after she ignored my pleas to postpone it (indefinitely) I grabbed my tea and headed upstairs.

We were opening the shop up at eleven – Mum figured dogs didn't want ice cream before then – so that meant under an hour to get to the supermarket and back. I couldn't skimp on getting ready, as not only was I going to "be the face" of GADAC, as Mum put it, but now I was also at risk of running into TMH. Saturdays were one of the days he was always at work. I had a spreadsheet. Password protected (Password: dontjudgeme).

I pulled on my stripey top. If I did see him when I was unprepared, I could lie sideways and pretend I was a barcode. I finished it off with the big B necklace Tegan and Rach had given me for my bday.

I shouldn't have worried though, because when Mum said she wanted "company", what she actually meant was, "someone to do all the lifting," and we semi-sprinted round Tesco, totally undetected.

RESULT.

However, as I was loading the boot, TMH walked past at the exact moment my necklace got stuck in the trolley's baby-seat, and he saw me almost choke to death.

UNRESULT.

We drove the whole way to GADAC with Mum saying she didn't know what my problem was, that things like that happened to her all the time. But coming from a lady who once ate the tooth I'd left out for the tooth fairy (thinking it was a bit of popcorn), this was no reassurance. And by the time we arrived at the shop, I was completely over the day already.

Luckily, I'd made a plan to make the most of it.

Morning: man the fort looking all young-entrepreneur-y.

Early afternoon: search Tumblr for quotes from Amy Poehler and Zendaya and Emma Watson and Mary Berry and basically all who are wise, to help inspire me for tomorrow's competition.

Late afternoon: dive back into the fandom entries for inspo.

Mum was going to be popping in and out to keep an eye on things, so all I needed for my masterplan was for the shop to be its normal quiet self.

Mum flicked the till on. "I'm expecting a really busy day today. I stuck a load of leaflets through doors advertising our first ever 'free human ice cream' day."

Oh well. At least I still had the internet.

"So listen up, cos you won't be able to just message me – the wifi's being fixed and the reception's terrible."

I looked at my phone. Not even 4G. Were people allowed to work under these conditions?!

"Oh yes – and I've got you a uniform." OH NO. Please not an outfit chosen by Mum. "Don't give me that look – Shay chose it."

Phew. At least I was going to do it in some sort of statement look – could be a good opportunity to replace my profile pics.

Mum dug around in the box behind the counter and lifted up a coathanger, on which today's outfit was dangling.

It really WAS a statement look. And that statement was "dog". A larger-than-human dog. A sort of a mutant King Charles spaniel. And even worse, it had a waistcoat. Dogs can't even do up buttons. IT MADE NO SENSE.

"Shay said it was would be a great publicity stunt."

I couldn't form words. All I could do was stare.

"I like to call it Gary Barklow. But you can be whoever you want it to be."

Still no words.

My screen lit up. A message from Jo.

HAVE YOU SEEN GARY YET?
SELFIE PLEASE.

So EVERYONE knew then.

She followed up with ten 😄.

This could *not* be happening. If I didn't totally owe Mum a massive apology I'd absolutely say no. But if there was one thing I was known for, it was sticking to my word. And being able to eat a packet of Quavers with no hands.

I lifted Gary off the hanger. He weighed a tonne. I was going to become two inches shorter just wearing it.

But Mum had places to be. And none of them were standing next to me while I moaned. So she whizzed through instructions about tills, customer toilets, and making sure I didn't jumble up which free samples were for which species, and headed out.

And then it was just Gary and I left alone to look after the shop. What could possibly go wrong?

CHAPTER

FOURTEEN

The first hour was quiet, give or take the twelve display tubs I knocked off with my tail, and someone coming in looking for a hairdresser. (FYI if I was going to ask anyone to recommend me a new hairdresser, I wouldn't go for the person dressed as a large dog.)

So I took some pics (surprisingly hard with paws), found my old *Game of Thrones* notes which dropped out of my bag (they were like a historic artefact from a past life), got carried away reading them in the loo (before remembering I'd left the shop unattended) and practised my best dog voice. Should I speak to customers as Bella or Gary? Barry? They all seemed equally scary.

Even though my reception was snail speed, I did manage to check the Helicans forum thread again. But they'd had over 7000 dilemmas posted so getting any clues was impossible. However, I did spot loads of replies from Lis, Amil and Rosie, which made me even more nervous about tomorrow. They really *were* choosing the questions.

The first customer of the day interrupted my research.

She was a chatty older lady, so I opted for Bella voice. When she heard it, she gave me a massive smile. "Ooohhhh it's you! How lovely to see you again, Bella!"

I nodded even though I had zero idea who she was. To cover my guilt I embarked (em-bark-ed) on a really long of-course-I-know-who-you-are-see-how-I'm-conversing-with-you conversation. She must be a friend of Mum's from Pilates. Or my doctor. Or physics teacher. It was quite hard to see through these dog eyelids. Still she bought a tub of ice cream, so that was good news.

"Can you let your mum know I popped in?"

I nodded. And came up with a cunning plan. I grabbed a piece of paper as if I was going to take a proper note of it.

"And er, how do you spell your name again?" Genius name-finding-out skills.

"P-A-T." Or not.

"Sorry – dogs are notoriously bad at spelling." I laughed. She didn't.

After that it was quiet again. I poked my head out of the door to try and see if any potential customers were around, but all I did was scare a small child.

Highlight was when a surprise visitor ran in. Tegan.

"Bells!?! Look at you?!"

I twirled. Then realized she hadn't even questioned whether it was me inside the suit.

She looked sheepish. "Didn't you see??"

Gary/me shook his/our head.

"Ah. Jo *may* have posted a pic and tagged you in it."

Oh well, isn't that wonderful? I checked my Facebook profile. Teeg was right – and to make matters worse, it was a pic Mum had surreptitiously taken that was out of focus and had a bit of her thumb in it.

Tegan rummaged in her tote bag. It had a new badge on it. "Blood, Sweat and Backflips."

"Cool, huh?" It couldn't be more perfect for her. "Mikey made it for me."

"Made?!" I didn't have him down as the craft type.

"Yup – I know! He's the best. Although his mum said something about their kitchen table never being the same."

"Not your fault."

"That's what I keep telling myself. Aaaanyway ..."
She put whatever she'd pulled out of her bag behind
her back. "The point. Dad was popping into town, so
I thought I'd cadge a lift and give you these..." She
plonked down a family-size bag of peanut M&Ms, some
Skips and my favourite magazine on to the counter.

"And THAT is why I love you."

"And THAT is also why the lady in the village shop
took one look at what I was buying and asked after you."

Ha! "What can I say? I'm a creature of habit."

She looked me up and down. "Well, you're certainly
a creature."

As we laughed, a real-life potential customer strolled
in.

I swiped my treats off the counter.

Teeg whispered, "And I will see you later..." and
headed out.

I paw-waved goodbye and tried to look as professional
as a giant dog can, which was a good job, as the customer
had loads of questions. Determined to do Mum proud,
I headed over to the main display by the window to try
and answer them.

As he asked about whether dogs could get brain
freeze, I spotted Tegan at the end of the street, looking up
and down the traffic. Was she OK? But when a car pulled

up, I realized she wasn't going anywhere. She was waiting for someone. And it *wasn't* her dad. It was a different guy driving – and as she climbed into the car, I swore I recognized him. . . Was it the guy from the bus stop?!

"So do you think the marrow would repeat on Colin?"

I landed back into the conversation with a thump. Before I could stop it, my mouth replied, "Who's Colin?"

The man looked deeply offended, and replied, "My dog – who we've been talking about for the past two minutes." And left.

EURGH.

How rubbish was I? I vowed to do better next time – and tried to make up for it by making more stuff for the GADAC social accounts. I filmed some excellent vids of me giving bark ratings for the different flavours, and came up with a hilarious comment about *serving suggestion: ice cream and woofles*. I was chuffed it got a like from 20% of our followers (Mikey, Rach, me and the account I just created for Gary). I was less chuffed that we still only had twenty followers.

In the afternoon things started getting busier. My Gary voice was getting pretty good, and I'd started to throw in extra-curricular barks to entertain customers. Or growls if I found them annoying. I'd also realized the benefits of being in costume – for the first time in weeks, when anyone I recognized from school walked past, they didn't even try to talk to me. If only this was acceptable school uniform.

But someone I did kind of recognize walked in.

She was tall, had perfectly blow-dried blonde hair, actual brand jeans that weren't saggy at the knee, and a white, oversized top, rolled up to show off her amazing tanned arms. OH MY GOODNESS.

One look at those beautiful wrist joints and I knew exactly who it was. Ska!

I gave my brain a big gold star for working it out, because it meant I was prepared when, seconds later, Luke traipsed in after her.

He looked round the shop as if we were selling small piles of dog poo.

"What the *hell* is this crap show?"

I wanted to shout, "Oi!" – but wanted to blow my cover even less. He made my life a misery enough for just being me; I could only imagine what he'd do if he knew I was a part-time hound.

Ska ignored him too. She was busy reading a tub, laughing at Mum's joke about eating too much and turning into a pup-sicle. But Luke's ego not getting the attention it demanded made it notch up an evil gear.

"Someone should have a word. This place is a joke."

I took a breath so deep a dragon sound came out of Gary's one nostril hole. Luke looked me right in the eye. Could he tell it was me? I didn't know what to do.

I panic-barked.

Luke laughed – and not in a good way – and kicked at the dog water bowl we had on the floor, splashing an innocent Affenpinscher and its owner.

I stopped keeping it together.

"EXCUSE..." But as Luke looked, I stopped. NO, BELLA. Gary voice for this. He *mustn't* figure out it was me. I dropped my voice as low as it would go. "...ME."

Luke fake smiled. "Soz. Didn't see it there."

We both knew he was lying. But I had to be nice, for Mum's sake.

I channelled my best I-don't-have-a-personal-vendetta-against-you-I'm-just-a-helpful-customer-service-dog vibe.

"Can I help you with anything?"

Ska stepped next to him, giving me a truly pitiful smile.

"Yeah, actually. I wanted to know – are these ingredients all organic? My dog is a show dog, you see."

Of *course* her dog was a show dog.

But I had to be polite. I mustered enthusiasm. "I bet she's wonderful."

Ska didn't even blink. "He."

Keep calm, Bells. Think of Mum.

"You can find all the ingredients here." I pointed to the sign with the url on. And hit them with a new catchphrase for Gary that I'd been working on all morning. "So... BONE APPETIT!"

Luke sniggered.

But it wasn't at me. It was at whatever Ska had opened up on her phone.

"Twenty followers? *Big time.*" He looked around. "I can er, I can help get those numbers up, you know." He dropped his voice right down, "For a fee. . ."

This time it was me who couldn't help but laugh. Which I had to emergency morph into an unexpected woof. Ha-oof.

"Sorry – I think you're barking up the wrong tree?!"

The Affenpinscher owner laughed, but tried to style it into a cough like he wasn't listening – or laughing. But the damage was done. Luke's pride was dented and he stormed out. Victory.

And Ska stuck around to make a purchase. Victory^2. I'd survived an encounter with my evil ex! I'd made a sale!

I was going to bask in this all afternoon.

Or not.

Because before I'd even sat back down, something much, much worse than the world's worst boy walked in.

The opposite happened.

The world's best boy arrived.

CHAPTER

FIFTEEN

Yup, Adam was officially in Give A Dog A Cone.

What *was* this shop? A ice-cream-based magnet to all significant guys in my life?

My heart did a temporary stop.

But despite me missing three to seven whole beats, Adam was his normal casual self. Just as happy and gorgeous as I remembered. Laughing and chatting with his best mate Marcus as if this wasn't the world's hugest deal.

As if this wasn't the *exact* day he said he was too busy and "long story" to see me.

As if seeing him in the flesh again wasn't so overwhelming I had to step on my own foot to check I wasn't hallucinating.

ARGH.

Why was I still getting all the feels (plus at least ten more) around him, when I'd been in training to feel nothing?!

And was it wrong that a tiny bit of me had hoped he'd died, just to explain his lack of contact?

I HAD to escape. But there was no way out. So... I did what any self-respecting dog-person would do. I crouch-hid behind the counter.

But what were they saying?

It was harder to eavesdrop than it should have been as I had a giant flappy ear over my actual ear. How on earth do dogs hear anything? Surely this is a major design fault?

"Mate!" Adam was deploying his boy-technique of "one word to mean ten things simultaneously". From his enthusiasm I think it meant, "Friend who I'm with – have you seen this? It looks pretty cool."

"Have you seen this? It looks pretty cool."

OH. MY. ACTUAL. DOG. I *still* knew what he was thinking. I couldn't hear what they said next but there was happy laughing like they were totally on-board with dog ice cream.

EURGH. How dare he be such a good customer, when I really needed to start hating him?!

"Hello? Anyone there?" His annoyingly fit voice came from the other side of the counter.

KEEP CALM BELLA. He might not see you.

"Oh – sorry. Didn't see you down there. . ."

OK, he's seen me. DON'T PANIC. Stay still and he might go away. Marcus might distract him any second.

But Marcus also peered over.

"You all right. . .?"

NO, MARCUS, NO! You were meant to distract him with something *other* than focusing on me. But I was in no position to debate this (unless the accepted arguing position was "sitting on your own heels").

Accepting defeat, I went to stand, but I was so freaked out seeing Adam that my wobbly legs got caught up in my own tail and I sort of splatted on to all fours.

Well, this was going well.

"Seriously – are you OK?" Adam sounded concerned, but I couldn't speak in case he recognized my voice. And nodding was not an option – I had to keep Gary's head on at all costs.

With zero clue of what to do, I froze. Unlike Adam, whose muddy trainers (and I assume attached body) were rushing towards me.

"Marcus – I think . . . think he might need help?"

Argh?! Why was Adam so caring? And why did he assume I was a he? #dogcostumegenderbasedassumptions.

And why was he now standing beside me?!

And why was he asking if I needed a hand getting this costume off?!

I HAD TO THINK OF SOMETHING.

HE MUST NOT DE-HEAD ME!

I would die of actual embarrassment – meaning I would style out him thinking I'm dead. By being actually dead.

What would Jo do? No. Scrap that. *What would Mumbles do?*

I only had one idea. And it would plunge me to a new low. Which, considering I was on all fours in fancy dress, was a big claim.

But with no other option, I went for it.

I spun Gary's bum round, square on to Adam. And did what any self-respecting dog would do.

I wagged my tail.

At the world's sexiest man.

"Oh." That's literally all Adam could bring himself to say.

RIP, dignity. Dognity. It was nice knowing you.

Dream scenario for this weekend: boy I can't help but think is amazing bumps into me, is dazzled by hilarious personality, tells me his long story was that he had to break up with Molly, realizes he thinks I'm great as more than a friend, professes undying love.

Actual scenario: wagging my own tail, while boy I'm obsessed with is warily patting me saying, "Good boy."

Official life rock bottom. And rocking bottom.

If I was witnessing this, my heart would melt with how Adam was going along with this deranged human. But seeing as I WAS the deranged human I just wanted to cry.

But nobody likes the smell of wet dog.

"Erm, sorry not sorry to interrupt whatever *this* is, but we wanted to get one of these." Marcus plonked a tub down. I looked up at it, grateful for this moment to end. Adam put his hand out to help me up, and for a beautiful moment we were paw-in-hand. Sort of like *Beauty and the Beast* except way more creepy and also THIS IS MY ACTUAL LIFE.

I took the money off the counter and, cringing so hard I swear Gary's furry face was blushing too, I turned to get their change. But as I handed it back it was Adam who put his hand out.

"Thanks, I cannot wait to see my dog's little face when she tries this."

"And I cannot wait to see your little face, when you see your dog's little face," is what I wanted to say. But instead I just passed him the bag.

The two of them turned to walk out, but Adam spotted the toilet sign and stopped.

"Sorry – would it be OK if I washed my hands, they're a bit. . ." He held them out. "Covered in your fluff" was the end of the sentence he was too polite to say.

I nodded and gestured towards the loo.

When he was out of earshot, Marcus politely filled the awkward silence.

"He's made up about finding this place. His dog's getting on, and he's been extra sentimental about her." It was weird Marcus talking to me like he thought I was a forty-year-old man. Still, probably better than him knowing the truth. "We've just been watching this, I dunno, dog display team or something, that practise near our football pitch. Ad always makes us stop and watch. He loves them. Anyway, it was them that told us about this place."

Well, that was nice of them. Must ask Mum if she knows them. But before I could figure out how to reply without words, Adam came back out. And he was clutching a bunch of paper.

PLEASE NO.

"Someone must have left these in there," he looked impressed. "It looks like the *entire* plot of *Game of Thrones*?!" Thank you, Lord of Pens, Queen Penelope, for not letting him recognize my handwriting?! "Whatever floats your boat, right?"

Little did either of them know that it was Adam who floated my boat. But all I could do was delicately nod my big dog head back. Marcus shook his non-dog one as if he couldn't believe what he'd seen and walked towards the door.

I lifted Gary's ear flap as discreetly as I could so I could catch every last chat morsel before they disappeared from my life for good.

"That was some seriously freaky fan stuff, dude." Marcus elbowed Adam. "Sure they weren't yours now you don't have that girl to talk to about it any more?"

Sorry, what?!

Was I *that* girl?! Was I sliding all up into their real-life chat like I had some significance?!

If only I could see Adam's face, not the back of his head. Reactions were a lot harder to tell from follicles.

Adam's head shook as he laughed. "Remind me why we're mates again?"

Noooooo. He'd moved the convo on. Hope of insight over. And in three steps' time they'd disappear forever.

"Cos who else was going to go to that weird festival with you? Although granted, whenever I'm with Molly, I do get waaaay more girls coming over."

OH GREAT. Could the world (or at least Marcus) just shut up about Molly already?!

But Adam swung his bag into the back of Marcus's knee.

"Oi, my dog is not your wingman."

OR NOT.

What the actual what?!

Molly, offa being my number-one most-envied human, was Adam's dog?!

And I'd been all jealous and frosty and, "No, I won't go on a date with you", because I thought she was his girlfriend!?

Bella Fisher, you are the World's Biggest Idiot! Why didn't you listen when he talked about her rather than just gormlessly stare at his beauty?!

But then again, why didn't Adam have an Instagram account for his dog like a normal person?!

But then again, again, why didn't you just say yes to Hillfest and find out live?!

Thank goodness Marcus and Adam had both cleared the shop because I had to temporarily de-Gary-head to get enough oxygen into my brain which was whirling so fast it felt like a fidget spinner.

The last five mins had had more revelations that a week of *Jeremy Kyle*.

I did a little doggie happy dance. Like doggie paddle but with no water. Adam *wasn't* going out with Molly. Other than in a "walking" sense.

And there might still be a glimmer of hope for us all?

And he'd just patted me?!

It was all too much.

I knew what I had to do. After I'd said no to Hillfest, I HAD to finish what I'd tried to start. Ask Adam one more time. To find out if he liked me as a friend – or something more. And this time I had to make it unique. Something me. Something he couldn't say no to.

But what?

I spent the rest of the afternoon serving what few customers we had, trying to think up ideas, until Mum arrived to pick me up for the dentist.

I couldn't run the risk of leaving the shop as me, so had to fold myself into her passenger seat as Gary.

She pushed my tail out of the way of her gearstick.

"Soooo, how was your doggie debut?"

What one word could sum it up?

"Eventful."

"And did we have many customers?" Her hopeful tone so desperately wanted the answer to be yes. I couldn't bear to disappoint her.

"Loads. Your free ice cream was a big hit."

True – I'd given away a hundred human ice creams. But I'd only sold ten dog ones. Mum beeped the horn with glee. OH GOSH. She'd changed it back to a cow sound. A confused old man stared at us as we mooed past. We must look quite something. A bellowing car with a dog shaking its head in the passenger seat.

"And sales?"

"Not loads," her face dropped, ". . . but lots of people said they'd be back, so I'm *sure* they'll pick up soon." I didn't want to tell her I'd only managed to add five new followers to the Instagram account as well.

Mum chewed on her bottom lip as she always did when she was genuinely worried about something. And for someone who giggled when a birthday-cake candle set fire to her hair, I knew this meant GADAC's slow start was really getting to her.

I put my paw on her hand.

"We'll get there, Mum. I promise."

As soon as I said it, I regretted it. I didn't like breaking promises – I just had no idea what I could do to help. But wait. There was *something* positive.

"Oh – meant to ask. Do you know an, erm, dog-display team?" It did the trick – her smile returned as she told me all about them. Apparently they were a "dog agility" team called the Furry Flyers and they'd been at the launch. And, as we sat in the waiting room, my appointment getting nearer, Mum turned the tables and tried to cheer me up by showing me clips of them in action.

Who knew dogs could look so happy bursting balloons?

Who knew there was a Jack Russell who had a genuine enthusiasm for zip wires?

And who knew that starting this conversation was going to turn out to be one of the biggest mistakes of my life?

CHAPTER

SiXTEEN

Whatever was in that sedative drink at the dentist they should put in drinking taps at school. I would never have to suffer a geography lesson again. Because when I finally woke up on Sunday I had three repaired teeth and zero recollection of it happening. RESULT.

So what with not having to face life semi-toothless, and the most amazing Adam development, I was on Cloud 9 for tonight's semi-final. Maybe even Cloud 10 because Tegan could make it, so we could finally tackle it as a three.

Yup, for the first time ever, I had a tiny bit of confidence we might get through.

What a time to be alive!

I was so happy that even when I discovered an

absolute shocker about one of the other contestants, it didn't phase me.

When the other two arrived I couldn't wait to tell them exactly what I'd found.

Letty, Queen of Evil, had struck again.

Rach tore open a bag of the Tangfastics she'd brought, put three in her mouth to channel her nervous energy and I explained.

"OK. So I was doing some last minute forum trawling. And surprise surprise, Letty had responded to one of Lis's comments." Rach grimaced. "But it wasn't just a suck up," I paused – I almost couldn't wait to see their faces when they found out. "... it was an attempt to get me kicked out."

Rach gasped so hard I think she swallowed all three sweets. Tegan just looked pure furious. I brought the page up on my laptop.

HI GUYS. LIS – LOVING THOSE PICS OF YOU AT THAT CHARITY GIG LAST WEEK. YOUR OUTFIT WAS TOTAL FIRE!!

Tegan shook her head, "Could she BE more obvious?!"

I'M REAAAAALLY LOOKING FORWARD TO THE SEMI-FINAL. BUT, I WAS CHATTING TO MY DAD* AND WE GOT TALKING ABOUT BELLA.

*HE'S A LAWYER

Rach was pink with rage. "Erm, excuse me. Why is she so obsessed with you?!"

I shrugged. "Exactly what I'd been wondering too."

OBVS I'VE TOTALLY LOOOOVED HER ANSWERS,

Tegan laughed. "Bet she has?!"

BUT IS IT FAIR THAT LAST ROUND YOU SAID ONE SENTENCE AND SHE BLATES USED TWO?

Tegan's laugh switched into a splutter. "Sorry, what?! Is she really going full grammar police in desperation?"

Rach stabbed at my screen, like she was somehow poking directly into Queevil. "Is it fair you've been

BRIBING STRANGERS to vote for you, you Queevilest douchebag?!"

I scrolled down. "There's more. . ."

SOOOO IF YOU'RE CHOOSING THE TOP
THREE ON SUNDAY, SHOULD SHE REALLY
BE ALLOWED TO BE IN IT?
JUST FOOD FOR THOUGHT!
LOVE YOU GUYS!

LETTY XOXOXOXOXO

I nodded along as the other two reread it ten times, just like I had earlier. It was satisfying that they were reacting just like me.

"Yup, not content with stabbing us in the ears with her terrible advice, she's stabbed me right in the back too. Well, sort of face actually."

"The only thing I can think of is that she considers you her main competition. And that's kind of great." Hell yes, Tegan. "And whatever happens . . . we *will* beat her."

I leaned over to high five her.

"In your face, Queevil." And I meant it. I *had* tried to figure out why she'd taken this swipe at me, but much like understanding why Mum kept a cheese grater in the bathroom, I'd come to the conclusion, ignorance was bliss. Instead I was going to put all my energy into beating her.

Although, who knew if I could? I lowered my voice as if whispering meant long-term memories couldn't hear me. "Guys, *pleeease* forget that I ever said this – but if, *IF* I don't get through, will one of you hide me in your wardrobe and bring me snacks till I'm twenty-three and everyone's forgotten?"

Rach nodded. "I've already cleared a space just in case."

OK, not as positive as Tegan, but good to know I had options.

Radio Shire was keeping us hanging, and every minute that passed meant one more gazillion incoming good-luck messages from school randoms. Although "Good luck" definitely felt like shorthand for "Don't mess this up, or I will hate you".

But I was weirdly calm. Cos with my friends beside me, a positive Adam plan to make and, thanks to Rach, two more bags of Haribo (Starmix AND Super Mix), I felt OK. I didn't even panic-hide anything when there was a knock at my door. Rach on the other hand was so on edge she rolled off my bed and on to the floor.

"Hope I'm not disturbing." It was Shay, and she was

holding what looked like chocolates. Double yes. Rach scrambled to her feet and smoothed her hair down. I could only make a generic "ymmm-hmm" noise as was mid-chew of two fizzy cherries.

"Bells meant, 'Course not, come in.' Right?" I nodded at Tegan. Our friendship transcended consonants.

"One more coming through!" Mum was in Shay's slipstream, three bowls balanced under her chin.

"Anyone fancy some ice-cream-cone flavoured ice cream I've been working on?" Mum passed them out. "Let me know what you think." She dropped her voice, thinking out loud. "It IS for humans this time... We really need something to help sales pick up at the shop..."

Shay stuck her plate out.

"Or you *could* try one of these? Somewhat healthier."

I peered at what looked like a plate of lumps of soil. "No sugar, no gluten, raw cacao balls." Tegan took one out of politeness. Rach took one out of deep love. I took one cos it was edible. But it was Mum's ice cream that was the clear winner. She looked delighted, but Shay looked annoyed.

"Fine, hint taken. I'll be downstairs if you need anything." She gave me a reassuring look. "And don't stress! You'll be totally fine." She paused. And winked. "I *did* mention Lis is really looking forward to tonight, right?"

CHATBOMB DETONATED.

Rach fell back off the bed. I was on the other side, so couldn't see her and shouted a concerned, "Are you OK?" A shaky mouse-voice wafted back.

"Diii-iid you t-ell her a-bout ussss??!"

Was she about to cry?! Shay batted her eyelashes in an innocent "What, me?" way. I thought I better clarify.

"Rach – in case you couldn't see that, Shay just batted her eyelashes in an innocent 'What, me?' way."

Rach made the sound a jelly should make when it melts.

But when she sat up, her face had changed. Like she'd seen a ghost.

"Erm, do I recognize those shoes?"

Shay lifted up one of her feet. Or more importantly, one of the brand new coral shoes attached to it. The ones from Rach's pic?!

"Oh, these?" She twirled it around. "Yeah. It was weird, I saw them in the shop and they seemed *so* much nicer. I meant to say" – Shay opened my door – "thanks for the recco – we're the same size, right? You can borrow them anytime..."

Rach's face was a mix of surprise, confusion and shoe-lust. She was like a living meme for "that time when you see the thing you wanted to buy on someone else and are kind of annoyed they have it and think they might have actually got the exact last pair you reserved, but are also impressed cos they look so great which proves you clearly did have excellent taste after all – in fact you have THE SAME TASTE, which is even better news – and now you've got the chance to borrow them, so feel conflicted."

It was quite a specific meme.

If it was me I think I'd be pretty annoyed, but Rach seemed happy to have yet another Shay thing in common.

But Modger had already left, and Mum followed soon after. And soon, full of ice cream, the three of us were alone listening into Jaz. But there was still no question. Tegan was seriously unimpressed, so I tried to lighten the mood.

"Teeg – did I tell you that you're basically a lifesaver? Cos after seeing Adam, the only thing that stopped me full-on fainting was that care package you brought."

She smiled. "No biggie. Seeing you in that dog outfit was 100% worth it."

"That's a thought?!" Rach looked like she'd had a great idea. "If tonight doesn't go well, you can always wear Gary full-time?"

It was worrying how pleased she looked with herself.

Tegan lay back on my bed. "Maybe drop the waistcoast in summer though?" I laughed. "I wish I could have stuck around longer, not dashed off to training. . . But next time, right?"

I nodded but I'd been hearing "next time" a lot recently.

EURGH. Brain, stop it. It doesn't feel good when you're negging on our best mate. I tried to de-guilt myself with something more positive.

"And hopefully this time next week you'll have your place too, so we can figure out how we're going to celebrate?"

Tegan's face scrunched. "Imma not so sure."

"Well *we* are, right, Rach?" With a slightly alarming screech Rach leapt like a flying squirrel on to Tegan and gave her a massive cuddle. "Damn straight!" But something Tegan had said was stuck on a loop. If she was dashing to training, why didn't she have her stuff with her? Where was she going with that guy? And why hadn't she mentioned him at all?

EURGH. What was up with me? There was probably a totally obvious explanation.

"Sorry I had to duck out to deal with that customer. Did you get to do much in town after?"

OMG. Was I really fishing for details?

Teeg shrugged. "Nah, just the usual."

Serves me right – if there was an explanation, I wasn't getting it. But Rach had no idea I was digging for info (thankfully), and was still fully focused on Radio Shire.

"How long do you think Jaz is going to be? Do you reckon it's too late to post a question?" She absently twizzled her hair, sticking the end in her own ear. "Cos what do you think the rules would be on me emailing in about this English essay?"

She'd restarted it five times already, and it was due in a week.

Tegan rubbed her arm. "Rach, you've GOT this."

She winced. "All I've got is being put down a set. It sucks." She huffed. "I suck."

OK, something about tonight had thrown the world off balance. It was like me being so positive had somehow stolen all the good vibes the other two normally had. And I wasn't going to stand for it. "Oi. The only thing that sucks is Mr Tucker making you stress like this."

Tegan wiggled her feet, clicking her ankles. "And Shay buying *your* shoes after persuading you not to."

Rach tilted her head. "People can change their minds!

And at least I can borrow them now. For free-sies."

Tegan shrugged and rolled back over to type on her phone. She'd been distracted by it all evening. Not that I had any idea who she was messaging.

But it didn't matter – because, for once, I DID have an idea.

"Look. Mr Tucker wants opinion. And passion. And knowledge . . . right?"

Rach nodded.

"Soooo, why don't you forget all those books he hinted at and do one you could write about for days?"

"Such as. . .?"

"Do I have to spell it out?!" Her blank expression meant yes. But Tegan jumped back in.

"OK, I only listened to the last two seconds of that and even *I* know." She threw a pillow at Rach. "Clue: It starts with H and ends with Otter."

Rach's mouth dropped open.

"What?! You think I could write about Queen Joanne of the Rowling?"

I nodded. "There's no one who knows more about the books than you – and I include JK herself in that."

A smile spread on Rach's face.

"I guess it IS defining. And he didn't say it couldn't be a modern*ish* classic?"

"Exacto!" THIS was more like it. Maybe I was OK at advice after all? "So, while I'm clearly ON FIRE, anyone got any other probs they need New Wise Bella to sort?"

Tegan propped herself up on my pillows. "Yeah – can you get Jaz to hurry up? I'm going to have to have to go... My cousin's picking me up at half eight."

Rach and I exchanged a quick look of, *Sorry, what? She hadn't mentioned she had to go, right?* With a dash of, *Did you even know her cousin was down? Cos normally we all hang out at least once?*

Tegan totally saw.

"Don't be like that. It'll all be back to normal once next Sunday is out the way."

Well, at least she was admitting that things had been getting a bit weird.

"Promise?" Rach sounded hurt.

But I knew it wasn't the training that stung. Cos we both only wanted Tegan to do her absolute best. It was something else.

The fact that somewhere, somehow, over the last few weeks, and without us realizing, Rach and I seemed to be last in line to know what was going on in her life. And when we normally knew every detail about each other (some would say too many, unless they thought Rach's updates on her verruca being burnt off were key to a good friendship), it felt extra weird.

Tegan reached over to hug Rach. "I promise."

She meant it. And I knew I had to push my weird thoughts out of my head, cos I had the best friends in the world.

But as the wait for the competition dragged on, and more messages came through, the more I worried that Tegan was going to have to go, and my nerves began to get the better of me. And when Jaz's question finally came it was ten minutes too late. Because the only one of us that was still positive, composed and confident was Tegan. And she'd just said a massive apologetic goodbye and headed off with her cousin.

Disaster.

Amil's breathless voice kicked it all off. "So sorry we're late. Our video shoot totally overran!"

I looked at Rach. "Toadally know the feeling?!"

She laughed. "Letty probably blagged a cameo to get more votes."

"Thank you so much for alllll your questions. It was SO amaze reading them all." He sounded genuinely touched. "I know it sounds cliché, but our fans really are the best. Seeing you all supporting each other with all your questions and advice? It's been immense." He waited a beat. "Helicaners ROCK!"

But Jaz was too focused on her script to pause for genuine emotion. Still, at least she hadn't mentioned Letty's attempt to get me chucked out.

"As Amil said, the response has been phenomenal. And thoooousands of people are tuned in right now to try get their school into the final."

I clutched my stomach as it had its 1032nd nerve spasm of the hour. "So, Amil ... what *IS* the dilemma you picked for today's question?"

He cleared his throat. "Well, here goes – and if you're on the Radio Shire Twitter, they're going to post a direct link to it too..."

Rach already had the profile up on her laptop. We were like a mission command centre.

As Amil read it out, we read along online.

vavavoom
Elite Poster

Hi, guys – hope you're "Beyond Incredible and Back".

Their last single – nice touch.

Here's the question I want to submit for the
semi-final. What one bit of advice would you
give the other competitors to help them get to
the final?
Or is that too weird?!
X

WOAH. This was like an actual RIDDLE.

"Tricksy, huh?" said Jaz, loving it. "And don't
forget – semi-finalists? You've only got till the end of
the song to send in your response. Everyone else –
that'll be your time to start voting! So get thinking
while we enjoy one of Lis's new favourite new bands –
Velvet Badger."

Lis *always* had impeccable taste.

But I'd got distracted reading the poster's follow-up
post below.

PS Thanks for being so awesome. When I feel
the most crap it's the Helicans that get me
through.

PPS Soz I'm being pathetic.

PPS No, scrap that. I'm just bored. Cos I'm

spending another lunchtime on my own. Again.
Like, will one person ever acknowledge me?!
Ambition or what?

PPPS Why am I posting this?! But what have I
got to lose – everyone hates me anyway!

I kind of wished *that* was the post we were meant to
be helping with. Cos I knew that feeling all too well from
last year, and it sucked.

But there was no time to waste. Rach was focused
and got stuck straight in with an idea.

"How about something like Tegan always says,
about 'sticking to who you are cos everyone else is
taken'?"

I wrinkled my nose. "Nah, I think we need to go big.
Go final worthy. Get those votes." Only problem – I had
no idea what that was.

Rach hmmmmmed. "Something about not bribing
your way along like Queen Be-at-ch?!" She was joking,
but the hate was real.

But a thought *had* come to me. And with time
against me (and also the "S" key which had a toast
crumb jammed in it) I typed as fast as I could. When
Rach approved, I pressed send – and instantly felt more

petrified than ever.

It only got worse when Amil came back on, and started reading out the five entries.

"Aisha has written, 'Just be yourself. And may the best person win!'"

Kind of sweet. Kind of boring. Obvs Amil was really nice about it anyway.

"Great job, Aisha – and good luck, Royal Orchard. Now, Letty from JOGS . . ." ("QUEEEEEVVVVIIILL," Rach and I yelled quickly.) ". . . has said, 'The best advice I can give is to. . . *Be more Letty*'." Despite trying not to give anything away, I'm convinced he sounded a bit grossed out. "Cos no one can tell it like it is like I can. . ." Yup, he deffo sounded like that combo of words had never come out of his mouth before.

I couldn't help but heckle. "Oh, come on?! As IF anyone will vote for that?!" But that's *exactly* what we wanted. Rach went off on such a long rant about how Letty was clearly not a true Helicaner that we missed the next entry from Blessed Trinity School entirely.

We caught Jaz reading the next one. "Saz from Malvern Academy has written that 'you should all just do your best, cos there's nothing more anyone can do than that'."

Amil gave a supportive "Aaaaah". Now – I'd liked all

Saz's other entries, but this one was a bit motivational assembly-y. Jaz carried on.

"And finally, Bella from St Mary's. Amil? You got this one?"

I grabbed Rach's leg. Total terror.

I pictured every single person I knew – and didn't know – listening.

Amil paused. *Had I messed up*?!

But, no?! He did exactly what I'd hoped. He laughed.

"Bella reckons you should all 'do a really good job of answering this question – and make it a better answer than this one ... if you want to win this round by being better at answering than this answer'." He made a sound like water spraying out of his mouth. "Meggaaa metaaaa!" He was laughing. "Peeeeeakkk meta."

WAIT. Had we made one quarter of the Helicans laugh?!

Rach and I spontaneously high-fived like we were in a cheesy American drama.

But Amil had more. "And, Bella – I totally saw your special message for vavavoom. So will v. quickly pass it on, if that's OK, Jaz?"

Jaz made an "ermyermnerm" noise like the answer was no, but she didn't want to say it. But Amil wasn't one for rules. "Mr/Ms Voom, Bella says, 'Hi, Vav. This is *me* talking to *you*. And technically one other person too, if someone is reading this out' – which I am?! 'So now two people have spoken to you, why don't you make the first move with someone else? Try a new seat for lunch or something?'. . . Hear that, Voom? Bella and the Helicans say go get 'em?!"

NOSTRIL FLARE. Amil just said my name like I was on their wavelength.

But Jaz was NOT impressed.

"Remember, guys, you're not voting for that, you're voting for the answer to the original question. Probably shouldn't have read that bit out, hey, Amil?"

Amil apologized. But I wasn't trying to get more votes. I'd just known exactly how vavavoom felt, from when I didn't have Tegan and Rach to talk to last term. And it totally sucked.

But there was no time to dwell on if I'd jeopardized our chances. All we could do was vote like crazy. We didn't have long. I yelled at Shay and Mum to remind them (although they could only text at old-person speed, so were only worth one fifth of one of us) and with shaky fingers sent in as many as I could. I'd roped everyone I knew into helping. Even Jo and her uni mates.

Which also meant literally everyone I knew was about to hear me succeed or fail.

By the time Amil came back on, I almost didn't want to know. Because there would be no going back. Ultimate hero, or public enemy number one?

He sounded uncharacteristically serious.

"It sucks to lose someone, anyone, at this stage, so I'm going to get it done quickly."

Pleeeeease let one of the next three names we heard be mine.

And let none of them be Queevil.

"In no particular order the three finalists are ..." He swallowed. "Letty."

NOOOOOOOO.

HOW COULD THIS BE?!

"Aisha."

Oh my hairy toe bushes. I'd messed it up, hadn't I?

Unless. Pleeeeeease pleeeeease let the final name be us?!

"and ... Bella."

Oh. My. Word.

We'd done it.

We were in the final.

CHAPTER

SEVENTEEN

My bedroom erupted with happiness. Rach was leaping round like the floor was too hot to step on, I was yelling so much I induced two accidental shock hiccups and Mum and Shay burst in full of hugs and congrats. Even my phone was on fire with 🎉 (and one 🍩 from Mikey).

If I'd felt popular earlier, now I felt like Emma Watson's more famous sister. What would it be like if I actually won?!

In the background Jaz was still waffling on, reading some of the emails she'd had in. There was fanmail for Letty (probs from her dad*)(*he's a lawyer). And some "We love you anyway"'s from friends of the two that had been knocked out.

"And 'scuse me if I'm not saying this right, but

Hitchhiker100 says, 'Yeaaahhhsssss! Come on, St Mary's – it's time the best band played at the best school in the local catchment area.'"

Amil snorted. "Love some good catchment-area chat!"

Jaz didn't laugh back. "So, on to a week Saturday... The final!"

Amil whooped. "Yesssss, sirrrrr. Letty, Aisha, Bella – we are SO LOOKING FORWARD to meeting you?!!"

WAIT. WHAT?! Did he say MEET?!

I, Bella Fisher, was going to meet the Helicans?!

Was this actually my life? Rach went instantly teary. "Bellss ... do you think..."

But she didn't need to finish.

"Rach – it's all three of us going or nothing, you wallyhead!"

She started to snort-laugh-cry so hard Shay stroked her hair to calm her down. But this just made her blub even more.

I turned my attention back to Amil. "Can't wait to hear what you all have to say in the live final?! Get your radio voices at the ready!"

It was all too much?! We were going to be live!

On the radio!

In thirteen days' time!

SORRY, WE WERE WHAT?!

I WAS GOING TO HAVE TO SPEAK LIVE ON THE RADIO?

The other three were still cheering like we'd won the lottery.

But I was silent. The realization hit me like a snowball in the face.

THE WHOLE HOPE OF MY ENTIRE SCHOOL WAS NOW RESTING ON ME GIVING ADVICE LIVE ON THE RADIO.

This couldn't be happening.

Rach was still yelling, "WEEEEE'RE GOING TO MEET THE HELICANS!" on repeat. Which wasn't really helping.

"I'm so proud of you, darling!" Mum planted a kiss on my head.

But how was I going to do well when I would be mute with fanic?! Argh, I meant panic or fear. Not both. See?! My mind had already stopped working with fanic?!

No one had noticed I'd gone the colour of Tippex – they were too busy celebrating. Rach was vibrating with excitement, already lost in preparing for the big day.

"We'll have to plan outfits carefully. Show Letty that Bella's got game?!"

Mum mumbled something about being sure there

must be something in my cupboard – but Shay snorted.

"Yeah – cos what you wear on the radio is *really* important." She immediately realized how bad it sounded. "Rach – how about you borrow the shoes?"

Rach nodded like today couldn't get any better.

But I didn't know if it could get more terrifying.

Still in silence, I made a mental list of petrifying things that were now looming.

- Representing the school (on live radio)
- Having the hopes of the school on my shoulders (on live radio)
- Speaking (on live radio)
- Meeting the Helicans (on live radio)
- Meeting Queevil (on live radio)
- Doing live radio (on live radio)

Could I think of anything positive to calm me down?! I racked my brain.

At least people can't see me go bright red/silently weep/run away (on live radio)

Cool. Great. Excellent.

"I'll drop you guys down there if you want? Be good to see what studio set-up they have." Shay looked at Rach. "Maybe catch up with the guys. . ."

SHE DID ANOTHER WINK OF INTRIGUE.

Luckily Rach nodded for the both of us. Having a pro

with us is just what we'd need. Jo had already messaged me with the same offer, but I'd stand her down.

After thirty more mins of pure celebration Rach had to head home. Keen to keep planning for Saturday I went with her. As we set off, Mum asked her to stop squeaking as it was frightening the neighbours' cats.

When we got level with the playing field Rach grabbed me.

"Bells. Why didn't you say?! We *totally* haven't written that Adam message?"

She looked horrified that she'd forgotten, but the truth was, seeing as both of us had experienced either an accidental dribble, or loss of speech in the last hour, I didn't really feel like we were top of our game. I'd decided to postpone till tomoz at school with Teeg.

But Rach had other ideas. She put her hand out.

"Remind me what you guys last officially said to each other."

I passed her my phone, and she scrolled down through the bazillion messages I'd received today.

But when she got to his name, I didn't recognize the message at the top. Had he sent me something I'd missed?! But, no.

The message was the wrong colour.

What the whatting what what?!

It was from ME??

What HAD I done?!

With my heart so far in my mouth it was basically a hat, I grabbed my phone and opened the thread.

I scrolled up to the first message I didn't recognize.

17:57 yesterday. When I was on the way home from the dentist.

Bella: 17:57

Hey Adam. A. Dam. (FYI DID YOU KNOW BEAVERS LIVE IN DAMS???)

Please, no. My big re-entry into his inbox was about animal habitats.

Why hadn't Mum confiscated my phone while I was in a vulnerable state?!

This was not OK.

This was not even OK's long-lost cousin.

Bella: 17:59

Anywayz, not the point. Do you want to go on TMUDE?

What did that even mean?! And worse, why had I used a z?!

But it got worse. Much much worse. Because what came next was a picture. Of me. In Mum's car, waving and smiling the world's happiest smile straight to camera – except one half of my mouth had drooped down and I had a cotton-wool roll dangling out of it like a fake cigarette when you're eight.

Did I think I was funny?!

Bella: 18:02
I'm so funny!

"Rach, please tell me this isn't really happening?"

She put her hand on my arm. "Calm down, Bells. It's going to be fine. . ."

But it already wasn't. Could I sue the dentist?

Still, at least I hadn't mentioned *TMUDE* again.

Bella: 18:03
You didn't answer!! Do you want to go on The Most Unforgettable Date Ever?!

Ah – so *this* was what this all about. Me arranging that date. And I'd used the forbidden D word?!

Could someone arrest my fingers please?

But Rach had started squeaking, because what came

next was a reply from Adam.

Adam: 18:05
Hello stranger. Are you . . . eating cotton wool?

Adam: 18:06
And it's a yes. To both TMUDE. And you being
funny xx

I gasped so loud a pigeon dived into a hedge. But I
was in utter shock. Shutter-ock.

I'd got a date (D-WORD DATE) with Adam?! And
two "xx"? And it had happened almost twenty-hour hours
ago. And I'd had zero idea until now.

Oooof. What a rollercoaster.

"Bells." Rach pointed at my screen. "I don't know if
you're in a fit state to deal . . . but there's more."

I wasn't in any fit state, but I NEEDED to know. I
strapped my life-ruining seatbelt back on.

Adam: 18:08
So what is TMUDE going to involve?

Good question. I'd been thinking about it all day
yesterday.

Bella: 18:12
I've chatted to my mum and we've got it!!

Yes, Bells, nothing says sexy and spontaneous like planning a date with your own mother.

Bella: 18:14
Sunday. My house. Be prepared for. . .

For what?! A meal with my fam? An awkward evening of soil balls and *University Challenge*? No good could come of this!

Bella: 18:14
DOG AGILITY!!

Oh.
My.
Holy tooth decay.
I HAD to be joking.
This was not a *thing*?!
Damn you, Marcus, for telling me Adam was a fan of it. And damn you, Mum, for showing me Furry Flyers in action!

Bella: 18:15
Mumbles and I are going to show you what
we're made of!!!! Bring a cushion. And some
Malted Milks.

The dentist must have drilled too far and replaced
my brain with toothpaste.

On top of *everything* else, there was NO world where
Malted Milks would be my first choice of biscuit. I
collapsed into Rach's shoulder.

"Tell me I didn't actually do this??"

She stroked my hair. "I . . . cannot do that. But – he
hasn't replied yet. We could suggest something else?"

But as she said it my screen flashed in real time.

Five words that meant all my dreams of Adabella
now rested on me and a dog that occasionally walked
into rooms backwards.

Sounds great. See you Sunday. xx

Plus side: at least I knew what it felt like to have my
worst idea ever.

Not plus side: this was my worst idea ever.

There was NO WAY I could go through with it.

So when I got back, as casually as I could I dropped

the whole Adam date thing into convo with Mum to get full deets. It was so cringe I almost crimbled (verb: to cringe in on oneself). But Mum just smiled proudly (hypothesis: she clearly never thought a real human boy would agree to spend time with me) and excitedly told me she'd already treated me to some "fun props" for it. And they were non-refundable. So whatever I did, "I couldn't change my mind now".

Even her guilt tripping was on to me.

What HAD I done?!

With my mind near melting, trying to take today in, I climbed into bed fully clothed.

But there was no way I could sleep.

Because all the things that a week ago had felt impossible – Adam wanting to go out with me, winning the competition, going from a nobody to popular – were suddenly the nearest they'd even been.

But something was troubling me. And as I shifted from pillow, to time-wasting on my phone, back to pillow, I tried to work out what.

Was it because I also felt like I was the nearest I'd ever been to screwing everything up?

Or was it because the one congrats I wanted the most this evening was the one that never came. Tegan's.

CHAPTER

EIGHTEEN

My walk into school the next morning was the kind of thing you'd see slow-mo in a music video – all high-fives and cheers from random groups of people (although if I *was* in a vid, I wouldn't be wearing tights that had lost their elastic, causing me to semi-waddle as they fell down).

As far as everyone was concerned, the final was now just a formality – in their minds St Mary's had already won the gig.

To say I felt under pressure would be like saying Zayn was a little bit fit.

Worst of all, Mrs Hitchman greeted me with an actual hug. Full boob-to-boob squash horror. I was so taken aback I'd stepped on her foot. And then was so taken aback-aback that it was wearing a Converse I'd stepped into a water cooler (which ironically made me a lot less cool than before I'd bashed into it).

But despite the competition being the only thing anyone was talking about, Tegan didn't ask a single question about it till Rach brought it up on Tuesday morning. And when I'd excitedly said all three of us could go to the final and meet the band, she'd replied with a half-hearted "cool".

It was rubbish to think about, but I was getting used to Teeg being a part-time friend. And, later that day, after a really honest chat with Rach, I'd discovered she felt the same. We weren't cross. We were both worried. Worried she was putting herself under way too much pressure about the try out, and even more worried that she was shutting us out of anything to do with it.

Even worse, we had no clue how to help. Everything we'd tried so far had backfired. So with no other ideas, and Tegan getting more distant by the day, we'd decided to have a quiet word with Mikey to see if he had any advice. It didn't help that Rach also thought it was weird that Teeg was being so cagey about "hot bus boy" (as Rach called him) after I let it slip about me spotting him pick Tegan up that day.

But finding a private moment with Mikey at school

this week had been impossible – I was never alone. People shouted my name when I didn't know theirs, and instead of pushing past me, strangers queued to ask how I was. Was this what life was like being Rachel? Even the dinner lady now chatted to me – and gave me the largest slice of treacle sponge pudding four days running.

I guess it *could* be fun if I wasn't so hyper-aware how it could all change if I didn't win the gig. It was almost too scary to think about.

Equally as terrifying was my date on Sunday. Prep was naaat going well. It had started on Monday evening when I'd got Mumbles to sit beside me as we watched vids of dogs running through tunnel tube things, and leaping over gates. I'd hoped she'd feel motivated to show the world what she'd got. But instead she'd fallen asleep with half a sock sticking out of her mouth. I'd tried to pull it out, but discovered it was mashed up with a dog chew she'd forgotten to finish eating earlier.

If swallowing was beyond her, I wasn't sure my future with Adam was in the safest hands. Or paws.

And it hadn't got any better.

Every inch of me wanted to cancel. But the others reckoned Adam was the kind of guy who'd be more put off by flakey-ness, than misjudged activities. Especially as he'd messaged saying he was "intrigued" (same) and "really looking forward to it" (not same). So, I was persevering as best I could.

My fear had notched up an extra gear on Wednesday when Mum's props had arrived. It was a "starter kit" (who knew?!) of dog-size hoop, two stands and two poles. Sadly, it didn't include a competent dog. In the two evenings since, Mumbles had only managed to clear one jump, and that was only because she spotted a particularly aggressive crow and was running for her life.

So what with "Sit!" still beyond us, I'd concluded any *actual* agility was going to be impromptu. I'd also concluded that my garden was a terrible location as Mumbles mainly stood staring at a fence because she thought there was a sexy dog the other side of it (sadly it was just a fake bark alarm the neighbours had installed).

After seeing me so stressed, like the wonder-saint she is, Rach had offered that we could do it all at hers. This was excellent for three main reasons.

1) It meant not bringing Adam into my family home aka Shame HQ, packed with pictures of me as a baby (I looked like a toe in a jumper), and my actual mother – who still referred to Adam as "That Man You're Going To Marry".

2) Rach had a range of statues and bushes we could make some sort of jumping course from. It was going to be positively Olympian.
3) Rach's entire life/family/snacks/even wallpaper were cooler than mine.

I was gutted Tegan was going to miss it, but it was the same day as her audition so it wasn't an option. She'd spent every waking hour this week training. Probably the non-waking ones too, as in this morning's assembly she was so sleep deprived, she didn't even notice Mrs Hitchman playing a Helicans song as the entrance music.

This was the exact moment Rach and I knew we *had* to speak to Mikey, and as it was Friday, we had to do it before the day was out. As much as Tegan was pushing us away, we wanted her to know she wasn't alone.

"Oh hi, dream team." Ava gave us a wave from a stepladder as we walked to class. She was putting up yet another "Vote Bella" poster. (Mr Lutas had let all classes design and make them instead of their normal art lessons.) She grinned at the poster. "Not long now. Just over a week before the actual HEL. I. CANS. Could be here?! In this very building?!!"

I "Ummm"-ed, feeling weird standing next to a giant picture of my face, which was bigger than my IRL face.

"Sounds ammmaaayyyyzzzinnnng – if you have zero standards."

Luke.

Tegan thrust a poster straight towards him. "You know you don't have to ask if you wanna give us a hand putting some up?"

I stifled a laugh – she might be a part-time pal at the mo', but her work was still excellent.

Luke glared like she'd handed him a bunch of dead squirrels. "I'd rather vom."

Rach sniggered. "That IS one of their singles. Glad you're on-brand."

If there was one thing Luke hated more than being called out in front of his mates, it was being called out by Rach – the girl everyone fancied and he could never have.

"Fit Rach, I DO NOT KNOW why you still hang out with these idiots." He looked straight at me. "Well, mainly THIS one."

I gave Luke a cheery wave. It's much harder to look like you care about being called an idiot if you're choosing to look like one. He rolled his eyes.

"So, Fishy." Oh good, he was back on the retro Fishy Balls nickname. "I came to say thanks for helping keep this whole Helicans thing going."

I smiled. "Total pleasure."

"It's made it a whole load easier to avoid the tragics." His mates all shrug-laughed – imaginative (except Boxer Boy who was pretending he couldn't hear). "Except Fit Rach, of course. She's always welcome, anywhere, any time."

"Dream on." Rach shook her head. "And if you're not gonna help, leave us alone."

Luke didn't move.

Ava stepped forward. "Errr, think she meant 'get lost'?"

Which he eventually did, but not till they made us so late we had to sprint just to avoid missing the start of biology. We then got shouted at for running. School life was no win.

Break time was another instalment of people hounding me with questions so by the time lunch came, it was fair to say that the comp was the number one last thing I wanted to talk about.

So I was relieved when we spotted Mikey. I waved him over and he plonked himself down.

"Did you guys see that Radio Shire blog about the Helicans?"

ARGH. Et tu, Mikey?

"Don't wanna talk about it."

Course I'd *heard*. But so far had managed to avoid the details. They'd revealed what order the three finalists had come in vote-wise. I was nervous enough already – and if I found out I was in last place I was not going to feel ANY more confident.

But Mikey looked put out. "But isn't it *better* to be David rather than Goliath?"

WAIT.

WAS HE TELLING ME I WAS DAVID?!

Rach, Tegan and I stopped chewing and stared straight at him. Realizing his slip, he gulped so loudly the next table turned round.

"I just meant hypothetically, you know." He pointed out of the window. "Look! Puppy!"

But even imaginary small animals couldn't gloss over what he'd said. And through a variety of nagging, poking and low-level threats about sharing the vid of him attempting Tegan's floor routine, he confirmed what he'd started to say. I'd come third. Aka last. And in first place was Queevil.

"OK, so, to recap," I put my hands on my face. "I'm going to lose. And be a massive loser – literally – in front of the Helicans. And live to the nation."

Tegan shook her head firmly. "Nope, course you're not. Knowledge is power, Bells. It just means we have to step up our efforts. Get EVERYONE ready to vote."

I kind of thought that's what we'd been doing already.

"Plus," Rach looked over her shoulders like we were in *Pretty Little Liars*, "the other finalists don't have our secret weapon..."

"A tiny catapult?" I quipped at Mikey.

"How many times. You are NOT David?!"

But Rach was full flow. "NOPE. Best friend to the band, and good word putter-inner... SHAY."

I knew what was needed right now was positivity so I gave Rach a "Hells, yeah!" Truth was, I wasn't sure what Shay could really do for us. And what I felt comfortable even asking her. I certainly didn't want to do anything that could jeopardize the final, not with Letty on the lookout.

But... I looked at Rach and imagined how destroyed she'd be if we didn't win. And how much every single person in this building would hate me. And ... well, maybe the easier option was chatting to Shay tonight.

"Talking of which, you guys want to come round for a bit later? Shout at a confused dog with me?"

Rach shook her head. "Soz, gotta do that essay so I'm free Sunday for..." She mouthed the last two words, "... the date". She knew I couldn't handle them with actual volume. I mouthed back, "Thank you."

"And T and I are off to see my brother's band play a headline gig." Mikey looked all uber-cool and mysterious like he was about to casually drop details of a Wembley slot. "... Aaaat my cousin's ninth birthday party."

Tegan's face fell. "Oh, Mikey. No *way*." She dropped her head into her hands. "It's the last time, I promise. PROMISE."

He finished what Rach and I knew was coming.

"... But you've booked in a last-minute training session?"

Tegan nodded slowly. "I'm SO sorry."

But Mikey wasn't cross. "Don't be – all we want is for you to nail Sunday. Whatever it takes."

Rach and I made noises of agreement. Teeg smiled at us all, embarrassed. "You guys are the best."

I didn't feel the best, because right now I was mainly feeling sad for Mikey. But Teeg didn't need to know that. All she needed to know was that we were on her side.

I prodded her arm. "You'll smash it. I know it. Just please try and not put too much pressure on yourself? For me?"

I smiled as I said it, but she glared back. "What – like you're *not* doing with this Helicans thing?"

Mikey rubbed her arm. "Teegs, c'mon. Bells didn't mean it like that." He looked at me. "Did you?"

Tegan didn't give me a chance to agree.

"It doesn't matter *what* she meant. I wish you'd all

just stop hassling." She slammed her lunchbox closed. "Support? Isn't that what friends, *best friends*, are meant to be for?"

"Teeg?" I pleaded. But it bounced right off her.

"See ya. I've got work to be doing." And like that, she stormed out. Something I'd never seen before. She was full of surprises these days.

And this latest one made me feel like I'd been thumped in the stomach. I gave up eating my lunch. Another world first.

Mikey gave me the most reassuring look he could. "It's just the trial, Bells. We'll have her back soon."

But the way he said it made it sound like a question, rather than a fact.

"You do know I was trying to help?" They both nodded, making me feel a tiny bit better. "I just can't stand by and watch her slowly implode."

Rach put her hand on mine. "Bells, I'm with you – all the way. But I have zero idea what to do either. She's just so on edge. All. The. Time."

I footsied Mikey under the table. "Has she said anything to you?"

He shrugged. "Nope. Other than the obvious." He thought a bit. "Although. . . I can't help but think a lot of it might be cos of this new Charlie from training."

Rach and I exchanged a look – we'd never heard that name before. Yet another detail we didn't know. "Some Team GB squad gymnast who Tegan's got friendly with. And now it's all 'hours in – power out', 'sleep is for second place'. . . I'm exhausted just listening."

That did explain a lot. And it had given me an idea.

"Charlie can drive, right?"

"Yeah. . ." Mikey nodded and got out his phone. "Elite gymnast. . . personal chauffeur? Hang on a sec, think there's a pic of them together somewhere. . ."

Mikey searched for the account to show Rach. But I already felt like a weight had been lifted.

"Rach – Charlie must be hot bus stop boy who we keep seeing her with?!" But Rach was doing tiny head shakes. She wasn't getting it. "You know – the one who picked her up last Saturday?" Rach's shakes got bigger. But it was too late. Mikey had turned his phone round.

"Bells – *this* is Charlie."

Oh. Tegan wasn't with the hot boy I was expecting.

She was with an even hotter person. All muscles and smiles.

"Ah," was about all I could say.

Charlie was a girl.

Mikey flicked the screen off. "Ah, indeed. So you were saying?"

Could I urgently retrieve my foot from my mouth?!
"It's nothing."

But Mikey's gutted face didn't look like nothing. "So there's a, to quote, 'hot boy', and you, to quote, 'keep seeing him' with Tegan? And ... she's never mentioned him to me?"

OK – this wasn't ideal. "I've made it sound worse than it is. It's probably just a, a training thing."

Rach was staring at a yoghurt, not blinking, like she was trying to teleport somewhere, anywhere, else.

"And you said they were together last Saturday – when she told me she was too busy to see me?"

I didn't know what I could say that would help.

"There's bound to be a logical explanation." Shame I didn't know it yet. "Like you said, it's just a weird time. She's being weird with ALL of us. You saw what just happened?"

Rach backed me up. "She didn't even hand in her homework this morning."

But Mikey looked heartbroken. I had to give it everything I could. Try and undo the damage. As weird as this whole thing was, Tegan would never hurt him. "We ALL know she's crazy about you. And you *know* you can trust her?"

He didn't look any happier. "Do you think I should

speak to her?"

"NO!" I snapped too quickly. "Sorry ... no. Please don't."

If Tegan was already mad at us – me especially – and stressed about Sunday, her thinking I'd dropped her in it with Mikey wasn't going to help anyone. But I got it. If I was him I'd want to find out who this guy was. I mean, I was *me*, and I wanted to know badly enough. "Can you wait till after the try-out? Then *I'll* speak to her. Properly this time." I owed it to her to be honest and explain the mix-up that had just happened.

He nodded. But with nothing but a Tegan-sized hole for company, we finished lunch in silence. We didn't manage to find her before the bell went either.

Sure, I was a bit cross at her for flying off the handle, but I was mainly sad that things weren't right with us. And I wanted to make it better. Rach and I messaged her and suggested meeting by the Bum tree (the tree that looks like a bum) to walk home. With my shift at GADAC tomorrow it'd be the last time we could all be together before her try-out. As the afternoon dragged on, I got more and more nervous.

Until finally, some good news: right on time, Tegan was at Bum tree.

Bad news: things were definitely still weird between us.

I was so worried about getting my words right, that the first half of the journey was just random chat to avoid talking about earlier.

I had to be brave. "Teeg."

She replied with an, "Uh-huh," knowing where this was going.

"I'm really sorry about earlier. The last thing I wanted to do was make this harder for you."

But it was met with silence. Just the sound of our steps for what felt like for ever.

"Look. . ." Tegan sounded serious. ". . . I'm sorry too." OH PHEW. She wanted us to be mended too. "It's just been so full-on, and I know it's a bit out of hand, but . . . but I shouldn't be taking it out on you guys."

She linked her arm through mine. Sealing the apologies in.

Rach joined in on her other side. "We just want you to know how amazing you already are."

But Tegan looked uncomfortable. "Not amazing enough, I think. Have I told you about this new girl, Charlie? Next to her I look like a total beginner."

I did a little smile to myself and caught Rach doing the same. So she'd finally mentioned Charlie. We were inner-circle again.

"Teeg, if you want to see *beginner* you should try

watching me do a handstand. I look like a wild donkey."

She laughed, although it soon stopped. "But quickly. While we're on the subject... Can I ask you something?"

I squeezed her arm. "As long as it's not about jumping dogs or the Helicans, fire away."

"Do you know what's up with Mikey? I tried to apologize to him twice this afternoon and he was really off with me."

Erm. What should I say? Tell her the truth?

Would she understand it was a mistake or fully freak out?

I knew I had to do whatever was best for Tegan, not what was best for me. Shame I had no idea what that was. I looked at Rach but she seemed as confused as me.

Luckily, Tegan didn't realize it was an awkward silence, and assumed we just didn't know what she meant.

"It's so unlike him. It was like he didn't want to talk to me..." She sighed. "Just what I *don't* need this weekend – wondering if my boyfriend's about to break up with me."

Hmmm. So Mikey had kept his word and not dropped me in it, but had made Tegan more worried in the process.

I had two options. Let Tegan sweat it out – which could distract her when she needed to be focused – or come clean – and run the risk of her hating me.

I knew how much the try-out meant to her. And what I had to do.

"OK, so promise you won't be mad?" I took a deep breath. "I mean, it's kind of funny."

She gave me a suspicious "Go on".

"Right. Yes. So … after that thing at lunch, Rach and I were wondering how we could make amends. Be better at helping you through this whole try-out." Yes, start strong.

Tegan looked confused. "And this has to do with Mikey ignoring me, how?"

OK. On to the tricky bit.

"Ah – well, we kind of got talking to him to see if he had any ideas…" Tegan's eyebrow raised. I looked away. This was already too hard to explain. "Which sort of led to us chatting about your training… Which sort of led to me accidentally thinking that when Mikey mentioned Charlie, he was talking about that guy from the bus stop."

Tegan stopped walking. "*What* guy from the bus stop?"

I had to carry on or I'd never get to the end.

"And then I *might* have said something to Mikey

about seeing you with him. Like … in his car last Saturday…" In panic I nervous laughed. But Tegan didn't look like she was finding this particularly hilarious. Furious was more accurate.

"Sorry, what?" She dropped her bag on the floor.

"It was just a mix-up, I promise?!"

"So Mikey's being weird with ME cos YOU once saw Liam on a video call and have been spying on us ever since?"

Ah, Liam. He finally had a name. But it wasn't really a victory when I could see the expression on Tegan's face.

"Not at all! I just saw you together – and meant to ask you about it. But you've been so stressed!"

"And you both thought going straight to my boyfriend to ask him about it was the best way to keep things calm?"

This was *not* going how I hoped. Rach looked mortified.

"It wasn't like that. I promise!"

Tegan took a breath trying to compose herself. "So let me get this straight. Now my boyfriend – who FYI I think is amazing – might finish with me cos you've made him think there's something going on behind his back?" She was getting more irate with every word. "With LIAM?! Who – incidentally – is my sports psychologist?

Who – oh also incidentally – comes to most sessions with his wife and children!?"

Ah. This was really not getting any better. And Tegan was in full rage flow, spitting her words out. "Who I didn't bother mentioning before, as he really was no big deal. LIKE I SAID. Plus, I didn't want to risk another lecture from you two on how I was overdoing things by having extra sessions with him." She was now full-on shouting. "But instead I'm starting the biggest weekend of my life justifying myself to you – and the rest of it sorting out your mess?!"

Well, this felt awful. And like maybe I should have kept quiet after all.

I didn't know what to say.

"I'm sorry – it really was an accident."

Rach nodded. "It totally was – I was there."

But Tegan looked like she was past caring. "I don't have time for this." She looked at me. "For you. So if it's quite all right, I'm going to leave before you make anything even worse than it already is. Oh – and if you speak to Mikey, can you tell him you're an idiot?"

And for the second time that day she walked off.

But this time I knew I'd really messed up.

NiNETEEN

Friday evenings normally feel like the start of a mini summer holiday. But this one felt like one big fat Monday morning. I was so desperate to take my mind off my argument with Tegan that, as soon I got home, I headed straight to the garden to practise with Mumbles in the last of the daylight, but she spent the whole time eating grass like she was having a cow-based identity crisis.

By the time Mum called me in for dinner, we'd achieved zero progress. Sunday was going to be a disaster. The only good thing had come out of this mess — Mum had picked up on my miserable mood and had made my fave. Broc 'n' cheese (a version of mac 'n' cheese, but with added broccoli). Dinner began with the usual disagreement over whether she should rename it "broc 'n' mac 'n' cheese", but as usual she argued then we'd be listing every single ingredient, and we might as well call it "broc 'n' mac 'n' butt 'n' salt 'n' garl 'n' must 'n' mil 'n' flou 'n' cheese".

It was delish, but as we ate Mum looked more glum than me – she hadn't been her usual chatty self for weeks. Next time it was just the two of us I'd ask her what was up. Whatever it was, I didn't want to add daughter-who-has-humiliated-herself-live-on-radio-so-much-that-she-has-to-live-out-her-existence-in-my-lounge to her woes. So, when Mum answered the phone to Brenda (so could be distracted for four hours plus), it was the perfect time to do what I'd promised Rach. Speak to our Secret Weapon.

Standing next to each other at the draining board, Shay and I looked like a real-life game of opposites. She was in a structured statement mini dress and hadn't taken her heels off, and a foot and a half lower was me, now in my burger pyjamas and horse slippers.

"So, Shayyyy."

"Soooo, Belllaaaaa," she replied, passing me a bowl. But I wasn't sure what to say next. "C'mon, I know something's up. You've been starting sentences, and trailing off all evening."

"Oh sorry! I didn't realize. . ."

She turned to wipe the table.

"See?"

"Ah... OK... Well... It's errrr, about next weekend... About the final."

She chuckled quietly. "Surprise, surprise."

I tried to sound as casual as I could.

"I just wondered if you'd heard from er ... the *guys* at all?" I'd totally overshot Casual Village and ended up in Cringetown. I scrubbed extra hard at a plate so not to see her reaction.

"If by 'the guys' as you say, you mean 'the band' then the answer's no..."

Oh. I *knew* that would be the answer, but couldn't help feel a bit sad she hadn't said, *"Yes, and they said they loved you and will do anything to help you win. And isn't Letty a total monster?!"*

"I don't like them to bother them when they're on tour, you know?"

She always said "y'know" when I really didn't.

Her arm went round my shoulders. "Bells. It *is* going to be OK."

I dropped my head. She didn't even know about the Tegan situation. Or the Adam one. Right now things felt very far from OK. "Look, I'll chat to them when we're at the studio. Keep it informal."

I smiled. At least there was a glimmer of hope in all this rubbish. Just having her around, on our side, was going to be such a boost.

My phone beeped. Had Tegan come round?

I'm at my little sister's Year 3 Spelling Bee.
Someone just got thrown out for not being able
to spell misspelt. Am so glad I've got Sunday to
be thinking about x

Oh my broccoliballs – an unsolicited Adam message. I was so excited I didn't even not-reply immediately to try and look cooler than I am.

It's going to be something! Prepare for slobber!

Followed by an emergency clarification:

From Mumbles.

Which, despite staring at my phone for the rest of the evening, he didn't reply to. Thinking of the thousand different things I *should* have replied with, I crawled under my duvet, promising myself I'd take off my make-up and clean my teeth in a second. But instead I got sucked into an internet hole trying (and failing) to find pics of Letty, studying recent photos of Tegan to see if she looked happier with her new training friends than with us, looking at Luke's new girlf's holiday pics from two years ago (She's so pretty! She has SO many followers! She really does have outstanding wrists!), and watching vids of small animals with hiccups.

But my bed must be like the Tardis, and seconds later it was nine a.m. and I'd woken up to the sound of a baby mongoose sneezing on my laptop screen.

The most important weekend of my life had begun.

CHAPTER

TWENTY

I started Saturday like I meant to go on – total power woman. YAS, BELLA.

I sprang out of bed, ate cereal that was brown (not rainbow), blasted the Helicans on repeat and said confident hellos to everyone I saw (including a confused bin man).

But sadly I soon discovered that the battery that powered my newfound power-woman status only lasted approximately forty-five minutes. And by the time I was halfway through another slow day at GADAC, I was on emergency power-save mode.

Maybe launching an ice cream place in the autumn wasn't the greatest idea? Still, as Mum always pointed out, "Anything keeps in the freezer!" (Followed by a more business focused, "And it's always the season for a treat".)

Today I'd brought Mumbles with me – maximizing bonding time before our big moment tomorrow – and discovered she was surprisingly good at smiling with her eyes. But after two hours of uploading hilarious pics – complete with more hashtags than I'd #everusedinmylife #cringe – we'd only added two new followers (and one of them was a naked lady "looking for good man fun". Not dog ice cream).

The shop was so quiet I FaceTimed Jo. She'd been in a mood with me after I chose Shay to give us a lift to the final. I wasn't surprised. Ever since the GADAC launch Jo had had it in for her. She blamed Shay for the fiasco and kept telling me she couldn't be trusted – and that she wasn't Team Fisher like she said. Even when I told her how nice Shay'd been with all her advice, and lifts, and help with the comp, Jo wouldn't have any of it. So I reckoned she was just jealous.

Jo's mood had upgraded into epically bad when she'd discovered Mum was away at a business workshop the day of the final, so she'd been drafted in to cover my GADAC shift.

So I thought I'd ring and clear the air. And it worked, cos when I told her about being patted by Adam leading to somehow now having to perform dog agility for him – she was too busy laughing at me to remember to hate me. A result – I think? I then fully repaired any damage by letting her enjoy a ten-minute mega gloat that Mum had said yes to paying for her athletics trip. Job done.

The afternoon was even quieter than the morning. It was pouring down and I only had four customers – so packaged up some online orders to pass the time. When Mum arrived to pick me up, I/Gary was sitting cross-legged on the floor by Mumbles.

"Hello, Little and Large." She gave us both a kiss. And a pat behind the ears.

"Maybe people'll think I'm her Patronus?"

"Maybe they'll think you've lost the plot." Mum opened up the till. "Have you already cashed up?"

I shook my head. "Nope. We just didn't get many people in today. Must be the rain."

She gave me the kind of smile that makes you feel awful, as you know it's done to comfort you, even though the smile-ee looks like they feel way sadder.

"Oh well, I'm sure it'll pick up, won't it, chickadee?"

I tried not to notice how little money she was emptying and took off Gary's head. I hung it on a peg, freaking out Mumbles, who stood and growled at it.

"Everything OK, Mum?"

She sighed. "Do you want the mum answer?"

"The real one, please." I didn't really, but without Jo around, sometimes I had to step up.

She leaned against the cupboards, weighing up what to say.

"C'mon. I'm fifteen. I can handle it." I couldn't, but this week couldn't get a whole load worse, so she might as well.

She took a deep breath. "I just don't think we've got more than a couple of months left here." She looked around the shop. "We're just not making enough to break even."

WOAH.

I had to fully concentrate on not looking as shocked as I felt.

I had no idea things were *that* bad?!

"I know you're doing your best on the internet with all your socializing." Not the time to explain social media again. "But it's just not enough."

Oh, man. She was on the verge of tears. And I didn't feel far away myself. I *mustn't* let her see. I put an arm round her.

"Thing is, Bella, I put all my savings in here. *Our* savings. And Shay's going back to London in a month.

And . . . and, if things don't pick up, I'm just not sure . . . sure what to do." As soon as she said it she buried her head in her hands. "Sorry. Bad Mumming. I shouldn't have told you that."

But she should. Because as terrifying as it was hearing things were falling apart, at least it meant now I could try and do something to help stop it.

I gave her the biggest hug.

"GOOD Mumming. I'm SO proud of you." I used Gary's paw to wipe away a tear. I felt like the parent. Well, a parent dressed as a dog. "We'll figure this out. You're not on your own, you know? You never are."

She held me extra tight. "Wonderful, wonderful Bella. I knew that from the moment I first clapped eyes on you."

That made me sound slightly adopted, but now wasn't the time to check.

"Better than Jo?"

She rolled her eyes. Normality had resumed.

"Joint wonderful."

And, despite my terrifying date being less than eighteen hours away, my best friend hating me, and my entire school life hanging in the balance of next week's final, when Mum and I headed home, we enjoyed the best evening I'd had in ages.

Snuggled up under a sofa-duvet, we watched Saturday night TV, ate so much popcorn I had to undo my jeans, and best of all, both pretended everything was OK.

CHAPTER

TWENTY-ONE

Mistake one was the home-made face mask I'd let Mum talk me into last night. There is a reason beetroot is a food and not make-up.

My look was fifty shades of pink.

Mistake two was THIS WHOLE DOG AGILITY THING.

I stood in Rachel's garden, looking at the course we'd created. I'd wanted "glorious sporting triumph". I'd achieved: "looking like the outside bit of a garden centre had sneezed on Rach's lawn".

Even *if* Mumbles did miraculously manage to impress Adam with an award-winning performance, I'd still be the girl who'd spent her weekend lugging around bits of decorative log and statues of small boys having wees (if that's not acceptable in public, why is everyone so into immortalizing it in stone?!).

For the first few hours, I'd been pretty proud of our ingenuity. Right up until HOB yelled out of the window, "What the HELL is *that*?!"

Turned out answering, "A dog-agility course," wasn't enough to stop him following up with, "What goes on in your head?!"

He was right. This was the worst idea I'd ever had. And I'd once thought it would be an OK idea to use Jo's razor to shape my eyebrow. I'd never *been* more grateful Rach's parents had gone shopping in Paris for the weekend and weren't here to witness it.

The *pièce de résistance* (retrospectively, *pièce I should have resisted*) was the "Tunnel of Terror" constructed from the big hoop Mum had bought, covered with a sleeping bag, all staked out into the ground.

We'd done it when I was sugar-high on three bags of Haribo, but now a slice of normal thought had returned, I realized I *had* to take it down. I pulled at the poles we'd used to wedge it in, like this was all their stupid fault. But they weren't budging. Damn Rach for putting them in with her superior upper body strength.

"Can't you just tell him I'm not in?! Pleeeeeease, Rach?"

Adam's ETA – ATA – was six minutes away.

"Bells. I sin-celery think I might have broken at least two toes when we dropped that statue." We'd definitely cracked two of *its* toes. "So if you think I'm going to let all my nice shoes go to waste for nada, you can think again."

BUMBAGS. It was so much easier backing out of plans if you hadn't talked the one best friend who still liked you into physically labouring on them for four hours.

Rach put her hands on her hips.

"Now, let's do last-minute checks. Dog choc?"

I patted my back pocket. "Affirmative." Mumbles came over for a sniff.

"Teeth." Rach peered in my mouth and gave a satisfied nod.

"Breath." I "huhhhed" in her direction. She passed me another chewing gum. I apologized.

"Conversation."

"His drumming, Molly – HIS DOG – *Game of Thrones*, world events."

"Yas. And in 'world events', feel free to include, 'have you got any friends/relatives/people you once met in the street who could vote for St Mary's next Saturday?'"

I laughed. But it was a throat-only nervous one.

I didn't want to admit it to Rach, but on top of

everything, I was worrying about what she would think about *him*. Yes, they'd met in a casual way, but this would be our first time together as a three. Four with Mumbles. If Rach didn't approve, then it was game over.

I looked at my phone.

ATA: two mins.

TERROR WAVE.

I would do *anything* to get out of this. Even swap with Tegan. But just thinking her name made me feel sad. She'd be at her audition right now. Rach and I had sent her a good-luck video this morning, but we hadn't had anything back.

ATA: one min.

Breathing and swallowing switched from automatic to manual.

My mouth was so dry I had to use my finger to nudge my tongue around a bit to unstick it. I needed someone to tell me it was going to be OK, but Rach had headed in for a wee, and there was only Mumbles left, and she couldn't speak, let alone guarantee her performance.

I called her over anyway. She didn't move. Excellent start. I walked to her and crouched down.

"Now then, Mumbelina." She panted and I almost passed out with her mouth-fumes. Adam was going to think we fed her on a diet of sewage and rotting meat.

But now was not the time to crush her confidence (although maybe it *was* time to look into whether chewing gum for dogs had been patented).

"It's just you and me now." She licked my face. Great. Now I smelt of sewage-death too. "Thanks for that. Now, listen. This is what's going to happen." She pricked her ears. I loved her – she totally knew this was important. "You and I are just going to spend some time jumping over these, er, obstacles." I gestured at the random collection of things. "Then you're going to play dead. Then run through that tunnel. Big finish. All things we practised, remember?" Key word was *practised*. Less accurate description would be "*achieved*". "We just need to try our best. And not do anything weird. . . OK?" That bit applied to both of us.

She looked at me with her lovely soft brown eyes, and for a moment I thought she understood. Then she let out a fart that smelt so bad my lungs tried to emergency eject from my body. My vision actually blurred. I fell back on the lawn wafting at my face.

"YOUR BOTTOM IS A WEAPON OF GAS DESTRUCTION." I tried to take in a breath without ingesting smell particles. "WHAT *IS* YOUR PROBLEM??"

"Always being one minute early for everything?"

Wait. What?! My vision un-blurred to reveal Rach

and an Adam-like specimen peering over me.

Oh please, no.

It wasn't Adam-like. It *was* Adam.

"Is that you?!" *Please let me be hallucinating.* I was NOT ready?!

"Erm, yes – although wouldn't everyone say that?"

He laughed, and put out his hand.

Sorry. Did he really think me touching his actual flesh was going to help me be more normal?! But I had no choice.

I grabbed it, and pulled myself up. As I did Rach's nostrils flared so wide, I swear her face became half hole. I had to look away before getting inappropriate giggles.

Not helped by the fact my hand was so sweaty that it made a weird hand fart.

What would Tegan say if she was still talking to me? *Confidence. Composure.*

"So, errr, thanks for coming to chez Rachel, for, errr, what I can assure you will be a, err, once in a lifetime experience." Not exactly a TED talk, but it was a start.

I swear Rach muttered, "You can say that again."

Adam looked around the garden. Make or break time.

"It looks really … *impressive*. You must have been

doing this for hours?!"

"Noooo," I said dismissively – just as Rach said at the exact time, "Several."

BUT he hadn't legged it at the sight of a sleeping bag flapping in the wind (currently billowing like it was the International flag for Sleepovers). RELIEF. If I could just get this section of the day out of the way as quickly as possible, we could move on to more traditional activities, aka anything other than performance-based pet exercise.

Rach leapt into action. "Before we start do you want a drink or anything?" Yes! Part one of our plan.

"Erm, a water would be amazing. If that's OK?"

"I'll go and fix ... you ... one," Rach said weirdly slowly, trying to subtly indicate to me "PHASE ONE ALERT!! QUALITY BELLA AND ADAM TIME!" It would have been more subtle if she didn't slow-blink with every word.

It was at this *exact* moment I realized I'd never mentioned there would be a third person on our date. This is *surely* the kind of normal thing a normal person would have done. Oh well. But Adam wasn't making a thing out of it. I hated (/absolutely adored) how able he was to deal with everything. He even spoke to Rach like she was a generic human – most boys just dribbled and stared.

As she walked away, I attempted convo.

"So how's the er..." My mind raced through the authorized topic list. Drumming, yes. "Drumming?" EW. It sounded too serious, like a teacher question. Be more chatty! "Done any good, er, banging?"

SORRY, WHAT WAS THAT, MOUTH?!

"Errr, lots, actually. This new football team's been full on, so it's been nice to let off some steam."

I nodded gormlessly. I *swear* I've had at least thirteen years of practising using words, so why was it always so hard whenever he was near? JUST SAY SOMETHING, BELLA.

"Steamy."

Not that.

"You *could* say that?!" Adam laughed to make it less awkward.

But, hold up. What new football team did he mean? This was the perfect opportunity for normal-person convo.

"I don't think I've seen you since you had a new team?"

He suddenly looked all embarrassed. "Oh yeah. I was going to explain... I had, er ... trials for the, er ... county team. South Worcester Reds..." I loved how he was trying not to brag, even though he totally wasn't. "And I found out when they picked the team last

Saturday." He looked back up at me. "*That* was why I couldn't meet up with you?"

OMG – had he just revealed his long story? Cos actually it was quite short.

"You should have just said?! And congrats, by the way."

He grinned. I auto-swooned. "Well, it seemed like you had enough on your plate with all that radio competition stuff without me going on about my drama too?"

As if?! I wanted to know ALL his drama. "Not at all?!" Too enthusiastic. "I love a full plate." What to say next? "And empty ones." He smiled. "Bowls too."

Oh. Help. I couldn't just list crockery for the next five minutes. Well, I could, because when you think about it, there's actually a huge range, but this probs wasn't the killer chat that would win him round.

As I racked my brains for something better, I spotted Rach peeking out from behind a hedge. I jerked my head up in a "quick, get here before I start talking about gravy jugs" way. Adam totally saw. I pretended I had a fly in my hair.

"OH LOOK RACH IS BACK WITH THE DRINKS," I said, loud enough to coax her out. She sidestepped her way across the lawn, and passed out the glasses.

"Here you go. Sorry it took so long. I . . . got a phone

call? An urgent one."

She laid out our carefully chosen snacks. Adam reached for some Monster Munch. I shot a look at Rach to say, "*SEE*. I told you: he IS my dream man."

I grabbed a couple too – look, Adam! We have things in common!

"Ummmm, these are totally my dave..." Now I wanted to say nibbles but was too worried I might say nipples. I needed another word. "Nipples."

Adam did an actual choke. How could I make this less terrible?

I laughed hysterically. "It's just what we call them." Hahahaha. "Nip-ples." I said it again. "Niii-ippp-pples." Why couldn't stop saying it!? "Cos we nip to the shop to get them."

Silence.

"Nipples." MOUTH, STOP OR I WILL PHSYICALLY HOLD YOU CLOSED.

I stared at the ground. Now would be a really great time for it to swallow me whole. I shifted my weight around to encourage it. But nothing.

"Yes, we definitely DO call them that," Rach said like a human robot.

Well at least we'd hit peak weird early on.

Adam mustered his best smile.

"Well, in that case. . ." He shut his eyes and breathed in as if giving himself inner strength. "Great nipples?"

None of us could make eye contact. Even Mumbles looked away. Probably because she had six of them, and no jumper on, and felt extra self-conscious.

I crossed my arms across my chest. And noticed Rach and Adam had done the same.

Well this was awful.

"Right then!" I clapped my hands desperately trying to end part one. "Let's get this show on the road!"

I walked away, grateful to put some distance between me and Adam, and all of our poor nipples. I was meant to be making him laugh *with* me not *at* me. Mumbles trotted over and sat at my feet. Maybe she'd sensed the importance and was going to pull this out of the bag after all?

I bent to stroke her, plucking up the courage to sneak a quick look back at Adam. Luckily, he was smiling.

"Ladies . . . er . . . lady and gentleman. Welcome to today's extravaganza! A visual feast of the, er, relationship between man – well wo-man – and dog! Who is also a woman. A woman dog." I did two-hand pointing. "It's. . . MUMBLES!"

Our audience of two clapped and whooped.

"For your delight we will be performing some of her

most agile feats. . ."

Rach and Adam did an excellent gameshow, "Woooooo!"

". . . including playing dead . . ."

More oo-ing.

". . . walking backwards . . ."

This time it was an ahhhhh.

". . . jumping these three death-defying fences . . ."

Even bigger, "Wooooh!"

". . . and crawling through this tunnel of doom!"

We got our biggest applause yet. Maybe this *could* be fun after all?

I grinned at Rach, so happy she was here. She smiled back and flicked on the music.

Adam drummed along on his deckchair. Fit. But I couldn't just stand here and perv (well, I could and currently I was). I turned my back on them, stroked Mumbles' ears, and whispered, "You've got this!"

"Soooo, let's start with one of the simple jumps. . ." I legged it to the far side of the first one, and yelled her name. And like a tiny furry thoroughbred stallion she galloped towards me and flew over it.

In my dreams.

In reality she didn't move a muscle.

I shouted again.

She lay down and started chewing grass.

I was being blanked.

There was only one thing for it. I ran to her, waved the dog choc under her nose and pelted it back as fast as I could, jumping over the fence with her running alongside me, like a graceful hairy best friend.

Well ... that's what I intended. What actually happened was that I ran towards the jump, slid slightly in a patch of water Rach had spilled, lost my balance, tried to take off anyway, tripped into the whole thing, put my hands out to stop myself falling and ended up sort of leapfrogging Rach's dad's compost bin. All while Mumbles stayed exactly where she started looking at me like I'd lost my mind.

If there's a Buzzfeed list on Top 100 Unsexy Things To Do On A Date, I'd just crossed off at least twenty-two.

But as I regained my balance there was a loud clap. And some full-on laughing.

"TEN!" Adam held up all his fingers. "Ten! For aerial skills!"

I had two options. Apologize. Or embrace the ridiculous. And based on the last fifteen years, I knew I only had one option.

I embraced my failure so hard, I did a little bow, and grinned at Adam. Who grinned at me (as did Rach, who was grinning at me being grinned at by Adam).

Mumbles and I then had two more equally unsuccessful attempts at the remaining jumps (I jumped one, Mumbles walked into the other whilst staring up at me) before it was time to move on to safer ground.

"Before our Tunnel of Terror grrrrrrand finale, we will now show you one of our best slash only skills... Playing dead!" True, it was our most successful trick (one in thirty-five success rate). I pointed to the ground and shouted, "Tragic sudden death!"

On the "death" Mumbles was meant to fall to the floor and shut her eyes. But as I shouted it, Adam did the loudest sneeze. And instead of remaining deathly still, Mumbles bolted the entire length of the garden and leapt into a hedge.

Erm ... could I style this out?

Nope. But I didn't need to because Adam burst into the sort of full-body laughter that's so extreme it sounded like he was getting a six-pack from it. No, Bella. Do NOT think about what lies beneath Adam's jumper. Today is challenging enough already.

"You guys!" Adam was physically bent over his knees, holding himself as he shook. "Tooooo good."

Rach looked at me, getting "Am I OK to laugh at this

too" approval.

But it was too late – I was already laughing so hard I'd done an accidental nose snort. Yup, after dedicating all this week to practising, it was fair to say Mumbles and I were atrocious. The only thing we'd actually learnt that was if in doubt – laugh at yourself. A lot.

But we had one more thing.

"Rach – please could you line up the finale song?"

She pressed play on the tune we'd chosen for the big finale. The Helicans, "Look What I Could Be To You".

"Mmmmmmm, nice choice..." Adam's drumming picked back up. He smiled, enjoying the song. I smiled, enjoying us enjoying the same song. Step one – like the same song. Step two – lifetime of happiness. Right?

But I couldn't just stop to witness the fitness. It was time to tackle the finale – the sleeping bag/hoop tunnel. I coaxed Mumbles from her hedge hiding place and she trotted over with the confidence of a dog that knew what her job was.

Adam gave her a welcome like she was a returning hero.

"So ... are you guys ready?!" I got a loud "YAASSSS" back.

"Mumbles, ready?"

She looked up from the stick she was now chewing. Probs dog for "Yaaaaassss".

"Let's dooooo this!"

Just like we'd practised earlier, Rach turned up the music, and I ran to the far end of the tunnel, waving the last of the treats, yelling, "Mumbles," before standing back proudly to watch the magic.

Finally, Mumbles did exactly what she had to do. Pelted at full pace towards the tunnel.

That's my dog.

But, no. NO.

Something was wrong.

She still had the stick hanging out of either side of her mouth.

Now, I'm no tree expert, but technically it was so big it was in branch territory.

Adam and Rach stopped clapping.

I started shouting, "Nonononnonono." Then a less generic "COME HERE!!"

But it was too late.

Mumbles dived into the tunnel.

And she didn't come out.

Because instead of it being a tunnel, the tube, hoop, sleeping bag and one of the large stakes had now effectively become the world's largest dog hat. And it was zigzagging furiously around the garden.

It was so big that I couldn't actually see any dog

underneath it, just a tail flapping out of the end, as it ran in panicked circles.

Rach and Adam stared in silent horror as the monstrosity pelted towards Rach's glass patio doors. It was like HatDog was being remote controlled by a toddler.

I HAD to stop it. Leaping into action, I sprinted as fast as I could after it and without a second to think if this was a good idea, launched myself at the pile of running sleeping bag yelling, "Noooo!" as I sailed through the air. It would have been impressive – if I hadn't missed entirely and hit the ground with such a thud I just startled her even more. Hat Dog was now bolting straight towards Adam.

Please, Mumbles. Anything but Adam?! I'd rather she ran straight through the patio door than him. Glass can be mended. Legs – and memories – are much harder.

But he was right in her path and in the potential splash zone as she careered towards the pond. "Loooookkk ouuuuuut!" I yelled.

Adam was so shocked he didn't move a muscle. In a last ditch attempt to save him from getting soaked, Rach leapt up and dived towards him to push his chair to safety. Go, Rach!

PHEW!!

Disaster averted!

Even better, the squeak of the chair on the paving stone had scared Hat Dog away from the pond!

BUT, NO!! Hat Dog was now heading straight towards Rach's dad's big stone statue?!

I held my breath (which is hard when also yelling "Muuuuuuumblllleees"). There was no way my shifts at GADAC would ever earn enough to replace that?!

BUT, OH, THANK GOODNESS. Mumbles missed it by millimetres.

BUT, OH NO, WAY WORSE THAN EVER BEFORE. The same couldn't be said for the end of the branch, which was sticking diagonally up. And as Mumbles skimmed past, it bashed straight into the statue's lower half. Stone dust flew everywhere.

And, like a killer shot at Wimbledon, the three of us watched as a large piece of grey rock flew through the air. Spinning in what felt like slo-mo, it headed straight for Adam, and landed with a thump into his lap.

I didn't need to look to know exactly what the offending piece of rock was.

But I did anyway.

And wished I hadn't.

Because what was there had knocked Hat Dog into

second place in the "weirdest sight in Rach's garden right now" leaderboard.

In Adam's lap was a tiny stone penis.

I couldn't take my eyes off it. And neither could Rach. Or Adam. Not that I could really see faces, as I was too busy staring at the area that shouldn't be mentioned.

I swear even passing pigeons were looking.

Through the silence, Lis's voice sang out, "Thiiissss isss whaaaat liiiifeee could be like with meeeeee."

For everyone's sake, I hoped it wasn't.

THWANG.

Mumbles ran headlong into the patio door, finally freeing herself from the tunnel hat.

But Hat Dog was old news.

We were all staring at the liberated peen.

Someone had to do something. And that someone had to be me.

"I AM SO SORRY RACH!!! I WILL TOTALLY FIX THAT."

But I also had to fix what was happening live.

I edged towards Adam, desperate to remove the appendage from his presence (whilst equally as desperate not to acknowledge it in any way).

The usually unflappable Adam had officially been

flapped. His freckly cheeks had gone redder than me when I'd been covered in beetroot face mask.

Nice one, Bella.

I reached out a hand.

"Am I, er . . . OK, to, er . . . grab the, er, *item*?"

He said, "Sure," in a way that sounded very unsure. Without making eye contact he retrieved it, and held it out.

I *really* didn't expect my first time touching a man-dangle for it to be a group activity. Or for it to be happening in Rach's garden with HOB staring from his room.

But there was no other option. With my thumb and first finger, I plucked it out of Adam's hand like it was a burning hot carrot.

RELIEF – it was out of his lap.

HORROR – I was now dangling it in front of his face.

Please let this nightmare/daymare be over.

With mutterings of, "I'll deal with it later," I stuffed it in my pocket. MUST remember to take it out before I put my jeans in the wash, or I'm going to get the mother of all creepy talks from Mum.

This. Was. Awful. I was going to need at least ten minutes without any human eye contact to recover. I ran over to Mumbles to check she was OK, leaving Rach to deal with the aftermath. But Mumbles had discovered a tasty bit of bird poo and had forgotten the whole ordeal already.

If only the same could be said for any of us three (not the bird poo eating bit).

Desperate to put the statue castration behind us, Rach suggested we all go in for milkshakes. Adam and I both reacted with such enthusiasm it was like she'd suggested we go on a free all-you-can-eat tour of America. *Anything* to pretend what had just happened, hadn't. Rach could sense my mortification, so to try and ease the mood, she chatted full on to Adam about who he could get to vote for St Mary's next weekend. I love this girl.

I let them plan away as I rustled up our drinks.

"Uhhh, hmmmm." I splodged peanut butter into the blender with a satisfying splat. "Peanut, popcorn and banana. Undisputed queen of all milkshakes."

Adam smiled and pushed his glass forward. "Bella's Bananutter Bonanza? I was BORN ready."

Was it wrong to fancy someone even more cos they named a drink after you?

Rach passed over the ice cream. "Seriously F— erm, Adam, you have NO idea. It's *immense*." She was still trying to keep extra convo going to help me out. "In fact, it needs some sort of patent. Right now."

She reached out for my phone. "May I?" I nodded, cos hers was charging next door. She brought up Google, Adam watching as I wrestled with trying to get a spoon through the ice cream.

Rach talked as she typed, "How ... to ... get ... a ... patent ... for ... Bananutter ... and ..."

But, on word three, my phone auto filled from my search history. And from the other side of the counter, I could. Not. Stop. It.

How to get rid of toe hair?

There was only one thing for it. I grabbed my phone. Turned it off, and blended the milkshakes for as long, and as loud, as was humanly possible.

Note to self: must urgently google how not to let Google show up googles. (Surely it's an extension of all the weird thoughts you have in your brain, and there's no way there should be a log of that ANYWHERE.)

I really hoped Tegan's audition was going better than this. But after the blender noise died down, we were soon slurping overly large glasses of Bananutter, asking about HillFest, looking at pics of Molly, telling Adam all about Tegan's try-out, and definitely not looking at my phone.

It was weird.

Because I'd so obviously failed at being impressive-and-cool Bella, I relaxed into being my normal, unimpressive-and-uncool Bella. And Adam and I had never got on better. Even when HOB came downstairs and immediately started grilling him. The flying peen must have sapped all of Adam's awkward, because he took it all with a smile, winning him round with sport chat, and their mutual love of a TV show that said a great way of starting a fire in the wild was to use belly button fluff.

And even though it felt like seconds ago that I was stressing about him arriving, way too quickly it was time for him to head home. As he disappeared into the hallway to get his coat, Rach gave me an encouraging thumbs-up. And a push towards the door.

It was time for the most cringe chat of all. Front-doorstep chat.

Running my hands through my hair to try and look a little better than when he remembered me from three seconds earlier, I headed out after him. And without letting myself have any time to think too much, I blurted out what I needed to say.

"Thanks so much for coming over. I've had a really nice day."

But Adam was bent double pulling his trainers back on.

"Sorry, did you say something?"

And as he stood back up, and looked at me all my confidence poofed away.

"Just, errr, thanks. For today."

"Thank *you*. Funniest day I've had in ages."

Well that was *one* word for it. I shuffled awkwardly. "Fanks." And remembered I still had to figure out reattaching the item that was in my pocket.

Adam chuckled to himself. "Who knew we both found dogs hurtling around so entertaining?"

Marcus, that's who.

"I'm sorry – blame the dentist. Her anaesthetic made me do weird things."

He smiled. Had he, against all odds, had a good time? I couldn't bring myself to keep eye contact, so stared at the floor like I'd never seen wood before. He shuffled his feet.

"So . . . how about the next one is up to me?"

I un-stared at the floor.

Next one?!

Next one!!

Adam wanted a next one?! Even my pocket-peen quivered.

". . . unless you're not up for it?" He paused. "Rach could come along?"

But he didn't need to talk me into it! "No?! As in YES! I am. Up for it. That would be. . ."

But I couldn't think of the word that meant all the amount of 'YES' that I needed, so instead I grinned at my lack of cool. Adam just grinned.

"Next Sunday then?"

I still had a chance with Adam.

"I wouldn't miss it for the world."

CHAPTER

TWENTY-TWO

It was Mikey who told us that Tegan's try-out had only gone "OK". They'd had a big chat on Saturday and sorted everything out. Now with training back to normal, they were better than ever.

But it was Wednesday now and she was still ghosting Rach and me big style.

I've read a zillion articles on dealing with love break-ups, but this friendship breakdown felt way worse than any boy ever could. Despite my sheer panic about the live final on Saturday, and worrying about Mum, it was the situation with Tegan that was eating away at me the most.

Yes, she sat with us at lunch, but that's because she was with Mikey – and he was doing anything he could to glue us back together. The most we ever got from her was shrugs and "uh-huhs". The only smile we'd achieved all week was when we re-enacted the flying stone peen (Steve the Steen as we'd started calling it) incident. To make her laugh, we even secretly dropped it into Tegan's blazer pocket for her to discover. We thought we'd all laugh about it later, but that later still hadn't come.

It sucked. My best friend was blanking me, while every single other person wouldn't stop trying to make convo. I'd swap all of them for Tegan any day.

And it wasn't just the students that were obsessed. When Mrs Hitchman saw us on Wednesday morning, she beamed and did the big "H" Helicans hand sign. I was so horrified Rach had to lift my elbow to help me wave back. Even worse, she'd then asked to speak to me at break.

It was the first time I'd ever opened the door to her office and been met with a smile. Unnerving. She gestured me to sit down, but glimpsing her Converse just freaked me out all over again.

"So first up – thank you. From everyone."

"I haven't won yet, Mrs Hitchman."

"Well, when you do" – she made an oops face – "sorry, '*if*'." She stressed the word like she was doing me a cute favour, not being factually accurate. "There's going to be a lot of people very grateful indeed."

She put her hand to the side of her mouth like she was doing a stage whisper. "And I *may* have already been in touch with the local TV news?!"

With an, "I'll try my best," that fell on deaf ears – except for her offering one-on-one practice rehearsals that I politely declined – I made as quick an exit as possible. I couldn't wait for all of this to be over, whatever happened. Rach was waiting outside to tell me it was going to be OK. But I knew she was feeling as lost as me without Tegan.

We trudged back to class batting away all the shouts and hellos (that had become normal) with half-hearted waves. The only person who wasn't celebrating early was Luke, who was loudly telling anyone who would listen that I didn't have a hope of winning. He meant to stress me out, but people getting their heads around this quite strong probability, was *exactly* what I needed.

The only other person who wasn't bouncing off the walls was Ava, which was weird, as she'd been the one doing the most to help get us this far. When she saw me sitting on my own in the changing room, killing time before heading to lunch, she walked over. But it was weird. The atmosphere felt like we'd gone back to week one of term. To strangers.

She sat and fiddled with the thumbhole she'd worn away in the cuff of her jumper.

"OK. I'm not sure how to say this. . ." She hadn't got any better at her hellos.

"After the week I've had? Nothing will surprise me."

"Yeah, you look like you could do with some cheering up." Was I *that* obvious? She chewed her lip. "Not that it's cheering. More weird, I guess. . ." Why was she being so shifty? "Anyway, yeah. It was . . . er, it was *my* question you answered."

Mind = blank.

"Soz – I've got nothing."

She wrinkled her nose. "Last show? vavavoom? Or as *I* would say, V-ava-voom?"

I was so shocked I grabbed her arm, even though our friendship hadn't reached that level yet. "YOU'RE vavavoom?!??!"

If I was a cartoon, a puff of smoke would have just shot out of each ear.

She shrugged. "I didn't think I had ANY chance of them picking my one, obvs."

Woah. It was one thing giving terrible advice, it was quite another being face-to-face with the person you'd given it to – who also knew I was the last person in the world to give life tips. Unless there was *any* possibility Ava didn't 100% already know that? She pointed at the side of my mouth.

"Bells – off topic – but have you been chewing a biro?"

She TOTALLY knew.

"Maybe..." I dabbed at the ink. "Slash yes. They taste nice! Anyway, er, well," I didn't know what to say. "I don't know what to say."

To my relief, she laughed. "Same. But I wanted you to know. So I could say a proper thank you – this last week has been the first one I haven't spent a single lunch on my own."

As soon as the words left her mouth, she looked a bit embarrassed.

"Gawd, this is so cringe. Sorry." She laughed. "Who *even* am I any more?!"

But she shouldn't be apologizing. It was the best thing I'd heard all week.

"Oi, I'm the one with pen on my face! And the talking to new people thing? That's all you. To be honest, I only said what I did cos of what happened in the canteen when you Diet Coke sprayed Tegan. And we got talking for the first time everrrrrr."

Ava smiled as she put the pieces together. "So you mean, I kind of helped with the comp?"

"Well, you or an exploding can?! Cos I'm sure that 'you can sit with us' bit was the only real reason anyone voted for me!"

She flung her arms round me. It was lovely. For 0.01 seconds. Until we both remembered that we don't really like personal-space invasions. And pulled back, laughing at what weirdos we'd become.

Together we headed to the canteen. Rach was nowhere to be seen. It wasn't like her to leave me hanging on my own. When she finally came through the doors, she was running. And waving a bunch of paper in her hand.

"I did it!" She slapped the stapled sheets on the table. "I got an A! I'm NOT being put down in English!"

Well this *was* excellent news. I gave Rach a massive hug (she always had a VIP pass to my personal space).

"Congrats, muggle!"

Adam would be happy too – he'd been asking about Rach last night when we were chatting online. Apparently he was planning a surprise for our next date. EXCITEMENT.

Rach shimmied her shoulders, so chuffed it was wiggling out of her. But someone was incoming on her right. Mikey – followed by a glum-looking Tegan. He stuck his finger straight into my custard. In retaliation I pulled the stool he was heading for towards me, tripping him into the table.

"Crimes against food must be punished."

I wasn't going to tell him he now had custard on his nose.

"You've got custard on your nose." Tegan was a better person than me. She sat down next to him without a hint of a smile towards us.

Mikey did his usual power-enthuse through the awkwardness. "Custard bonus!" He wiped it off and ate it. "So Bells, what's it like being the most Fay Mousse person around here?"

I blew on my nails. "Exhauuusting, but I'm holding up."

I looked to see if I'd made Tegan smile – nothing.

Rach fake pouted.

"AnddidImention I totally nailed my English essay too?"

She swished her long red hair with an OTT hair flick. Luke wolf-whistled from across the room. He had a knack of sensing where he wasn't wanted, and turning up right there.

Mikey glanced at Luke, then back to us, and lowered

his voice. "Did you see what *he* did last night?" I shook my head. "He was all over social media encouraging people to vote for one of the other schools." Mikey scrolled on his phone. "See?"

Under Luke's username was a big pic.

A black square with big white letters.

He really was such an idiot.

"Jay and I reckon it's his way of trying to get in with the JOGS girls."

Ava looked grossed out. "Well his personality's *certainly* not going to do it."

This was normally the joke Tegan would have made, but she was busy staring into middle distance. I was also distracted – thrown by the amount of likes Luke's post had. Over a thousand. A "Vote Bella" one would get nowhere near that.

"Go back to his profile, Mikey. . ."

Mikey brought up the grid of pictures. A real bumper selection of snaps of BMXs and his mates doing moonies (aka a normal person's deleted folder).

But something was niggling at me.

Luke had 4.6k followers.

Surely not even 4.6 people could be interested in badly framed pictures of bikes?

I asked Mikey for his handset and scrolled down as Ava fessed up her vavavoom revelation, and they moved on to talking about getting votes for Saturday. This nagging feeling about Luke's profile was exactly the kind of thing I'd normally talk to Tegan about. She always knew when I was overreacting – and when I was on to something. But right now she wouldn't even make eye contact.

Whoever said "Time heals" lied. This felt worse every day.

"Bleeee!" Rach was peering over my shoulder.

"I know, right? And does this seem weird to you?" I showed her his follower number.

"Reckon they're all bots?"

"I'd bet my final mouthful of sponge they are." She shoved her spoon in her mouth.

She stopped chewing. "Who's that mega bayyyybe?"

She was pointing at a pic of Luke and Ska. How had he managed to not put her off yet?

"Ahh – that's Ska I was telling you about." And like prodding a bruise, I couldn't help but click on it. The two of them were arm in arm, sitting on a posh sofa, black-and-white pics behind them, both smile/pouting/smouting up at the camera.

I put on my best Luke voice to quietly read what he'd written.

NBD when your girl signs her biggest modelling contract yet #fit #rich #fitandrich #shesmine #london #youknowit

I checked Luke wasn't listening.

"I mean, as if his face and personality weren't sufficient to put her off him, surely this comment alone would be enough?"

She really *must* be as gross as him to actively want to spend time with that kind of #idiot #loser #idiotandloser.

Rach put on her best *Made in Chelsea* voice to read what Ska had replied below. The first bit was just kiss noises.

⬦⬦⬦

Then:

And thanks @legalmark for being the best dad
in the world & 🚐 us to LDN to make it happen
👄 👄 👄

I was so tempted to post a 😁 but Mikey would kill
me.

Grossed out, I switched the screen off. But
something was still bugging me.

It was like I had all the pieces of something.
Something important. But I couldn't work out what.

TWENTY-THREE

When I'd got home that night, I'd done all the things I usually did to make things OK – ate unnecessary toast, binge-watched *Master of None*, and chatted with Shay about Adam. But even good stuff didn't feel as good when I couldn't talk to Teeg about it.

I was so desperate for something to feel normal again, I rang Jo. The last thing I wanted to talk about was how much I'd messed up with Teeg. But my brain had its own plan, and it was the very first thing I'd mentioned.

Jo couldn't believe we'd fallen out. She was right to be shocked – saying it out loud made me see how bad things had got.

So after I put down the phone, I picked it back up to Rach. It was time to sort this out once and for all. We agreed whatever happened the next day we weren't going to leave school until we'd properly spoken to Tegan. And apologized one more time. I even messaged Mikey to check she was free at lunch.

Look out, world. Mission: Repair Us Three was on.

I could do this!

Or could I? Because when I woke up the next morning I felt sick with nerves. But my freak out was interrupted by the doorbell.

With my hair dripping wet, I flung the door open.

I didn't expect to see who was standing there.

"We need to talk."

It was Tegan.

Without bothering to brush my hair, and with legs that were actually wobbling with fear, I grabbed my stuff and yelled bye. I then dashed back in, grabbed the two bits of toast I'd already made, and ran back out.

"Apology bread?" I held out a slice for Tegan.

"Wow. You really *must* be sorry."

She knew nothing normally came between me and Marmite.

We walked out on to the street, chewing in silence.

But what could I say? "Erm, so thanks for coming."

She shrugged, "Mikey *may* have given me a heads-up that I was going to get hunted down for this chat today.

So thought I'd at least make it somewhere private." Oh. I was hoping she was here cos she wanted to sort things out, not just avoid attention. "And don't be mad at him – he was trying to help."

But I was done being mad at anyone. I only had one priority. Trying to make things up with her.

I took a deep breath. And almost choked on a toast crumb, so had to wait a bit longer.

"OK. Well, let me start. . ." But where to begin? "I'm sorry. Sorry for talking to the others *about* you. I should have just come *to* you. . ." I knew at the time she'd hate it, but was too much of a wimp to just ask her. "Sorry for being a crap friend." I tried to make her smile. "And er, sorry for slightly perving on your married gym teacher who is an actual father."

She did a tiny nose laugh. This was a good sign, right?

"It wasn't *slightly*, Bella. It was full on. And you missed the part about somehow putting it all together to wonder if I was having some kind of, I dunno, *secret affair*?" She shook her head. "Oh – and then telling my boyfriend about it."

"Yeah. I know. Awful. I'm awful." I certainly felt awful. "But I never thought you were cheating. Just, I dunno, something weird. And then it all came out in one big accident."

She softened a little. "Yeah, Mikey told me. Backed up what you said at school. I just. . ." She searched around for the words. "Well. . . I guess I'd just felt a bit pushed out."

"Woah," *She'd* been feeling pushed out? But that's exactly how I'd been feeling? "I had no idea."

"Do you not think all these weeks I'd *much* rather have been hanging out with you guys than stuck in that gym hall? Chatting about the Helicans, rather than being yelled at to do repetitions?"

"Guess I'd never thought about it like that." I always felt like she was the one abandoning *us*. Maybe even a little jealous of it all. "But whenever I tried to talk about it, you shut me down."

"It's cos I didn't have a choice. I had to do it and it seemed like you were secretly mad at me for it." Ouch. I'd kept telling myself I wasn't, but maybe she was right. "Sooooo. . . I stopped talking about it. And at the same time, got used to not knowing what was going on with you guys any more so it didn't feel as crap for me."

So *that's* why she'd backed away. Not cos she was bored of us – because she missed us. Eurgh. Hearing it so black and white made me realize how tough it must have been for her. If these guys nagged me every time I mentioned the Helicans, I would have zero people to help take the pressure off. And that's exactly what had happened to Teeg. Instead of resenting her not being around, I should have realized she needed us more than ever.

"I'm sorry. I really am... I guess, guess we just missed you." I tried to think of something more positive. "So, er, did you get the good-luck videos we made? We were thinking of you ALL day."

She nodded. "Yeah, thanks." Well at least that was something.

"When do you find out?"

She shrugged. "Soon."

"I've been hitting you up for updates every day?"

She nodded. "Yup. I know. I guess I just wasn't ready to be friends then."

"And now...?" My question hung in the air. "Cos, lemme be clear, this week has totally sucked without you." Was she starting to smile? "And lemme be also clear – you may have a stone penis in your pocket."

She put her hand in and pulled out Steen.

"What the heck?!"

"Well, exactly." I unzipped my bag. "Oh, and we spent all night making you this..."

I presented Tegan with the fruits of mine and Rach's Photoshop marathon last night: Tegan's face added on to the Team GB squad, printed and made into a brand-new badge for her bag (I KNEW there was a reason I'd hoarded my BadgeIt under my bed).

"Woah," Tegan tried to take it in. "I mean ... *speechless*?!" Yup, it was a monstrosity. But it was the thought that counted and I was happy she pinned it on to her schoolbag.

"So, what's it to be ... apology accepted?" I grinned. "Cos if no, don't think I'll reveal if there are any more appendages hidden about your person."

This time I got a proper laugh.

"Friends." She put her hand out to shake mine, but snatched it back quickly. "Although, there's something I want to say first."

Uh-oh.

"Bella, I'm sorry too – I've been acting like a right weirdo. If I hadn't been so stressed out then you would probably have just talked to me like normal. But..." She shrugged. "The audition's out of the way, and I'm never going to get like that again." She grimaced. "Or should I say, pleeease never let me get that way again?! Moody Tegan was no fun. And storming out is hard work!"

This time she put her hand back out and kept it there. And with a firm, "Promise!" we both shook.

Which turned into a hug, which turned into a massive, relieved laugh.

The team was back in action.

But the good mood didn't last long. Because as we ambled towards school Tegan explained the other reason she'd wanted to talk to me this morning.

And by the time we got to school I was fuming.

TWENTY-FOUR

At first Rach hadn't understood (especially as she was mainly focused on hugging Tegan and telling her how she happy she was we were all friends again). Then she didn't think it was possible.

But when we'd showed her what Tegan had revealed to me, we had all the proof we needed. Tegan had worked it out after hearing our lunch chat yesterday. Even when she was mad at me, she was still secretly having my back.

Why were things always so obvious *after* you needed them to be obvious?

So many things had to happen.

The final was only three days away and we needed to act fast. Step one was confronting the person behind it all.

And as scary as it was, because I was at the centre, I knew I had to do it. Alone.

So that's why after school, I found myself sitting on the bench near my house, on my own, waiting. (Tegan and Rach lurking within shouting distance.)

I was petrified.

But it had to be done. And it was better now than Saturday, live on radio.

I wiped my clammy hands on my jeans trying to gather my thoughts. Deep breath. Keep calm.

Teeg had said it had all fallen into place yesterday after I'd left. Mikey had asked who it was in the pic of Luke's girlfriend which I'd left up on his phone. Tegan had replied, "Apparently she's a hot model called Ska. Let me see..."

Mikey had misheard. And thought she was called Skalett. Scarlett. And with another click on her profile, Tegan had realized she was. And with one more click on her dad who she'd tagged, it didn't take long for Tegan to get confirmation he wasn't just *legalmark*, he was a lawyer. Who sent his daughter to JOGS.

Ska was Letty.

Ska was Queevil.

I was so furious I knew I had do something. But as the expected mix of footsteps and bike wheels got closer, I wasn't sure I was brave enough to go through with it.

I tugged on Mumbles' lead, happy not to be on my own (although she was scared of falling leaves and puddles, so in our relationship, I was more of a guard-human than vice versa).

The approaching figure was in the shadows, but I was certain who it was. I took a deep breath and channelled my inner Tegan.

"Luke."

My heart was beating so fast my voice sounded like I was sitting on a tiny washing machine.

He stopped. "Fishy Balls." He was closer to me than I felt comfortable with. I *mustn't* let him intimidate me. I stood up.

"I'll keep it quick."

"Thank God."

"I *know* what you're up to..." Yup, I was doing it. "And it's not going to work."

He laughed. "Speak English, not Netflix drama."

So he was going to be difficult. No surprise there.

"OK, I'll spell it out ... I know who Letty is. I know you've been helping her win. And I KNOW that it STOPS NOW."

I'd practised that line at least twenty times, but was

still impressed I'd managed to say it right. If only I felt as brave as I sounded.

Luke sucked in his cheeks.

"You mean those Instagram posts? Nothing stopping me supporting her."

"No, Luke. I mean hacking the votes. Don't even *think* you can get away with it in the final."

I'd always thought it was weird that the person with the worst advice had kept getting through – was now in the lead. And after Tegan's Ska discovery, I'd worked it out. It had been rattling round in my head ever since Luke had said that thing in GADAC about getting followers up. Then it had got retriggered when I'd seen the numbers on his profile. Luke, the same guy who'd hacked the school directory to change my name. Who loved nothing more than causing trouble with his computer.

He laughed again. He was actually *enjoying* this.

"Oh, yeah, cos of course they're going to believe the person who's in last place, who suddenly wants to take out the favourite." We both knew he was right. "Who also has how much proof? Ummm, that's right, zero."

He'd been clever – covered his tracks. So I had to make him believe I had more than I did.

"That's what you think."

But he wasn't buying it.

"That's what I *know*. No one likes a sore loser, Blob. So if you're going to come last, don't make yourself look even more bitter while you're at it."

But little did he know, I *did* have an idea.

When we'd worked out the full scale of what was going on, Rach, Tegan, Ava, Mikey and I had discussed what we could do. Try and get official proof? Tell Jaz? Confront Letty? But we'd come to the same conclusion. It was too risky to do anything official. Luke and Letty had no limits, and I couldn't jeopardize my place in the comp. If I wanted to win, I was going to have to do it the only way Letty and Luke couldn't. Fair and square.

Well. Fairish and squareish. Oblongish maybe.

Because I did have Shay. And I did have a plan.

And it was time to activate part one of it. For it to work, I HAD to sound as casual as I could.

"Mrs Hitchman's going to be gutted if St Mary's lose."

"Detentions for life, probs." He said it with absolute delight.

"Bet the headmistress of JOGS doesn't even care?"

He grinned, happy to break even more bad news.

"You'd be surprised. She's been coaching Ska every week – but I'm not an idiot, Blobfish. If you think emotional blackmail will work, think again. As if I care about what happens at school."

Him being so cross with the world was really so boring.

"Yeah yeah, or about the Helicans, or anyone. I get it, Luke. You're so cool, we're not. Repeat to fade."

"Glad you've worked it out."

"Well it's been a total pleassssshure talking to you."

"Same."

"Send Ska my love."

He rolled his eyes and without another word, except "Get a life" under his breath, walked away.

But he'd given me exactly the info we needed to try and stop him in his tracks.

I headed straight to the others to update them. It was time for part two of the plan.

Yes, it was risky, but it was all we had.

CHAPTER

TWENTY-FIVE

The horn was beeping, but final mirror checks couldn't be rushed.

This was it. The final. A LDD. Life Defining Day. My jeans, trainers and Jo's star top looked as good as they were ever going to. There was nothing more I could do now.

REALIZATION. The next time I looked in this mirror, I wouldn't just be "Bella". I'd be Bella who had met, and maybe even made slight-friendly-hand-greeting-based physical contact with the Helicans. *Fingers, are you ready for the greatest moment of your life?* But it didn't seem phased and calmly opened up a message of a hundred 💪 from Mikey.

I needed them, cos this morning was meant to have

been a peaceful haven of mental preparation.

However, it had been a total last-minute scrabble to get ready, as at approx 11:08 p.m. last night Shay had messaged. I thought it was going to be some Helicans good news. I couldn't have been more wrong.

Bells, don't hate me, but I've gotta work tomorrow. I'm presenting so can't swerve it. It sucks. Am SO sorry. Know you'll smash it though xoxoxoxo

I told her it was all right. It really wasn't. More than our lift there, she'd been our secret weapon. Our being-friends-with-Lis trump card to freak out Queevil.

In times of crisis I do weird things. And with Mum away, this time it was to call Jo. She was meant to be covering my GADAC shift from midday, but when I explained, (and she'd ranted about Shay for ten minutes), she'd offered to set off from uni at five a.m. to give us a lift instead. GADAC was going to have to stay closed. Mum agreed to it all on condition I worked tomorrow to try and make up any money we lost. It was the least I could do for everyone putting themselves out, even though it meant sending Adam a message just now asking if we could rearrange. Luckily he'd replied with, "Good luck for today. Can you do next Saturday instead?" Which, when I had more free-brain, I'd reply to and explain everything, even the truth about GADAC.

Shay's bombshell meant I'd had about twenty minutes sleep and was in a total flap. None of it was helped by getting more notifications and messages than I'd received in my entire life. I got actual thumb cramp trying to keep up.

Right on time at nine a.m., Jo arrived. She looked exhausted. And it made me more determined than ever to do her – and everyone – proud.

By the time Rach and Tegan were on the backseat, my nerves were at an all-time high and it was all I could do to whimper. Rach was so excited she kept yelping, making Jo slam on the brakes thinking something was up. But even with twelve emergency stops my sister's efficiency meant we still arrived early.

She waved us bye, and as the three of us stood under the giant RADIO SHIRE sign, I couldn't believe this moment was finally here.

I pulled my shoulders up and looked at Rach and Tegan. "Right – let's do this." Yup, this was the start of a new Bella. One that could handle stuff. Win this competition.

Following my lead, we walked in to the huge reception and I strode up to a friendly looking lady to ask her which way to go. The security guard then loudly (too loudly) shouted that she was a hologram, which was when a person not that much older than us, but wearing more lanyards than I'd seen in my life, came to greet us. I hoped she hadn't seen what had just happened.

"Don't worry – loads of people think she's real." She thought a bit. "I mean, mainly old people, but whatever."

She gave us each a lanyard and pass of our own (with our own names on?!) and ushered us into a room with biscuits and free tea and water.

Our passes said VIP. We were VIPs!

There was Helicans merch EVERYWHERE.

It was heaven (if God or whoever needed you to sign a form and wear ID around your neck to get there).

None of us said anything – we just stood there, trying to get our heads round it all. But as we did, the door opened, and in walked Lis, Amil, Rosie, The One With No Name, and Pastry.

Oh. My. Extreme. Gosh.

We were officially breathing the same air as the Helicans.

And all I could do was gawp.

They were even more amazing in real life than on the

internet. Even Pastry looked like she was wearing extra cute fluff implants.

OUCH.

Rach jabbed me in the thigh as if I might not have seen the four people and one dog, who were two metres away, smiling straight at us, watching her stab me in the leg. Could humans malfunction or was that just robots?

"Are you guys here for the final?" Lis broke the silence.

But none of us could muster words, so we accidentally mended the silence straight back, gawping like she'd grown a unicorn horn. Unihorn.

Amil stepped forward, ignoring our version of musical statues. "Hi, I'm Amil."

He put his hand out. Towards me. INCOMING!! Hand, it's your time to shine!

"What's your name?"

OK – at least I could answer *this*.

But as I went to say, our hands made contact.

I was TOUCHING A HELICAN.

"ElleasemeeyounamBell . . . ah."

He grinned awkwardly. "Sorry, I didn't realize!" He spoke slower. "Do. You. Speak. English?"

All I could do was nod. Extra confusing, given that

the answer should be yes. I side-eyed Rach for help, but she was pointing at my hand.

I was still hanging on to an exceptionally confused Amil. Maybe he'd think it's customary in my country?

Luckily Tegan had my back. It would have been more helpful if she'd had my hand, but whatevs.

"Yup, this . . ." she pointed at me, ". . . is Bella."

He smiled (maybe because I finally managed to let go of his hand), and with loads of chatter and hugs, the rest of the band introduced themselves, including Lis (like I couldn't identify her, her dog, her mum, even the socks she wore on stage, at fifty paces). "You've been amaaaazing. So happy you got through. Your last answer was. . ." She kissed fingers and popped them apart.

Sorry, was this real?! Was I being complimented by *Lis*?!!

Tegan picked up on my involuntary nostril flares like they were tiny radio masts broadcasting distress signals straight to her brain.

"Bella's saving her voice for the final."

The One With No Name murmured as if this was incredibly wise, not an obviously massive lie. With me off the talking hook for a bit, we huddled round for some group selfies, Rach beaming so hard her teeth threw the white balance off.

I couldn't believe they were talking to us like they were normal people too. Just like Shay said they would. I was in two minds whether to say hi from her, but she'd told me she'd message them instead, and I didn't want to look desperate. Plus I still couldn't form sentences, which cemented my decision. So I listened as the band chatted away about how they loved Rach's shoes, asking Tegan about the Team GB badge they'd spotted on her bag, and saying how cool it was that vavavoom had messaged saying things had really picked for her. They didn't even seem phased when *Team Bella* (as they called us) actually squeaked (positive: a least I could now make sound) when they played us the demo version of their new single. It was the best thing I'd ever heard. And when we told them that, they seemed genuinely made up.

Ears, LISTEN TO ME (and that should be your strong point). You are the coolest you are ever going to be right now.

Rosie then dug out a limited-edition hoodie for me, which they'd all signed. I didn't want them to think I was ungrateful, but after a very enthusiastic "thank you" mouthing I gave it to Rach. I knew she'd wear it 24/7 for at least the next two years (including at parties and maybe even in swimming pools). When the band saw her swoon-flop on to a beanbag, clutching the hoodie to her like it was a newborn child, I think they totally got why I'd done it.

Sadly, the perfectness of being alone with them couldn't last.

Because in a burst of perfectly waved hair and heels we could hear a full minute away, in walked Ska. Aka Letty. Aka Queevil. Aka the one we had to beat.

The band did a double take, not sure if she was a presenter, popstar or both.

Unlike us, Ska didn't need them to make the first move, and jumped straight in with the most relaxed round of "Hiya"s. Without even acknowledging us, she opened up a massive paper bag she'd carried in and passed out posh-looking boxes to the band. "These are for you guys."

Lis did a genuine, "Aaaaah!" as she opened hers to reveal a head-sized marshmallow printed with the cutest pic of Pastry, a miniature Fez on her head. They must have cost a bomb. The One With No Name, Rosie and Amil made similar sounds as they discovered the thoughtful pics Ska had chosen for them.

HOW DARE SOMEONE SO EVIL BE SO NICE! And excellent with print deadlines.

Rach threw me a satisfied smile. I knew *exactly* what she was thinking.

Mistake one. Ska had just proved she wasn't as big a fan as us. Even entry-level Helicans fans knew Rosie, Amil and Lis were vegetarians.

But Ska caught our silent exchange and smiled at the band. "They're vegan, *obvs*."

Lis and Amil made an impressed "oooh" noise, as it obscured the "Queevil" Rach mixed in with a fake-cough. But before Ska could produce any more nicely evil (neevil) gifts, Lanyard Girl rushed back in and, with friendly waves goodbye, bundled the band out.

Then it was just us four. The last thing I wanted to do was be nice to Ska. Being civil was hard when she was pure evil, had rigged the votes with my eviler ex and had tried to get me kicked out. But part three of the plan was crucial: don't let Ska see anything was up.

"Fancy seeing you here." I laughed to show her it was a joke.

Instead of answering, she tapped at her phone screen, and with the most sickly, "Hiii, baaaabes," she answered a call and strutted out of the room.

Tegan waited for the door slam before she spoke. "Anyone notice anything odd?"

I looked around. "The band forgot their marshmallows, yet not one of us has suggested eating them yet?"

Tegan shook her head. "Nope." She held out her

phone. "No reception. Which would make taking a call kind of tricky, right?"

Rach grinned. "Unless it was a call with your BIF . . . Best Imaginary Friend."

Ha. So Ska wasn't the mastermind she was pretending. She couldn't even handle being in a room with the three of us.

Knowing that she had a chink in her armour put us all at a bit more at ease, and soon we were flicking through our photos and taking even more with random things we found in the room. (Lamp! Sofa! Water cooler!) By the time Lanyard Girl came to take us through to the studio, I'd almost forgotten how terrified I was. But as soon as she said the words, "Phones off, it's time to start," I remembered so hard, my right knee gave way and I wobbled into a large pot plant.

We made our way through a gazillion heavy doors, stopping under a big ON-AIR light. It might as well be flashing BELLA'S PANIC ROOM.

I stared through the huge thick glass window underneath it. Jaz and the band were sitting opposite each other, giant blue microphones hanging above their heads. Ska was already on a chair, her elbows on the mixing desk as if it was her second home. Another girl was sitting at the back of the room, looking a lot more like me i.e. petrified. That must be Aisha. Jaz winked through the glass and, as she pressed play on the band's last single, beckoned us in.

Tegan pulled the heavy door open – but Lanyard Girl pushed it shut.

"Soz – it's too small for all of you. Which one's Bella?"

I raised my hand. Lanyard Girl's smile faltered as she realized the person about to go live on their radio station was the one couldn't use words.

"You guys can watch from here, OK?" She gestured the others to some seats where a couple of people I didn't recognize were whispering amongst themselves, and bustled me through the door, shutting it firmly behind me.

Woah.

The final was finally happening.

Success or failure.

It was all down to me.

CHAPTER

TWENTY-SIX

Everything that made me feel better – Rach, Tegan, free biscuits – was now on one side of the door.

I, however, was trapped on the other side, with only EVERYTHING THAT MADE ME FEEL TERRIFIED for company.

Being in a confined space with the Helicans. ✓
Being in a confined space with Jaz. ✓
Being in a confined space with Ska. ✓
Being in a room that could broadcast any
accidental hiccup to the world. ✓
Being in a room where in a matter of seconds
I would be representing St Mary's. ✓

C'mon, Bells. Deep breath. *You can only do your best.*

Is what I *should* think. But who was I kidding? Doing my best wasn't going to be good enough if I didn't win! An entire school wasn't going to NOT hate me just because, "I'd really had a very good go." The fear was real. I HAD to win.

Jaz gestured me to sit alongside Ska, beckoning Aisha to do the same. Aisha waved a hello, and I waved back – both clearly relieved to have a fellow non-presenter, non-band, non-model person in the studio.

"Soooo..." Jaz jumped straight in with chat. It's what Shay said – radio people ramble on with small talk to help get people's confidence up. "Our final contestant Bella is in the hizzzzz-ouse!!!"

Everyone except Ska whooped. For the thirtieth time today I nodded.

"For everyone at home, that was a nod!" Ska laughed louder than necessary.

"So why don't you tell everyone at home a little bit about the reeeal Bella Fisher?"

Jaz?! What are you doing to me?! Sometimes I have to build myself up to saying my chocolate selection at the front of the newsagent queue, let alone attempting a standing start at making hilarious conversation on live radio?!

"Erm, I'm Bella Fisher and. . ." This was my time to make an amazing, aloof, cool, first impression. I needed to focus. But instead I pictured everyone listening. My whole school. Adam. Ava. Literally everyone. "And I, er, like dogs. And crisps?" Silence. "And Daim bars?"

Jaz glanced around the studio not sure what to do with me. "Riiiiiight." When she saw Amil giving me a thumbs up for managing words, she opted for general enthusiasm. "LOVE IT! Shall we crack on?"

The band cheered. I smiled back, grateful for their niceness. Outside Tegan and Rachel were waving enthusiastically like we hadn't only been apart for fourteen seconds. But there was someone missing. Someone who should be sitting near them. . .

Luke.

When he wasn't here today to support his girlfriend we *knew* we had it right.

He'd stayed at home to be with his laptop – to make sure she won.

But I HAD to stop worrying.

We'd put our own plan in action. Done all we could. And soon I'd find out if it had worked.

TWENTY-SEVEN

Jaz played three songs back to back so she could step out and chat in secret with the producer. When she came back in it sounded like drama was going down.

"So, guyyyyys, we'll get stuck into the final in just a sec, but before we do, it's time for some DUH DUH DUH breaking news...!" I gulped so loud that Jaz had to temporarily mute the mics. "As you know . . . we like to keep things fair, here at Radio Shire."

Unless . . . *could this be to do with what we'd planned?*

Outside, Rach grabbed Tegan's leg. They were thinking the same thing.

"This morning we got an email in from one of the head teachers of the finalists." Jaz waved a bit of paper into the mic (no one at home would know it wasn't the email, but a baked potato menu for the local café). "Who rightly pointed out that the three schools in the final aren't anywhere near the same size – which kinda gives a couple of our finalists an advantage..." Jaz looked apologetically at Aisha and I like we were about to be massively disappointed, cos our schools were both huge. But Jaz couldn't be more wrong. Because it *might* have been Tegan's bright idea to put this very thing on the radar of the Head of JOGS. A little email from an 'anonymous concerned parent' to say if they *really* wanted to win, it might *not* be an advantage that their school was so *very* exclusive.

Luke had confirmed they were taking it seriously when he'd bragged about them giving Ska extra tuition for it. Thanks, Puke.

"So, what with such an *intimate* Helicans gig up for grabs, we thought who better to judge the final than ... the band themselves!"

Amil and Rosie "Ooooh"-ed. But I wanted to *YEEEEE-HAW* (Argh! The cowboy noises had returned!) around the studio whirling a victory lasso in the air. We'd done it! The public vote was off! Plan *Stop Luke* had worked and it had been Ska's very own head teacher that had made it happen. And Ska was *fuuu-ming*.

This couldn't have gone more to plan. I did my best

discreet air-high-fiving at Rach and Tegan who looked as happy as me.

"So down to business. Final question time. Letty, Aisha, Bella, write your answers down then we'll get you to read them out one by one, OK?"

I took the paper Jaz handed me, my hand trembling more than in the last five mins of an exam when I still had a billion words to write.

"Lis you ready?"

"Sure am. It's so great to finally meet you guys." Lis smiled at us, like we were all just round a mate's house. "Ska – thanks for the marshmallows, obvs I've already eaten mine."

Ska purred, "No probs, babe."

"Aisha – can I just say I *need* to know where that scarf is from – I've got envy for days." Aisha looked like she was going to hyperventilate with glee. And Bella. . ."

OMG LIS WAS TALKING TO ME AND PEOPLE AROUND THE WORLD COULD ACTUALLY HEAR.

"You've got a friend for life in Rosie."

OMG, LIS JUST SAID ROSIE WOULD BE MY FRIEND.

"On tour I swear she sometimes *exists* on Daim cake."

OMG, I DIDN'T KNOW DAIM CAME IN CAKE FORM.

Life = peaked.

Thank goodness Mikey had promised to record this.

"So we thought hard about a good final dilemma."

I crossed everything I had, including my legs – which made me almost fall off my stool – that it was something I could answer.

Amil jumped in. "And we've gone with one we get *aallll* the time. . ." My heart was thundering in my ears as Amil read it out slowly. "How can we reply when *yet* another journalist asks us, 'Can girls and guys ever truly be friends?'"

Woah. So THIS was the grand finale.

What a weird question. I'd never even thought about it?

The other two had already started to scribble stuff down. But no words were coming to me. The band gave me an encouraging smile. As if the Helicans smiling at you would calm anyone down?!

But I HAD to think of something good. I HAD to win.

Can girls and guys ever truly be friends?!

Of course! The question was too simple. There *must* be more to it.

I stared at Teeg, trying to channel her amazing ability to know what the secret complex meaning is in stuff. But the soundproof studio was blocking our vibes out and all I had in my head was radio silence (which was about to lead to an even worse IRL radio silence).

EIGHTEEN, SEVENTEEN, SIXTEEN.

My brain felt like a wordsearch.

But, WAIT.

Amil had said it was all about what the band *could* say, and considering two of them were guys and two were girls, they already *proved* the answer was, "Of course, duh." So the question wasn't really about *if* people could be friends, it was more about other people reading into it.

Yes, brain! I knew giving you an extra slice of toast was a good idea.

So what could my answer be?!

Ska suddenly sat up, smiling.

"Nailed it! I'm ready to go!" Trademark hair flick/deliberate interruption to throw Aisha and I off.

But there was still time. I had to ignore her. DO me.

And with a couple of seconds left I scribbled down what I could.

But would it be enough? As Jaz hit zero, and the studio broke out into "woooh"s and "let's gooooo"s, I pushed my paper back and tried to remember how to breathe. As she'd done best in the semi, Ska was up first. She shone a megawatt confident smile round the studio.

"So ... my answer is." It was like she'd already thought she'd won. "Next time someone asks you if guys and girls *can* be friends, your answer should be a massive, big, fat..." (*Please say "no" and annoy the band!*) "YES."

Oh.

She winked at Amil. "And if your friends just *happen* to be extra hot, then they can soon become friends with benefits. If you know what I mean?"

Er, no. The only benefits I'd ever want from my friends were for them to carry around spare biscuits.

Surely the band were going to hate this answer? But annoyingly they didn't look at all revolted. Instead they had a quick whisper to themselves before Lis leaned back to the mic.

"Thanks, Letty – good to see you're a believer in keeping your options open. Aisha – what do *you* reckon we should do?"

I hadn't heard Aisha speak yet, and when she opened her mouth, her voice was so fragile I was worried it wouldn't make it all the way to the microphone.

"Not to copy, but I'm with L-Letty." She held up her paper as proof. Letty winked again, as if this cemented her victory. "I s-s-said: 'Anyone can be friends, cos it's about personality, and looking out for each other, not...'" She paused. But Jaz encouraged her on. "'... What's in your pants?!'"

Aisha flung her hand over her mouth as if she couldn't believe her one moment of fame involved talking about trouser-contents. She dropped her paper and nervously freestyled. "I'm sorry?! I couldn't think of another word for it. And anyway, and this isn't my answer, cos I didn't have time to write it, but I wanted to say, you guys already totally prove it, cos you formed six years ago, and have been through break-ups and make-ups and record deals and world tours, and are total friendship goals, so if anyone even *bothers* to ask you that again, you can just be like, *duh-dah!*" Aisha flung her arms out, almost hitting me in the face. "And all, 'Why don't you come expand your tiny minds by hanging out on our tour bus for a bit?!'"

She said it all without taking a breath, and when she got to the end, was so shocked by her own outburst she physically crumpled her head down on to the desk. But the band laughed, clearly on her side, and after a quick confab, it was Amil who responded.

"Nice, Aisha. Though I'm not sure anyone who wasn't paid to be there would want to step foot on our tour bus.

Rosie's trainers are *something* else." Rosie punched him lightly on the arm. "Obvs by 'something else', I mean beautifully fragrant and a joy to have under my nose. Aaaanyway, Bella? You ready to bring home the final answer of the whole competition?"

Short answer, no. Long answer, noooooooooo.

Everything rested on this.

I opened my mouth. Took my word handbrake off.

"Thanks for having me. It's been an amazing day."

Rosie pulled the mic her way. "No! Thank *you* guys for helping us out with all your amazing advice."

"Don't speak too soon?!"

The One With No Name laughed.

Phew. But I couldn't delay it any more.

"I guess my answer was kinda the same as the others'." Well, that sounded lame. "Except obviously different, and unique."

Gulp.

I stared out at Tegan and Rach who were nodding and waving and sending every bit of physical encouragement.

"I think it's not about whether people *can* be friends, it's about what other people think about them being friends."

Because while I'd been watching Tegan trying to keep up with Rachel's two-person Mexican wave, they'd made me think of someone else. Mikey. My friend Mikey, who had been voting like crazy to get us in the final. Who hadn't dropped me in it with Tegan. Who'd helped us patch things back up. Who'd worked so hard at the GADAC launch. And when he'd found out about Shay, had offered to cover my shift even though he was meant to be going to Birmingham with Jay.

"One of my most awesome friends is a boy. He's been an amazing friend to me – helping out with this comp, looking out for me and my mates. . ." I looked up from my paper. "Shout out to GIVE A DOG A CONE – shout out to Hamster!" The studio looked understandably confused. I looked back at my scrawled writing. "So, my point is that people are just people. And if you find a good one, hang on to them. Who cares if one of you has more face hair? So if someone asks you that question again – maybe just ask *them* why they think it matters."

Woah. I had no idea where that had come from.

But did it sound OK? I'd never really thought about any of that stuff before. I didn't even really think of Mikey as a boy. Just one of us, who had a really different opinion of how funny farting was.

But the band weren't giving anything away. Unlike Ska, whose furious face suggested she thought I'd done OK. Good. Most importantly, Rach and Tegan looked happy. But would everyone listening in from school would think the same?

Jaz ushered the band out to chat in private and played song after song. They were gone so long I swear I witnessed my own fingernails grow.

"While they figure out the winner, let's read out some of the thousands of messages we've had in. . ." Jaz flicked through the ones the producer had just handed her. "A Mrs Hitchman's been in touch." Oh GREAT. "She says The Helican's new single is a, and I quote, 'a complete slay fest'."

OMG. Surely behaving like this when you ran a school was a sackable offence?!

"Although she did spell it like Santa's sleigh."

OK, that was a *tiny* bit better. "Moving on, we've got a lot of love for Aisha – and a lot of people who want to come and hang on the Helicans tour bus! Oh and one more quick one, South Worcester Reds are listening in. . ."

OH MY WHATTING WHAT? Adam's new team?! Please let me have just thought "swoon" and not said it out loud.

"They reckon all the answers were bang on. But are rooting for Bella – cos apparently she's the best TV-chatting, milkshake-making friend a guy could have."

Jaz smiled at me like she'd done me a favour, and pressed play on the next song.

But had she just said "friend"? Was this seriously happening? Had Adam confirmed to me and the whole world simultaneously, that's all we were? Just as I thought we were finally becoming more?! This COULDN'T be happening?! How was I always getting it so wrong?!

But there was no time to even try and deal, as Jaz was reading the latest email she'd been passed, and it was clear something was up. After the song finished she let the studio fall silent.

"Before we get the band back in, an important message has come from an eagle-eared listener. He's got a valid question. Luke..." OH NO, wherever this was going, it wasn't going to be good, "wants to know if it's true what Bella said earlier..." Jaz looked straight at me. "That she'd got help from her friend with this competition?" Did I *really* say that? I looked down where the words were still written on my paper. I had. But I only meant with voting?! "Cos that's against the rules."

Jaz paused. "Bella ... *has* this competition been all your own work?"

This time she didn't need to play any tension sound effects. The silence was loud with it. But what should I say? What *could* I say?

Mikey hadn't helped with any of the rounds. But I hadn't been alone either.

I tried to ignore Ska's smirk. If only I had proof of what she and Luke had actually done to rig the competition. I looked out at the others – they were pressed up against the glass, tiny breath circles forming around them.

What *was* the truthful answer? I hadn't *meant* to break the rules. But that wasn't the question. The question was whether I'd done it on my own. And the truth was the rounds had been a team effort, between Tegan, Rach and I. Even Jo at the start. But if I admitted that I'd be out the competition.

And so would my St Mary's.

And Ska might walk off as the winner.

If this was *Hollyoaks* the episode would end.

But then I'd also have perfect lip gloss on, and not be sweating in places I didn't know had sweat glands.

Not sure of what to say, I pulled the mic towards me. And began to speak.

CHAPTER

TWENTY-EIGHT

"The friend I was talking about, he didn't help with any of the rounds, no."

Jaz looked relieved.

So did Rach and Tegan. And Aisha, which I thought was kind of lovely.

But I hadn't finished.

"But it'd be a lie to say I did it all alone . . . because the stuff I sent in for the other questions was something I wrote, my friends alongside me." I looked towards the window. Rach's breath circles had stopped. "I didn't know that was breaking the rules, but if it was . . . I'm owning up to it."

Silence.

And not a dramatic one. Just Jaz not knowing what to say.

Ska slow clapped. "Nice work, Bella. Sooooo brave."

But I didn't feel brave. I felt stupid. Why didn't I just say "no"?! Had I messed up everything? If I had, Rach and Tegan would never forgive me. Nor would anyone at school. Mrs Hitchman might even expel me. And I bet Adam, along with the rest of the world, probably now thought I was a cheat. I bet Luke was LOVING this. What had I done?! But I'd wanted to win so badly – and with Luke and Ska looking for any excuse to bring me down, I really thought honesty was the only way it could be possible.

When the band finally walked back in, none of them made eye contact. Was I disqualified? I felt sick.

Lis cleared her throat. "So we've got our decision." Her bandmates grouped round her.

Amil dropped his voice. "We obviously heard all the answers ... and the drama too." He gave me a sympathy-smile. This was like being told your homework was disappointing by the one teacher you think is OK, except it's actually the coolest band ever, and it's all live on the radio and the guy who has just half-dumped you is listening.

Was I out?

"We spoke to the producers, and they said our decision was final. So, we've decided ... to ... allow Bella to stay in the final three, as we could see that everything she said today was deffo her own work."

Yipppeeee!

This was AMAZING?! I said the biggest thanks, and smiled wider than my actual face. The Helicans laughed, but in a way that felt with me, not at me. They were being *so* nice. Had Shay got something to do with it?

I looked to see if Ska was giving me evils, but she was reading the notes she'd made for her winner's speech.

"So, cracking swiftly on, let's find out who has won. In a very respectable third place, it's ... Letty!"

Ska dropped her notes. Dropped her perfect smile. And dropped a massive swear.

Jaz pressed the emergency beep. I tried not to LOL. After all her tricks, I'd beaten Ska fair and square. And now the Helicans had a 50/50 chance of coming to St Mary's.

Aisha looked even more shocked than me – like a waxwork version of herself.

"So who's going to be the overall winner?" Amil took a deep breath. "Will it be Bella for St Mary's, or Aisha for Royal Orchard?"

Lis chuckled. "I feel like I should have a big gold envelope to open."

Amil nudged her. "It's radio, so just pretend like you have?"

"Have it your way!" Lis air-opened an imaginary envelope. "The winner is. . ."

The oxygen supplies of Worcester dropped as everyone took a massive gulp in.

Please say Bella, please say Bella, please say Bella.

Please let me have pulled this off.

Please let the Helicans be coming to St Mary's.

"AISHA!"

Oh.

In one word, the dream was over.

Aisha started vibrating, a tear rolling down her face.

I felt like I also might cry, but for opposite reasons.

I was gutted. Totally gutted.

I'd failed.

I tried to smile as best I could and put my arms round Aisha. "You totally deserved it. Well done." But she was quickly bundled in a way-better Helican hug. All I had was cold reality.

And I was left alone with the cold reality of how scary life was going to be once I stepped out of this studio. Back into real life. Back to school where everyone was going to hate me. Back home with Mum who I'd disappointed. Back with Rach – who was going to put on a brave face that I was going to feel for ever guilty about.

I looked out of the window to see if they were both OK. And panicked. They weren't there. Had they walked out? But as I frantically searched for any sign of them, the door flung open, and bursting past Lanyard Girl came my two best friends, greeting me with the biggest, squashiest cuddle.

"You don't hate me then?" Tegan snorted.

"Hate? We are *so proud* of you!"

And despite not winning, for the first time I knew everything was going to be OK.

CHAPTER

TWENTY-NINE

"Loser."

"Why didn't you just say no?!"

"Have you got Lis's number?"

"It's that weird radio girl."

"I hate you."

Were just some of the things that got shouted at me on Monday. I also got an, "Ouch, that's my foot," but that was valid, as I did accidentally stand on a corridor warden.

Rach and Tegan promised me the groups of people crying were not crying because the Helicans weren't coming to St Mary's. I would have had an easier time believing them if my locker wasn't covered in ripped-down posters, one scrawled with, "We're crying cos of YOU."

If fake-popular last week had been bad, anti-popular was worse. People couldn't get away from me quick enough. It was like my failure might be contagious. They only dared come near me to tell me how much I'd let them down.

It had started yesterday, when I'd spent the day stuck working at an empty GADAC, with nothing to do except try (and fail) not to see what everyone was saying about me online. When I wasn't doing that I was wondering whether to message Adam. But what was there to say?

Even the drive in this morning had been depressing. Mum had given me a lift as she knew I didn't want to go to school and "face the music". I'd pointed out not having any music to face was the problem. But she had bigger worries of her own, because as she was driving I'd seen a calendar alert on her phone that she hadn't meant me to see.

11.15 Alliance & Shire Bank. 253 High Street.
Notes: Bring all documents. Decision Day. Good luck me!

Which made sense of the fact that she was wearing a shirt and skirt that almost matched. It also explained why her driving was more terrifying then usual, as she had a pair of Jo's heels on. It *had* to be about the business loan she'd mentioned. Maybe *that's* why she thought she could afford Jo's trip after all?

"Anyone sitting here?"

Ava pulled up a stool. So she was still speaking to me. Mikey bounced on to the empty one beside her. That made two.

He put his finger up to his bottom lip.

"The question is – *can girls really have lunch with people who are guys?*"

I laughed. He was the first person who had made me smile about the whole thing.

"Soz – was I a bit cringe?"

"Nah – I felt kind of chuffed." He ruffled his hair as if basking in the fame. "Although I guess it did lead to all that drama from Luke, so maybe I should retract my chuffing?"

At the mention of his name, we all unsubtly looked over at Puke. He held up a big L finger. If only there was a hand gesture to say, *I might well be a loser, but I still beat your girlfriend, and your terrible attempt to get me disqualified, so who's the biggest loser now?* But seeing as there wasn't, I just took an extra big bite of my crisp and cucumber sandwich. Jo was still home and had made them for me as a treat. Shay had said it looked like she was trying to kill me with carbs, which had just made Jo add the entire packet in protest.

"Er, Bella?" I looked up. Boxer Boy. Weird. "Heard you got one of those limited-edition hoodies?"

I nodded as he nervously looked across at Luke. "OK, well, just wanted to say, do not wash it. Like ever. Cos my mum annihilated my one." He rolled his eyes. "Gutted."

As if giving out garment care tips was not really massively weird, he scurried back to Luke before they spotted he'd crossed enemy lines.

But before I could try and deal with the dealing of this, my phone buzzed.

STOMACH LURCH.

Adam. Our first message since the final.

I beckoned Rach and Tegan to look as I opened it. A message shared is a message third-ed.

Hope today's OK. Sorry I couldn't help more.

Eurgh – I didn't even want a third of that message. What did that even mean? Except for we were no longer putting "x" or talking about another date.

I didn't know what had changed, but something really had.

No one said anything. There was nothing to say. I had to accept how he felt.

Rach gave me a squeeze. "We'll get through this."

Tegan nodded. "We always do." And she was right. I felt better just being around them. So Tegan went to the water cooler, I went with her.

"Any news about your audition yet?" Her face flinched.

"Nope."

"Feeling positive about it?"

"Nope."

"C'mon – I'm the loser round here, not you?!" It was meant to make her laugh, but it didn't. "Teeg . . . are you sure you're OK?" She was still nodding, but it felt like a no. "C'mon – after everything, you KNOW you can talk to me about this. I'm on your side, remember?"

She took a deep breath. "OK. For your ears ONLY. . . I. . . I didn't get a place. I blew the try-out."

What?! This was awful.

"Teeg – I'm SO sorry. I had no idea." I wanted to give her a hug, but knew she wouldn't want to alert the others, so I secretly squeezed her hand. "When did you find out?"

"Promise you won't be cross?"

"Promise."

"On the day. They told me on the spot."

Woah. And she had been dealing with it on her own for over a week?!

I felt awful. I *really* hoped our row hadn't had anything to do with it.

As usual, Tegan could read my mind.

"Don't worry – it wasn't our stupid argument that caused it. It was all me. I messed up my routine." Well that didn't exactly make me feel any happier. "You guys were right, it was too much. I burnt out."

This was one occasion where I really didn't want to be right.

"Why didn't you say something?" I felt guilty. "Well, y'know, once I'd stopped being a massive idiot?"

She just shrugged. "You had enough going on with the final, and Luke and Adam and everything." She fiddled with a thread in her jumper sleeve. "I guess I didn't want to bring anyone down."

Eurgh – and we'd even made her that stupid badge, that she'd still stuck on her bag, despite probably making her feel worse?! It was too much. I had to hug her. Even on her worst days she still put us first.

I wasn't sure how you could make someone a saint, but I was totally going to find the application form.

"Teeg, you could NEVER bring us down. You are the

glue that sticks us all up!?" She smiled, half-heartedly. "Plus you're the most talented person I've ever met. Total inspo."

She shook her head. But I wasn't stopping.

"No lies, remember? It's a promise. Did they give any reason?"

She shrugged. "They thought maybe I should try and focus on one discipline."

"There you go, then! You can't help being too talented and amazing at ever-reey-thang for them. This time next year they'll be *begging* you to accept a place."

Small traces of a proper smile began on her face. "Next time, whatever happens, *whenever* it happens, you tell us, OK?"

For someone so sensible, she really had no clue what friends were there for sometimes. "Now, how about you go tell the others? They'll be raging if they find out any later. And Rach will deffo buy you sympathy pudding."

She chewed her lip. "I guess so."

"I *know* so."

Protesting slightly, but not enough to not actually do it, she headed back towards them. I watched her telling Mikey and Rach, both of them reacting exactly how I did – shock followed by big unauthorized hugs.

I was *so* certain that next year we'd be hugging her to

congratulate her. And this time, we'd be able to support her properly to get there.

I sat back down trying to take it all in. What. A. Day. Tegan's news really put my moans into perspective. At least being the most despised person in school meant I got space at the bathroom mirror, and didn't get stopped by anyone handing out flyers. Plus I finally had some peace and quiet, because the only person, other than Rach, Tegan, Mikey, Ava and Boxer Boy, who made any effort to speak to me was Mrs Hitchman.

She summoned me to her office that afternoon.

I thought I'd be nervous when I walked in, but I was too surprised to fret. Had she been crying?

Mrs Hitchman saw me eye the box of tissues on her desk and swiped them out of view.

"I just wanted to say thank you." She sniffed. "I know you tried your best."

I checked under the table, and took comfort from the fact that normal footwear had resumed.

"Sorry it wasn't good enough."

"Trying your best is always good enough." She didn't sound like she believed it, but she smiled a little. "Was Lis as *captivating* in real life as she seems?"

I nodded. "Even more so."

But that made Mrs Hitchman blink even more

furiously. She spun round and walked to the window. When she turned back, her normal hard stare had returned.

"So yes. Thank you. And I've cancelled the TV crew. And . . . that's all." She waved me to the door.

She got more confusing every day.

Getting back to the safety of my home couldn't come quick enough. Despite Tegan's news, my two amazing friends walked me all the way home and didn't leave me till I was on the sofa, a Tunnock's Teacake in hand. Rach, who had wanted St Mary's to win the gig more than anyone, even unwrapped it. I just about managed my own chewing. And when they had to head off for their tea, Tegan made sure Jo tagged in on Bella-sitting.

Even though I only had half a bedroom when she was home, I was glad she was sticking around for a few days.

"C'mon," she hit me in the stomach with a cushion. "At least you didn't do anything *that* embarrassing. I've heard your hicburps – it could have been way worse."

Shay looked up from flicking through a magazine that was thicker than my biology textbook. "Think they would have turned her mic down if that happened."

Jo raised an eyebrow. "Not that you were there to offer that advice when it was needed." Yup, Shay had officially replaced me as the person who annoyed her most in the house. It was liberating. But Shay wasn't having any of it.

"Not that you students would know what it's like having a proper job that you can't say no to." In fairness, I'd hardly seen Shay since Saturday, but whenever I had, she'd apologized on repeat. "Oh ... Bells." She pulled something out of her bag. "Meant to give you this. To say sorry. Again."

Woah – it was a new bottle of the gold nail varnish she always wore that I loved.

I gave her a thank-you hug, blocking out Jo's eye-roll in my periphery. It was now or never to ask Shay the question that had been on my mind.

"Shay – did you ... did you have anything to do with the band keeping me in the comp, even after I said I broke the rules?"

She looked up with a naughty look in her eye. "Well, *that* would be telling?!"

I didn't know if that made me feel worse or better. Yes, it meant the band had been willing to do me a favour, but it also meant I hadn't got second place on my own merit.

BLEURGH. Why had I asked?

I gave up putting on a brave face. The only face I

could manage was my real one – and it was thoroughly fed up. I headed to the kitchen to see if there were any emergency crisps left, but it was like a crime scene. All the pots and pans were out, and Mum's bag was thrown on the table. But there was no actual mother.

Something caught my eye. A letter underneath her bag.

Although I get mad when Mum even sets foot in my room without asking, I figured this only works one way (surely mums don't have anything interesting enough worth hiding) and peeked inside the envelope.

And wished I hadn't.

The bank's logo. I'd been so wrapped up in my stuff I hadn't asked Mum about hers. Still, that's what I could do right now.

First thing on my Fixing My Failure Of A Life list. I sat and waited. But five minutes later there was no sign of her.

Swinging by the lounge to double-check she hadn't been camouflaged with a cushion the whole time (she's got a kaftan in the exact same floral) I headed upstairs. A light was on in her room.

Tiptoeing to the door I heard a sniff, and a quiet voice doing the thing I always did: a self-pep talk when I needed to pull myself together.

Using her own technique against her, I knocked and walked in.

And wanted to run straight back out.

Mum was sitting on the edge of the bed, tissues in hand, mascara running down her face.

She looked at me like I look at her when she walks in to my room and catches me playing *Puppy Dash* when I'd promised her I was doing my homework. Total innocence.

"You all right, love? Dinner won't be long." She tried to secret-sniff. "Fishless fingers and chips."

She wasn't fooling anyone. I sat down and put my arm around her. It was meant to cheer her up, but just opened the floodgates on not-so-secret sniffing. Crying like I'd never seen her do.

First Mrs Hitchman, now this.

It was way weirder seeing a parent cry. And by weird, I think I mean totally and utterly horrible.

When she finally caught her breath, she looked more frustrated than upset.

"Sorry, you shouldn't be seeing this." She dabbed away at her eye.

"Is this GADAC related?"

She nodded. And cried some more. I guess things at the bank hadn't gone so well.

"I think I owe you both an apology." She glanced at the photo of Jo and I on her bedside table. "I've really messed this one up."

I squeezed my arm tighter. "Jo'll understand about the trip."

Mum turned to face me. "It's not even that. . ." She was looking from eye to eye, as if trying to work out if I could handle what she wanted to say. I probably couldn't, but I knew I needed to.

"You can tell me, Mum."

She took my hand in hers. She hadn't done this to tell me news since Granddad died. "Unless things change in the next three weeks. . ." Her voice wobbled. "The shop . . . the shop will have to close."

OOF. I hoped more than anything it wasn't going to come to this.

"But you're getting more followers online? And we had people in yesterday?"

"Oh, Bella. Thank you. But. . ." she paused. "It's not enough."

"I can work extra shifts?! There must be something?"

She squeezed my hand. "Bells, sweetheart, it's not something an extra shift or two can change." She exhaled like someone stuck between the biggest fight of their life, and giving up entirely. "And if I don't figure it out, we might have to. . ." The sobs started again. "We might have to. . ."

She never finished her sentence. Instead she looked around the room and muttered, "What have I done?"

I knew what she was going to say. We might have to move house. Where I'd lived my whole life.

I knew the mortgage had been tight which is why Shay had moved in. And she was off in a month.

If Mum hadn't already used all the tissues, I might have joined in with the blubbing.

I wished Jo was up here, not down there, to handle this better than I was.

I wanted to tell Mum how proud I was of her. That she had nothing to apologize for. But all I managed was an, "I love you, Mum."

She did an almighty snort and shook her face out. "Sorry, Bells." She was managing her normal, breezy-chat voice. "I don't know what came over me?" She jumped up. And with a let's-pretend-that-didn't-happen-isn't-life-great cry of, "Better get that oven on," headed downstairs.

I stayed sitting in the low light of her room, listening to Jo shouting anagrams at the TV and the clanging of baking trays in the kitchen. If we were going to lose everything we weren't going to do it without a fight.

I'd had enough of seeing everyone so miserable. I was NOT going to stand by and do nothing. Let something else go wrong.

I might not be able to undo what had happened at school, but no one could stop me putting everything I had into trying to fix things for my family.

CHAPTER

THIRTY

I knew one thing: as unlikely as it seemed, I needed the Helicans.

They'd helped me out before – *maybe* they'd do it again?

And I knew the exact person that could try and make it happen.

I ran a brush through my hair and blinked through some mascara. If I was going to call in a favour this big, I needed to look serious – and on trend.

Before I could run through all the reasons this was a terrible idea and wimp out of it, I marched out of my room and downstairs.

Mum was still in the kitchen. Good. I needed her to not know what was happening.

I strode into the lounge. Because I knew what I was about to do, it felt like a dramatic entrance. But Jo didn't look up from the TV, nor Shay from her magazine.

I cleared my throat. Still neither of them acknowledged me.

Nice to know what authority I commanded.

I went for a more direct approach and sat on the arm of Shay's chair.

She finally got my hint and closed her magazine.

"There's no easy way to say this..." I started. Although there was. WhatsApp. But I had to be brave.

"What have you done *this* time?"

"Nothing. But I WANT to do something."

Jo muted the TV. Now I had an audience of two.

"Go onnnnnn." Shay said it in a way that sounded like she didn't really want me to.

I took a deep breath and, with half my brain trying to stop my mouth, and the other half willing it on before it chickened out, I explained my plan. And that for it to work, it all rested on Shay getting back in contact with Lis to ask a massive favour.

Jo did an impressed whistle through her teeth.

But Shay said nothing.

Please let her be thinking I was worth it.

Please let her be thinking my family was worth it.

But I wasn't expecting what she said.

"No can do."

Just like that. No sorry. Or explanation. Or tiny slither of hope that, in some alternate reality, it could work. That was it.

"Well, thanks anyway," I mumbled. But she was right. What had I been thinking?! As if failure me could have pulled something like this off.

I headed towards the door trying to not finally give in to the burning feeling of wanting to cry.

But Jo shouted after me. "You stop right there, Bella." She sounded annoyed. I shouldn't have asked Shay in front of her. Now I was going to get an earful from her about "overstepping boundaries" or whatever this week's bee in her bonnet was.

I didn't want *both* of them mad at me. I turned back.

"I literally cannot believe you sometimes." Jo was doing the aggressive one-finger pointing like she was conducting half of a tiny orchestra. But it wasn't pointed at me – it was pointed at Shay?!

"How *hard* would it be for you to send one email?"

Shay gave her a dead stare back. "How *hard* would it be for *you* to mind your own *business*?"

They locked eyes so hard that if Mumbles stood

up on two legs and started doing the Macarena they wouldn't notice.

"Would it really have killed you to not let my sister down ... *again*?"

Shay shrugged. "Would it kill you to try to understand how this industry works?"

I'd never heard anyone talk so condescendingly to Jo, and fifteen years of experience meant I knew what would happen next. I braced for an outburst. A shoutburst. But instead Jo calmly looked at me, and micro-smiled. "Bells, could you give us a sec?"

I nodded, grateful to be excused, and headed to my room.

Well, I pretended to head to my room, but actually tiptoed straight back to the door, and pressed my ear to it. Jo didn't waste a second before she unleashed everything.

"Have you got *ANY* idea how much everyone's put themselves out for you?" She was spitting her words out. But Shay wasn't phased.

"I'm paying good money, aren't I?"

"You're paying for your room – not to make my mum put her stuff in boxes. Not to give her even more hang-ups about her life than she already has." Jo lowered her voice. But as it was already really loud, it was still totally hear-able. "Not to kick my sister when she's already down."

I looked around the hallway. The familiar life-size cardboard Benny from ABBA *had* been folded away (Shay had said it was weird. She was right). Mum's childhood dreamcatcher *had* been taken down (when Shay put heels on, it did risk removing an eyeball, and they are quite important things to not take out of your head). The bed Mum had knitted for Mumbles *had* been replaced by a clean plastic one (Shay had made a good point that maybe not everyone loved the smell of woolly wet dog).

Hmmm. They'd all seemed like good ideas when Shay had suggested them. But maybe Jo was right. It *did* look a little less like our home. And a bit more like anyone else's.

I drifted back into listening to the argument. Shay was now accusing Jo of being jealous. Jo was saying that Shay believed her own hype. Shay retorted that everything was great when Jo wasn't around. Jo told Shay she'd had enough and was leaving to talk to her sister.

Which I almost-too-late realized meant me, and had to frantically tiptoe-sprint up the stairs, and dive under my duvet.

When Jo came in I hoped she couldn't see how fast

my heart was beating under the covers. She looked all pumped up like she did when she finishes a race.

"Sorry about that." She looked embarrassed. "I shouldn't have flipped out like I did."

"You don't have anything to say sorry for?! Although, Shay probs wouldn't agree."

Jo rolled her eyes. "She had it coming." But I wasn't so sure.

"She's not *that* bad, Jo. Just a bit flakey." She *had* helped with the Helicans, just not the way we thought it was going to happen.

"Nah – she's been winding me up something chronic."

"Maybe it just doesn't get to me as much – you've given me years of practice."

"Oi." Jo poked me in the ribs. I leapt back as much as you can do when you're lying down. "I won't tell you the thing I came here to tell you then."

"Well, you're here now..."

Jo gave me a mischievous smile. Uni was really bringing out a new side of her. I liked it.

"What with everything else, I forgot to mention it before..."

She dug around in her jeans pocket and pulled out her phone.

"C-L-A-R..." She began to spell. I stared at her blankly.

"Don't give me that look. Write it down!"

I scrunched my face up. Write *what* down?!

"The email address. For Clare... The Helicans' manager."

WHAT THE WHAT?!

Jo laughed at my stunned gawp.

"Long story short, I lent her some cash for the car park at Radio Shire. We got chatting, turns out she did the same course as me at uni. She said I should get in touch if I ever needed anything and we ended up swapping emails."

THANK GOODNESS I WAS ALREADY LYING IN A FAINT POSITION.

"I *was* going to save it for seeing if she had free band merch and getting you birthday presents on the cheap ... but figured this could be an early one instead?"

MY BRAIN WAS. NOT. DEALING.

Was Jo really showing me an arrangement of letters that meant I could get in touch with the inner Helicans circle? I gave her a hug that was so violent she asked me to stop.

"This is between you and me only. Agreed?" I nodded. The fewer people who knew what I was up to, the better. And after her reaction to my plan, that meant Shay too.

Did I owe it to Jo to tell her why I was plotting so hard? To admit how bad stuff had got with Mum and the business? No. Not yet. I had to see what I could make happen first. Mum had trusted me.

But did I trust myself?

Because this was my biggest idea yet. But the only thing I seemed to be any good at lately was getting things wrong.

THIRTY-ONE

If the start of the week had been bad at school, today achieved the impossible and got even worse.

It was Friday. The day the Helicans should be playing St Mary's. But instead they were at Royal Orchard. Giving some other school the best day of their life. All I was getting were the kind of evil looks from my classmates that should be reserved for the person who actually invented school.

At lunch I'd hidden out in the library – the rest of the school was either in the computer room, or huddled round phones (special permission granted from Mrs Hitchman) to watch the live stream of the gig. Apparently it "looked and sounded epic". Two people at Royal Orchard had to get emergency oxygen, it was that good.

When I'd bumped into Mikey later he told me that Boxer Boy had been spotted giving Ava a hug after she'd run to the bathroom in tears at missing out. Mikey realized too late that I probably didn't want to know that detail.

But I couldn't feel any worse about everything than I already did. Not helped by the fact I'd still had zero contact from Adam.

The only thing keeping me from joining Ava blubbing in the loo (other than the sanitary towel bins which take up most of the space) was focusing on channelling what little energy I had into my plan. Later today I was going to find out if my last ditch plan to Fix My Fam had worked. Despite all the work I'd put in, I had no idea if I'd done enough.

At least the Mum bit was sorted. She'd replied to me at lunch.

HELLO MY DARLING DAUGHTER I GOT YOUR
MESSAGE IS SOMETHING WRONG YOU
MUST TELL ME IF IT IS THAT IS WHAT MUMS
ARE FOR TO ANSWER YOUR QUESTION I
HAVE CANCELLED MY YOGA WITH BRENDA
AND CAN BE THERE AT FIVE THIRTY LOL
YOUR MUMZZZ

One day she'd accept that LOL wasn't lots of love. And that messages weren't meant to be full life histories. And incorporate full stops.

But today wasn't that day.

Today was the day I needed her to not ask questions and just turn up when I needed her. And when the final bell went, Rach, Tegan, Mikey and I ran straight outside and into Jo's car. Not only was she on time, but she'd done her bit and swiped the spare GADAC keys without Mum noticing. Within minutes we were inside the shop, unpacking the props I'd been making all week.

It was like we were doing a reverse robbery. A yrebbor.

A hand rested on my shoulder. Jo. "Have you heard back from your last email?"

I shook my head and tried not to notice her wince. Not a good sign. Made more painful as we were surrounded by actual good signs that we'd just stuck up everywhere. I *knew* my sister studying graphic design could pay off (for me) one day.

But I didn't have time to worry. Tegan needed a hand setting up my camera, and Rach needed a hand pinning up the big "Follow @GADAC" arrow we'd made. It was all hands on deck until a knock at the door brought us to a halt.

It was a man in a red cap.

"Delivery for B. Fisher?" I nodded and peeked inside the box. It was exactly what I wanted. Even though I *still* couldn't believe I'd put all my hard-earned GADAC wages towards it.

But having it here meant it was time. I headed to the back room to get ready.

Would the next knock at the door be everything I dreamt of? Or a confused Mum and a whole heap of explaining to do.

CHAPTER

THIRTY-TWO

Was that a scream?

I was only half changed, but rushed out to find Rachel looking whiter than what I was wearing.

Tegan was calmly pointing at the door "Bells. It's for you."

Giving me a firm nudge, I stumbled towards it and stepped outside.

The blacked-out people carrier still had its engine running as the door slid open.

I couldn't actually believe it.

When Clare had replied saying the band 'might be up for popping in for a few photos if their schedule allowed', I had no idea if it was a brush-off or she meant it. Shay was always saying how flaky music peeps were.

But, no.

It had happened.

THE HELICANS HAD COME.

To Give A Dog A Cone.

Lis was the first to get out. She gave me an actual hug, like we were friends. (Note to self: track down the street CCTV and secure footage of this moment.)

"I CANNOT believe you came?! Thank you sooo much!" I couldn't help but stare at her like she was an apparition.

She just laughed. "No biggie!" We obviously had very different definitions of "big". "Plus this one," she pointed at Pastry who was running back and forth through our legs, "would never have forgiven me if we'd deprived her of getting more Give A Dog A Cone treats! That tub your sister gave us in the car park? She wolfed it down."

Woah – I had no idea Jo had done that. She really was a proper genius, not just one of those people who does well in exams.

"Oi." I felt a prod in the arm. Amil. He reached out for a hug. "Long time no see!"

"You too – and today I can do sentences and evvverythang."

He laughed – and looked down at what I was wearing. "Loving the Pritt Stick look?!"

Ooops. I'd forgotten I only had half of my new costume on. Hopefully it'd make more sense when the top bit was on. Not exactly my *dream* look for the only time in my life where I was going to hang out with actual famous people, but every little bit of GADAC promotion helped.

Rosie held her hands out. "I nabbed this from the tour bus. You want?"

Oh my days, AS IF IT WAS A DAIM CAKE. She'd remembered our convo!?

I took the box from her like I was a Wise Man being passed the Baby Jesus in a nativity. But dressed as half a Pritt Stick.

The One With No Name stopped at the step. "Congrats, Bella – your mum's done an awesome job! No wonder you wanted to help out."

I blushed, unsure if it was because of the endorsement for my mum, or because it meant Clare must have told them everything I'd written in the email – and they'd remembered.

I'd been totally honest. I'd told them about Mum's business. About how it might be about to go under, and how I wanted to do *anything* I could to help – especially as it supported the local dogs' charity – and that if there was *any* time at all could they come by after their gig, even for just one photo outside... I *may* have also offered a lifetime supply of ice cream for Pastry (the one and only time I was happy that dogs didn't live as long as humans).

But even though I'd sent it – I never thought it could really happen.

The last person to clamber out of the backseat was someone I didn't recognize. Huge smile, hair piled on her head. She caught Jo's eye and waved.

Ahhh, this must be Clare.

Without meaning to, I ran over and flung my arms around her.

"THANK YOU, THANK YOU, THANK YOU, THANK YOU."

She just laughed. "Well, we had some time to kill before the bus heads up to Birmingham for tomorrow's gig, so the guys thought it'd be nice to come and show some support."

Woah. Shay had made out everyone in The Industry was like a Disney villain, but Clare was *lovely*. The band were *lovely*. They were all so *lovely*.

"Honestly, I cannot thank you enough."

Clare leaned in. "Between you and me, I think you were their joint-favourite to win, so they were happy they could sort something out." My jaw fell open. "And stuff like this makes such a nice break from the usual press."

Was she really chatting with me about the inner workings of the band?! This was too much. "Oh, and we thought it could be a good opportunity to try out some acoustic versions of a couple of new songs, if that's OK?"

OK? OK???

It wasn't OK!! It was un-bee-leeeeee-vable. My wildest dream.

(Previous dream = the band turning up for one picture. Maybe retweeting one GADAC's post – and now they were giving me a world-exclusive gig?!)

"Sorry it's gross, but we had to bring some security, just to be on the safe side."

Clare nodded at two enormous guys who were helping carry in black and metal boxes. They both shouted, "Hiya!"

"We've got a couple of journos on the tour with us. Is there enough space for them too?"

I needed to think another way of saying, "Yes, thank you," and, "You're amazing." And also – "OMG is this an entourage situation!?" But instead let out another, "Yes, YES! Thank you, you're amazing, thank you."

Clare laughed at/with me again and headed in to help set up. This was *actually* happening. I messaged

Mum and reminded her to brush her hair.

The next thirty minutes were a weird mix of being frantically busy trying to help the band set up, while stopping every twenty seconds to deal with the fact that the Helicans were in my mum's shop. Hanging out with my friends.

They were as chill as the ice cream – even when I tried to take a covert pic on my phone, but left the flash on, and got totally rumbled. They especially loved Pastry's VID (Very Important Dog) bowl I'd made.

Mikey had done an amazing job of tracking down all the contact details of the people we wanted to be there. He'd even found HitchHiker100 on a Helicans forum.

Right on time, the guests started to arrive. It was only a small space so we'd had to be really careful. Proper supporters of the band or GADAC only. We hadn't been able to be honest about what was happening, as I wasn't sure myself – so I'd kept it vague with a "Give A Dog A Cone and The Last Band To be First need your help" message. The reference was to a hidden Helicans album track, so we figured only true fans would turn up.

Ava arrived first. She was wearing the Helicans T-shirt I'd seen so often under her school shirt. I ran outside to meet her. Her mascara was still smudged from crying earlier.

"Bells – what are you doing here?!" I was too excited to speak. "If you wanted to start a petition couldn't we have done that at school? I was saying earlier tha—"

But mid putting in her ponytail band, she froze, arms in the air.

If I'd ever wanted to know what would happen if you dipped a person in liquid nitrogen, I now had a fairly good idea.

"Is . . . that. . .?"

I nodded. "Uh-huh."

"What. The. Actual. . ." But she didn't get to finish, as Tegan came out, clipboard and pen in hand.

"You made it! Great! First one ticked off." She spotted Ava was having trouble functioning, and physically pushed her in. "In you go."

Ava walked forward like each limb was being remote controlled independently. I wished I could see her face as Amil headed straight over, admired her T-shirt and began chatting away.

Tegan squeezed my hand. "Bells – I'm so proud of you."

Even though she was one of my best friends, I felt weirdly embarrassed.

"Total team effort."

"All your idea though." She held up the list. "Now, do you reckon these randomers are going to show?" She ran her finger down the names, which included people we hadn't ever met. Although. Wait? There was someone on the list I hadn't put there. It wasn't a name, just three initials.

TMH.

Tegan shrugged. "Don't look at me!"

"Aka *do* look at Rachel?"

She double shrugged, which totally meant *yes*.

"Apparently she saw him with a Helicans tote once? You did *say* we needed mega fans?!"

"But we don't even know his name?!"

"Oh we do. Mikey found out. Apparently it's Colin."

"Think I'll stick with Tesco Matt Healey."

Teeg laughed. "Same!"

I looked over at Rach, who was polishing one of the glass freezer doors with both sleeves of her hoodie. Whilst wearing it. It was impossible to ever be cross with her.

"Right, so five mins before Mum gets here."

"Thank goodness she's spent enough time in your room with the posters. Imagine if she was all like, 'Who are your new friends and why are they in here?' And, 'Isn't that one cold with her stomach showing?'"

I gulped. I hadn't actually thought through the prospect of my mum actually *being* with the band. She was bad enough at parents' evening, and I absolutely don't care what teachers think.

But there was no more time to panic, as the trickle of people turned into a full avalanche of all the names on the list arriving. The room was packed, and everyone was buzzing, especially the handful of people from school we'd invited – the only ones who had carried on being nice to us even after I'd lost the comp.

It was like normal rules were off – strangers all chatting to each other as if the fact we all had the Helicans in common was enough to know we could all get on. Rach was having proper goss with Tesco Colin Matt Healy. And Mikey and Boxer Boy were laughing like they were old mates, as opposed to people who shared the same school space daily but didn't acknowledge each other's existence.

As Clare promised, even some press turned up – and they weren't scary at all. They were in trainers and had messy hair and were genuinely interested in GADAC. Tegan made sure they all had lots of tubs to take home.

Suddenly a shout from Jo filled the room. "Everyone. SHUSH! She's about to arrive!" She flicked off the big lights. Mum must be coming. I felt a new wave of worry. Please let her be pleased!

Rosie and Lis picked up their guitars and shuffled up on to their stools. The rest of the audience gathered round, not sure whether to look at them or the door.

I took a step out into the cold evening.

Mum was bumbling towards me, chatting to herself. She was hurrying, but her shoulders were down and her hands were clenched. I hadn't picked up on it before, but she looked more stressed just being near the shop. Not noticing anything untoward, or the fact I was wearing half a fancy-dress costume, she gave me her normal kiss on the cheek.

"Now then, flower face, what was this thing you so needed me to be here for?" She put a hand on either side of my face. "Should I be worried? You are such a mysterious sausage sometimes, aren't you?"

Memory, please delete the time when a whole room full of the coolest people I'd ever met just heard me get called a "mysterious sausage" by my mum.

"Erm, it was this, Mum."

I pushed open the door fully as Jo flicked the light back on. The room erupted into cheers.

Mum stared like she'd seen a ghost.

Well, *another* ghost, as she said she'd encountered one when she went on a camping holiday in Scotland.

"What . . . what?" She staggered back.

"All publicity is good publicity, right?"

She looked at Lis and Rosie. "Aren't they. . .?"

I nodded.

"From your wall?"

I nodded again, although that wasn't their *key* achievement. "Also known as the Helicans. They wanted to help out. So let me take your coat, and you get inside and enjoy."

Jo took Mum's hand, and pulled her into the crowd. And with camera flashes going off, and cheering louder than ever before, Lis counted down from three, and the Helicans began to play.

THIRTY-THREE

They sounded AMAZING. Even better live.

The best thing I'd *ever* heard.

Mum was still in such shock Jo had to hang on to her throughout. She could've toppled like Jenga – Mumga – at any second. Everyone else was equally as hyped – all swaying, clapping and singing along to the ones they knew, and loving every second of the new stuff.

Finally, with no more running around to do, I pulled on the top half of my costume. Finding a human-sized bone outfit had been hard, but as I bounced along to the music, human-arm in bone-arm with Rach and Tegan, posing for photos, I knew it would look great. And as pics started landing in people's feeds, I was proved right. I just had to cross my fingers something would make its way into the papers tomorrow – that we could finally get the GADAC word out.

My phone buzzed in my bra where I'd stuffed it.

JO: You did good, Sis xxx

Across the room, I gave her my biggest smile – then remembered my face was entirely hidden behind a giant bone costume.

It really was more amazing than I could have ever imagined. Clare was even live streaming little teasers of the new songs, tagging GADAC in *everything*. Our followers had gone up by a thousand before the third song had even finished. I couldn't *wait* for Shay to arrive. She was going to be so impressed, and it would be an awesome surprise for the band to have their friend here.

It was the best I'd felt in forever. I had no idea if it was going to be enough to help save GADAC but I'd definitely given Mum a night to remember – and put a smile back on her face.

But as I was taking it all in, Rach started pointing at the door. I turned to see a very unexpected person arguing with the bouncers and headed out, Tegan following behind me.

"Er, hi, Mrs Hitchman."

She gave me a confused look. "Bella?! Is that you?!"

I nodded, which in my costume had to happen from the waist upwards. "I didn't know you were..." I stopped myself before I said "invited". If there's one person you don't want to sound aggro with, it's your head teacher.

"Invited?" She finished my sentence.

"No, no. Erm, free? I thought you had a, er, teacher thing?"

Was she one of the randomers who had turned up after seeing all the chat online? The bouncers were doing a great job at keeping them outside. There must be fifty already.

"Oh no! I cleared my diary for this! Just in case!" She ran her finger down Tegan's list.

"HITCHHIKER100. There I am!"

What the what? She'd been the one emailing Radio Shire, and posting all over their forums? Thank goodness I was in a costume so she couldn't see my look of horror.

But she'd already pushed past me, and was stomping her Converse all the way to the front. Tegan leaned over.

"So none of us are EVER getting a detention ever again, right?"

We looked inside – Mrs Hitchman already had her hands in the air. I swear Lis was trying not to giggle.

Tegan took her phone out. "I'm totally getting video in case!"

We headed back inside, but less than two songs later one of the bouncers came and got me.

"We've got two people outside who say they're regular customers, and a 'big deal on Instagram'. They're desperate to get in but I can't see their names. Any ideas?"

I stood on my tiptoes, but what with the crowd outside and in, I couldn't see who they were.

I went outside to discover the most beautiful girl looking furious at being made to wait – but not as annoyed as her boyfriend, who was loudly telling everyone he was friends with the band. When he saw a person in a Giant Bone costume, he looked apoplectic with rage.

"I said I wanted the manager. What are you, *stupid*?!" He was right up in the other bouncer's face. "I'm telling you – you are going to get *fired* when they find out you made us wait!"

The outside crowd were starting to film it, loving the drama. The guy was loving the ego trip and his girlfriend tossed her hair and pouted extra hard for anyone who was watching.

As quickly as I could, I pulled off the top half of my costume.

"Sorry, guys – your name's not down, you're not coming in."

Yup, there was NO WAY Luke or Ska were having *anything* to do with this night. And the looks on their faces made every second of hard work worth it. Thank goodness so many people were filming so I could enjoy this moment on demand for the rest of my life. I turned to the bouncers. "Good call, guys. Thanks for your help." I gave Ska and Luke – who were still open mouthed in horror – the sickliest sweet wave I could muster, and pulled my costume back on, walking back in to a shower of high fives from Tegan and Rach. Together we carried on enjoying the best gig of our life.

Sadly, in no time at all, it was almost over. The band finished the set with an amazing version of "Bucketlist Blues"– which they played twice after they couldn't stop the chants of "Again, again!"

"So, we'll be hanging around for a bit now, but before we do, we wanted to say a huge thanks to Bella for making this all happen."

Amil yelled, "THREE CHEERS FOR BELLA THE BONE!"

As *if* this was my life.

But it really wasn't me who deserved the thanks.

As scary as it was I pushed my way through the

crowd and pointed at the mic. "May I?"

Lis nodded. "All yours." She passed me the microphone.

"So, er, if it's OK, I wanted to say some thank yous?" It felt weird standing next to Lis and Rosie, looking out on all these people in Mum's shop. I couldn't believe I was doing voluntary public speaking, at least wearing a costume made it easier.

"The biggest one is for the Helicans, obvs." I didn't need to prompt anyone to start whooping. "Uh-huh! AmIright?!" The cheers went on. "Cos not only did their new stuff sound *TOTALLY AMAZING*, but they've taken time out of their tour to be here. And to support someone they hardly know."

This time they got an even more heartfelt clap from everyone. Lis smiled awkwardly at her feet. "Our pleasure. Seriously. There aren't enough women in business as it is, so what with dogs *and* food *and* charity, it was a no-brainer." She started clapping towards my mum. "The world needs more Bella's mums!"

Mum blushed and giggled. Jo yelled, "Tooooo right!" and Pastry howled as if she'd been training all her life to take excellent comedy cues.

But I had something else I wanted to say.

"So, if you don't follow us on social media already,

you can check out our accounts." I pointed at all the posters we'd made. "And stock up early for Christmas. And, er, dog birthdays. And basically do whatever you can to support this local business, because my mum has put her heart and soul into this, and I'm going to do everything I can to help it be the success she deserves!"

Moving at a speed I'd never seen from her, Mum pushed through the crowd and gave me the most massive hug.

"I love you so much, Bellington Boot," she whispered into where she thought my ear was, but accidentally said it right at the mic so it echoed round the room.

Luckily, I was too distracted to be embarrassed. Cos a face I recognized was peering in through the glass.

Shay. But instead of coming in, she spun round and hurried off.

Weird.

Was she cross I'd contacted her friends and not told her? Or didn't she want to see her industry pals when she wasn't prepared? I'd have to ask later, because right now there was too much going on. Including getting loads of pics of Mum as she chatted away to the band, the press peeps all taking notes.

All too soon it was time for the band to head off. After the biggest thank yous it was possible to give them (and as much ice cream as we could fit in to cool bags), Rach, Tegan, Mum, Jo, Mikey and I waved them off.

With everyone else now gone, we went back inside and shut the door, each of us having our own moment of wondering if it had all been a dream.

"This calls for," Jo dug in her bag, "a little something I got earlier."

Woah. An actual proper bottle of champagne?! I'd never had that in my life.

"Jo! You shouldn't have?!" Mum was that fake-cross parents sometimes do when they're secretly happy. It normally happened when you bought them a present. Jo grinned.

"I maaaaay have been given it when I won Athlete of the Season, but for reputation's sake can we pretend I bought it because I'm both wealthy and generous?"

She popped the cork, and in the absence of proper glasses, we had a couple of sips each out of ice cream cones. My head felt weird, like when you bend over for too long then stand upright.

"Here's to GADAC, and" – Jo looked at her phone – "hitting five thousand followers on Instagram, and yup . . . we're actually trending right now."

Mum smiled. "Well, isn't that something?"

Jo and I laughed – that was what Mum always says

when she doesn't have a clue what we're on about.

"And something's happened that I think you will like. Bella?" Mum held out her phone. "If you look in my hair drop, apparently it's all in there."

I think she meant Airdrop. I opened the files.

And gasped. It was full of professional photos, of Pastry and Lis and the band, standing around Mum, all looking amazing under the GADAC sign. And, in the middle, like Gigi Hadid but with fur, Pastry was eyeballing the camera as she licked an ice cream. So fierce.

"Mum, this is SO COOL! You look so A-list!"

"It was Lis's idea. After chatting about how I started the whole business she suggested that we do a collaboration. Pie-cecream and Pastry flavour. She hoped it could help raise even more for the Bark Shelter?" She flushed red. "Apparently the band are going to post it on their Facebook tomorrow."

Rach's jaw had dropped. "That's freakin' brilliant!"

"A total scoop!" I laughed as I held my hand up for a high five. But this called for more than that, and the five of us – me, Mum, Rach, Tegan, Mikey – ended up on the floor in a crumpled, celebrating heap.

"Sorry, you are *how* old?" Jo heckled from the side.

I grabbed her ankle. "Oi, this is how us Fishers do

it." I tugged at it, and without too much resistance she fell on top of us all.

And, out of all of the incredible moments that had happened tonight, this was my favourite.

THİRTY-FOUR

The house was quiet. Weirdly quiet: just the faint hum of Mum singing along to Radio 2. She hadn't had that on since Shay had made her switch to something cooler.

Jo had got up hours ago, so I was making full use of having my bed to myself, lying starfished, enjoying some peace after the manic-ness of yesterday.

My phone was still buzzing – a bit like me – but it could wait.

"OI. SNORE-BALL. PHONE FOR YOU." Jo opened my door and lobbed the house handset at me.

Or maybe it couldn't.

Someone had gone full landline on me. Something was up.

I used the shouting already coming from the phone to track it down in my duvet folds.

"BELLS!"

It was Rach, and she sounded excited. How could anyone be this excited about *anything* SO EARLY in the morning?

I squinted at my clock. 10.54 a.m. Hmm, still counted as morning.

"FINALLY! Guess where I've just come from?"

She was breathless. I hadn't even said my first word of the day.

"A puppy breeder's?"

"Nope."

"J.K. Rowling's kitchen and she cooked you pancakes?"

"No!!!" She was getting impatient.

"OK – Immagonna need some help."

"TESCO."

She announced it in the same way I'd expect the first person to land on Mars would do (landing on Mars – not going to a supermarket).

But why was this so earth-shatteringly important?

"Were they giving away free crisps?!"

"Better!" She squeaked like she was a human metal detector and it was getting nearer The Point.

"Free trolleys to take home and ride?"

"Better-er!!" She was so excited I knew if I held out another second she'd totally burst the news out.

Tick.

To—

"TMH!!!"

Ah. I got it. I'd seen the looks she'd been giving him last night. Had Colin achieved the impossible and managed to land a date with Rach in the romantic surroundings of the canned-food aisle?

"OMGHASSOMETHINGHAPPENED BETWEENYOUANDTMH?"

She made that No-how-dare-you-even-imply-it-but-you-can-totally-hear-I'm-smiling-even-down-the-phone snort that meant she was totally into him.

"NAUGHTY MINX FIEND!!! You should have said!!!"

"NOTHING'S HAPPENED!" She laughed. "Promise."

I knew there was a "but" coming.

"Buuut – something *has* happened . . . with you. . ."

What. WHAT?! I sat upright. Then lay back down. Too much braining for this early/10:56 a.m. "Well, technically between TMH and your mum. . ."

Nope. Rach and I had discussed the shortlist of people we'd allow to become my stepfather, and Fit Boys

Our Age were very much NOT on it.

"Rach, stop being so weird?! Explain thyself!!"

She took a deep breath. "Well I *may* have *kind of* been chatting to him last night... And then this morning." KNEW IT! She *was* totally into him. Name me a more iconic duo. I'll wait. "Anyway, not the point. The point is there's a reeeeason he works in Tesco."

"Tell me it's to earn money? Or are you about to inform me it's the world's weirdest hobby?"

"No, Bells." She spoke slowly, "His. Dad. Is. The. Manager."

Sorry, nope. Still nothing.

"And when TMH told him about last night, he said he wanted to chat to your mum?!" She'd given up not shouting. "ABOUT STOCKING GIVE A DOG A CONE IN THEIR LOCAL PRODUCE SECTION!!!!"

Oh.

My.

Holy Mozzarella balls.

Who knew inviting good-looking people you hardly knew to totally random evening events could have such amazing results?! This must be what Shay always meant by "networking".

"RACH THAT IS AMAZING! YOU ARE AMAZING!!"

"And *you* are most welcome! I'll send you his dad's number now!"

I took a second for the news to sink in, then asked if I could go and tell Mum the good news. Rach put the phone down on me while yelling bye.

I ran down the stairs so fast I accidentally sock-skiied the last three.

But Mum had popped to the shops, and Jo was quietly flicking through the Saturday papers. Not exactly the scene I wanted for Best News Of the Year.

"Notice anything?" Jo sipped on her tea.

"You never make me tea?"

"I dispute that. There was that time when . . ." She thought back. ". . . you were eleven."

Fine, I'd make my own, but when I sat back down, Jo kept casting her eyes into the hall.

Was something going on? Was it a hint? I couldn't spot anything?!

Except. . .

"BENNY'S BACK!"

There he was, being all cardboard and creepy again at the bottom of our stairs. Just the way I hate-liked it.

"Exacto." Jo sounded pleased, like I'd solved an episode of Sherlock. She turned her newspaper page over extra slowly, as if this was a very important moment. But

I had no idea what the moment was about. Until Shay walked in, saw us, and darted back out.

"Ahhh, Shay." Jo closed her paper. "Nice of you to join us." I hadn't seen her since outside GADAC yesterday – not that she knew I'd spotted her.

Shay yelled back from the hallway. "Just on my way out."

But Jo waggled something in the air. Shay's car keys. Shay ran back in, rummaging round the work surfaces. "Hey, have you seen my keys?" She didn't even look at me. "I swear I left them here."

Jo gave them a jangle. Shay spun round, and went to grab them, but Jo snatched them away.

"Jo, I haven't got time for this. I'm going to be late for work."

Jo just pushed out a chair with her foot, as if Shay should sit down.

"Important meeting, is it?"

Shay glowered at her. "Something like that."

Well this was weird.

"Maybe you've got time to have a quick chat about why you weren't there last night?"

Shay pushed the chair back in. "I was busy. Like I told Bella." Hmmm, not *quite* true. Luckily I'd forgotten to tell Jo I'd seen her arrive and disappear, cos she was already being weird enough. "Anyway, I really haven't got time for this . . . whatever *this* is."

I slurped my tea like I was watching something I didn't quite understand on TV, rather than thirty centimetres away in my kitchen.

Jo lent back and smiled. "Lis says hi, by the way."

Shay put her hand out for the keys. "Cool. I'll text her later."

But Jo shoved them into her pocket. Was I being caught up in a low-level hostage situation?! I did *not* want to be in police photos wearing pyjamas?!

"Maybe you could send her this. . ." Jo put her phone on the table. "It's amazing what you can find on the internet when you know what to look for."

It was another picture of Lis and Shay – like the one she'd shown me way back. A selfie of them lying on the floor, but in this one Lis looked a bit more awkward while Shay was grinning so cheesily I almost didn't recognize her.

Shay clicked the home button making the picture disappear. "I'm out of here."

Jo stood up. "Not until you tell Bella the truth."

Truth about *what*? "C'mon Jo, do NOT bring me into this." I knew they hated each other, but I'd tried hard not to take sides.

They both ignored me. Standard.

"Shay – tell Bells how you *really* know Lis." She crossed her arms. "Or I will."

Shay narrowed her eyes. "You've always had SUCH a problem with me."

Jo just blinked calmly. "Tell her."

"Why can't you just keep your nose out of other people's business?"

"Tell. Her."

Could I creep away? Probably, they'd seemed to have forgotten I was here.

"You *seriously* think this is a good idea?" Shay had raised her voice.

"TELL HER." Jo raised hers even louder.

Shay slammed her hand down on the table so hard, my tea bounced into the air. "FIIIIINNNNEEEE."

Then the weirdest thing yet happened.

Shay took a step back, and for the first time since I knew her, her whole body language drooped.

"Bella. . ." she looked around the room, anywhere but at me. "As your sister is so *desperate* for you to find out, I know Lis from, er. . ." I had no idea where this was going. "From . . . working together."

Oh? I already knew this. But Jo was shaking her head. "And by working together, you mean. . ."

"Yes, Jo," Shay hissed. "I'm getting there." This time Shay looked at me. "By working, I mean my job."

Again, old news.

"Working in . . ."

But I knew. *TV.*

". . . carpet fitting."

Sorry, what?!

"I'm a carpet fitter."

I put my tea down. "A high-level TV-producing carpet fitter?"

Shay shook her head. "A normal carpet fitter."

But Jo wasn't done. "And where did you get these pics from?"

Shay shrugged. "From a shoot we did when we re-carpeted their record company's floor. . ."

Thank goodness I was sitting down so it didn't matter if my legs buckled. But Shay hadn't finished.

"We gave them a discount in return for promo shots for our website."

Jo muttered, "Yup. Wefitanycarpet.com."

"And full disclosure . . . cos why not." Shay sighed. "I'm up here cos we're redoing the Midlands TV office."

I was almost speechless. But not quite. "So the high-pressure industry you're always talking about. . ."

Shay nodded. "Is the carpet-fitting industry." She picked her bag back up. "You happy now, Jo?" She looked furious. My sister was loving it.

"Almost. One last thing. Last night Lis told me that she'd never met a Shay."

"Yeah, yeah. You *know* why." Shay paused. "Cos my real name's Sheila. Not that she'd even remember me. . ."

This was all too much. So Shay *wasn't* friends with the band after all?!

I didn't get it. We'd spent so many evenings chatting about her work, her life, and it was one big lie?

"But why, Shay? Sheila... Whatever. I don't understand?"

Shay shrugged. "You don't need to make a big deal out of it. I just thought it sounded good." She swiped the keys off the table. "No harm done. And I *certainly* don't need a lecture from either of you about it."

And with that, she stormed out.

Jo took another overly loud sip of tea, knowing full well I was doing my accidental goldfish impression at her. "So, all this time. . .?"

"Yup. All made up."

I let the last few months flick by. The fake stories. The humblebrags. Making out she was bessies with the band. No *wonder* she didn't come to Radio Shire. I bet she never even meant to. And of course she didn't give me their details – she never had them!

But that also meant she couldn't have messaged them to help me stay in the final after all!? I *had* done it myself. And all of this while making us feel like we were in the presence of greatness. In the presence of a media genius. Not a shag-pile expert. I'd have to break it to Rach gently.

"How did you find out?"

Jo rocked back on her chair. "Accident, really. Was making small talk with Lis, telling her we'd had a lodger she might know, but her name didn't ring any bells. So I showed her that pic of them I had on my phone from when you sent it ... when Lis remembered who she really was I thought I'd better check before I said anything."

No wonder Shay had run off when she'd seen the band in the shop.

Jo looked a bit sad. "I mean, I totally don't care what job anyone does – I work with slugs for heaven's sake – but just don't lie about it."

I couldn't agree more.

"I get paid to dress up as a dog – and as a bone in my spare time."

"Yeah, but you're incredibly uncool, so that doesn't count."

I couldn't be bothered to think of a comeback – I was too busy thinking of all the times I'd hung off Shay's every word about "the industry" and how Rach had spent hours thinking up "insider" questions, and we'd all tried so hard to impress her, when all along she was making up a fake life to try and impress *us*, the least impressive people ever. Who probs would have thought Sheila the carpet fitter was way more fun. I made no sense.

When Mum came back from the shops, I was still getting my head around it. But Jo had said not to say anything yet. So I went with my GADAC-based news instead.

Mum gave me a kiss on the cheek and dropped her post in front of me.

"Morning, Beautiful Daughter Two. Nice of you to join Beautiful Daughter One!"

She unfolded the local paper to page two. "VOILA!!"

And there she was. Mum with the Helicans and Pastry, the GADAC sign stretching right across the page.

She began to read. *"Ms Fisher, 40,"* Jo and I looked at each other. "Oi! Age is nothing but a number – so you might as well give them a number you like! Anyway, *'packed out Give A Dog A Cone, her innovative new dog ice cream business, as she announced a brand-new collaboration with chart-topping band the Helicans. Revellers partied to an exclusive acoustic set, as the business looks set to take Midlands dog lovers by storm. With the internet ablaze with talk of her healthy dog treats and philanthropic work, there's no better time to announce Ms Fisher as the first finalist of our Forty and Fulfilled: Businessperson Of The Year award, to be announced next month."'*

THIS WAS IMMENSE!!! Mum couldn't take it all in and reread it out loud at least three more times.

"Forty and Fulfilled: Businessperson Of The Year. Little old me. Can you imagine?" I nodded. I really could. "They give the winner £20,000, you know." She looked lost in the enormity of it. "The Helicans must have really said *incredible* things last night. Such wonderful people!"

I winked at her. "Well, I don't put just *anybody* up on my wall, you know? Anyway – is now the time for some more good news?"

Mum closed the paper. "Go on. . ."

I opened up my phone contacts and scrolled to what I needed.

Mum's phone beeped. She looked at it, confused.

"Tesco Colin Matt Healy's Big Cheese Dad?" Her smile fell. "I'm not going on one of these internet dates, Bella."

"Sending you a number isn't an internet date, Mum.

But that's not what this is." I slapped the table. This was meant to be a dramatic reveal.

"Rach sent it. Cos guess who might want to start stocking your ice cream?"

Jo whistled, getting the connection. Then kindly spelt it out for Mum who really hadn't. She sat down with a plonk. "Is this a joke?"

"Nope – and he's expecting your call." I assumed, cos that's what they always said in movies.

Mum was so overwhelmed it took a minute before she whispered the nicest "Thank you" I'd ever heard. Checking Jo was distracted reading the GADAC article again I whispered back, "Do you think this means it's going to be OK?"

She smiled. "I think it means we definitely have the best chance we've ever had. And it's all thanks to you." She sniffed at me. "So, how about you go get in the shower, and we go and celebrate?"

Jo saw the sniff. "Yes, great unwashed. Go get clean. Then we can celebrate *everything*. The three of us."

Too happy to procrastinate, I jumped off the table.

"By the way." Mum looked suddenly serious. "Shay text a minute ago, saying she's got to head back to London today. Bit of a shock, eh? She's going to pack up later and pay up for remainder of the time."

414

I smiled. "Woah – that's totally *floored* me."

Jo laughed. "Better roll out that red carpet for her brief return."

Mum had no idea what we were talking about. "Well, as long as you're both OK about it?"

I nodded at Mum. "Absolutely fine. In fact, never been better."

But seconds later, something happened that propelled things into a whole new stratosphere.

THIRTY-FIVE

Nothing this dramatic should ever happen when you are sitting on the loo, naked except for a pair of socks, waiting for a shower to run hot.

It was a notification. Of a repost of Mikey's picture. Me as a giant bone, the head bit folded down, Pastry licking the bit of my face which was sticking out.

It was so mortifying I should really put in a request to get it removed.

But I didn't care about *what* was in the picture. I cared *who* had reposted it. @lildrummerboy100. More commonly known to me as Adam.

And underneath it was the second best comment I'd ever seen on the internet.

It's official. @bellingtonboot is the coolest.
Couldn't be prouder.

Yes. It was great that he'd broken the silence between us.

And *yes*, it was brilliant that he knew about GADAC being my mum's shop – and was into it.

And *yes*, it was amazing that he thought I'd done a good job last night.

But what was more awesome, more surprising, than all of this put together was the comment underneath it.

Well I could be prouder... if @bellingtonboot said yes to being my girlfriend?

THiRTY-SiX

Two hours later, I was on my way to the park to meet him.

Luckily Mumbles was trotting alongside me, helping me keep my balance, as every time I thought about what Adam had posted I almost wobbled over into a hedge.

As soon as I'd read it, I'd messaged him to suggest we meet.

I had questions. All the questions.

And he'd suggested now.

And I'd suggested the clearing by the bridge.

And he'd said yes.

And now I was here.

And he was walking towards me.

And I was petrified.

But this time he looked as nervous as me. Still

unbelievably fit obvs, but nervous too.

"So you said to meet here. . ."

"I did. Yes. Hello." Conversation gold, Bella. Well done.

Adam shuffled next to me on the log. As always happened around him speaking suddenly felt like my second language. But this was important. I was confused. Maybe cross. Maybe happy. I didn't know until I found out what was really going on.

I took a deep breath.

"So, err, I wanted to talk about what you posted earlier." Concentrating so hard made me sound way more serious than I meant. But I needed to know once and for all why he was always so up and down with me.

He put his head into his hands. "Oh no. I've made a total idiot of myself, haven't I?"

I shook my head, but due to his head being in his hands he couldn't see.

"I shouldn't have posted that stupid comment, should I?"

My heart dropped. I didn't think it was stupid. I thought it was the best thing ever. Unless he didn't really mean it? Or had had a change of heart. Again.

But he carried on.

"You just want to be friends and all summer I couldn't take your hints, and now look what's happened." He went to stand back up. "I'm so sorry. I should go. . ."

Erm, what?! All summer? My hints? What was he talking about? Was he getting *him* confused with me?!

"Sorry? *My* hints? But it's *you* who keeps only wanting to be friends?"

"Na-huh?" Adam looked confused. "That's all you?"

Everything on my face popped more open – eyes, nostrils, mouth.

"Me?"

"Sure," he nodded, as if it wasn't him with totally the wrong end of the stick. "Where do I start?"

Erm, literally anywhere – cos I had *zero* clue where he was going with this.

He drummed his fingers on his knee. Yum.

"How about – well, the other week when I saw you hide behind a car when you spotted me on the street?"

Oh – during my anti-stalking days? I thought he hadn't seen me. I also thought he was dating Molly. But if he had seen me, I could appreciate it might not look great.

"I think I was doing up a shoe?"

His nose wrinkling suggested he wasn't buying it.

"Well, what about me being all happy you arranged that amazing date at Rachel's – only for you to end it by telling me you only suggested it in the first place because you were under the influence of heavy medical anaesthetic?"

No no?! That's not what I'd meant?

"I didn't mean the *date*. I meant my totally terrible idea for it."

He looked unconvinced.

"And bringing a friend along? Aka – world's biggest hint?" Ah. Yes I could see that might be confusing. "Even if we did have the best time ... or so I thought until you cancelled the next one last minute."

The emergency Sunday GADAC shift.

"It was a work emergency!" It was also radio final morning – so my brain had forgotten how to use words to explain properly. And then what with friend-gate I maaaay have forgotten to ever tell him what happened. Ooops.

"And then the same day you made it pre-tty clear when you told everyone on live radio what a great *friend* I was?" He scratched his cheek, embarrassed. "I even made my new team listen in, cos they knew how much I, y'know ... liked you and then you said all that about your 'friend'. They're still taking the mickey out of me for it now."

Hold up. What? He thought what I'd said about Mikey was about him?!

And he'd told his football team he liked me?!

And he'd just told *me* that he liked me?!

Oh. My. Cod.

Adam. Likes. Me.

I should never second-guess this person again. Or third, or fourth, of fifth-guess.

"But that wasn't about you. That was about Mikey."

He scrunched his mouth up. "Ahhhhhhh. So the message I rang in with, that Jaz read out probably didn't help?"

Understatement alert.

"The one where *I* thought *you* were making clear we were mates slash friends? Yeah, not so much."

He squirmed. "Well there goes my attempt at trying to show you I was respecting what you wanted. Not wanting to pressure you into anything."

So he'd only acted like we were just friends cos he thought that was what I wanted?! And I'd only done the same back to him cos it's what I thought *he* wanted? When in reality seeing him buying frozen peas was the highlight of my summer? This was. Too. Much.

"So when we were hanging out, you *didn't* just want us to be friends?" My brain was having trouble keeping up.

"Well I always *hoped* you wanted more... Until that happened."

I was speechless. I'd spent so long trying to come to terms with him only liking me as a friend, my mind was having total engine failure trying to three-point turn to any other possibility.

"Bells..." He dropped his voice. "Isn't it *obvious* I've been trying to be more than just friends this whole, entire summer?"

Erm, no?! Or I wouldn't have spent the whole, entire summer doing in-depth investigation into whether he might want to be more than friends.

"But you told Nate that's what we were?"

He shook his head as if he was having as hard a time as me taking in everything.

"Isn't it polite to ask someone what you are to them before declaring it on public transport?"

Damn him and his respectful logic. I threw the friend-ball back into his court. "But *you* were the one who went all weird when I mentioned meeting up after Pasta La Vista?!"

"You suggested going to the animal park! Where my dad spends his weekends. Running a miniature railway. As a hobby." He shook his head, as if he couldn't believe he was telling me this. "Wearing an actual hat my mum made for him."

Oh, hello, hindsight, aren't you a wonderful thing? (And also, I really want to see that hat.)

"Well *my* mum's the one selling dog ice cream."

He laughed. "Yeah, I figured. You should have said?!

She's a legend! And you HAVE to tell me who she gets to dress up as that dog I met there. *Such* a method actor."

Hmmm, maybe some things were best left unsaid. I moved the convo on.

"So why now?"

He kicked at the floor. "Who knows? Maybe it was seeing all those photos from the Helicans gig. It was such an amazing thing you did. And I just ... oh I dunno."

More than anything I wanted him to finish what he was saying.

"Go on. . ." I encouraged, hoping he was braver than me when it came to finally being honest.

"Well, I just knew then that I couldn't just give up on you ever being my girlfriend. I *had* to try one last time."

OK. Something in me just melted. Had to hope it was a gall bladder or something.

"And you thought posting it on the internet was the safest option?!"

He grinned. "Well, it got your attention." (And Rach's and Tegan's who I'd instantly sent it to, not that he needed to know.) "Plus trying to tell you in person didn't seem to be working out so well!"

He could say that again. Or maybe he couldn't, considering all we seemed to do was confuse each other.

"Right ... OK." Adam stood up. It felt symbolic – like

getting down on one knee, but going up on two feet. He chewed his lip, building himself up for something, then took a deep breath.

"I really hope I'm not getting this massively wrong ... but, well, it's now or never."

He grinned nervously. I tried to smile back but was mainly concentrating on remembering to intake oxygen.

He looked me right in the eye.

"After me clearly being a bit of an idiot, I think, well, hope, you finally know how I feel about you..." He laughed, suddenly looking awkward. "Which TO BE CLEAR, is that I think you're all kinds of excellent."

This time I couldn't help but smile. And also put out my right hand out to steady myself in case I joy-fainted and fell off the bench, crushing Mumbles. But Adam hadn't finished.

"So, sorry if I've been giving you mixed signals. Because, er..." He paused. "The point is..." I swear he said a "C'mon Adam" under his breath. "Bella Fisher ... would you like to be my girlfriend?" He shrugged as if not sure how I might be reacting. "Have me as your boyfriend? However you want to put it..."

He shuffled, nervous. His brown eyes waiting for an answer.

Time to play it cool. Make him sweat it out.

Oh … who was I kidding?! It was what I'd dreamt about for months.

"Yesssss. Yes. IT'S A YES."

Adam's whole face lit up. I think he even did a mini air-punch. He looked as happy on the outside as I felt on the inside. Which was pretty mega happy.

"Well that is THE best news I've had all day." He laughed. "Scrap that. All year?!"

Funny, cos him saying it was the best news he'd had all year was the best news I'd had all lifetime. I couldn't stop smiling.

But what was meant to happen now? This was uncharted territory for me. Thank goodness I was sitting down.

I grinned up at him from the bench. Adam grinned down at me. Mumbles hic-burped. We both ignored it.

Adam – or should I say, MY BOYFRIEND – put his hand out. "May I?"

And as worried as I was about managing to both stand – AND SIMULTANEOUSLY BE ADAM'S GIRLFRIEND – I nodded.

"Yes, you may." I put my hand into his (obvs after a quick secret de-sweat-wipe on my jeans) and stood up. Yes, World. Fadam and I were officially holding hands.

And it felt ace.

Even better, when we made full eye contact, we had a millisecond of silence before both cracking up, laughing at what a mess we'd made, relieved to finally have everything out in the open.

When we managed to get our breath back I used my non-boyf holding hand (aka the hand formerly known as "left") to pick up Mumbles' lead. Slowly we began to head towards the playing field, chatting through a gazillion examples of all the times we'd managed to get each other completely and utterly wrong (I actually spluttered when I discovered he'd been revising Game of Thrones trivia as he thought I was a mega-fan and wanted to impress me?!).

We had way too much to say to each other, but equally kept going happy-quiet as we took in what was happening. I couldn't believe after everything, he liked me just how I liked him.

Hand in hand, we strolled to meet Tegan, Rach and Mikey at the bench.

The bench where I used to sit with my friends and watch Adam play football.

The bench where I used to imagine that in a dream world, one day my life might actually be as amazing as it is right now.

ACKNOWLEDGEMENTS

Acknowledgements is a weird word. I don't really want to acknowledge most of these people. I want to give them a massive hug and thank them for how amazing they've been to me.

Gemma Cooper – knower of everything, helper of all. I knew I was lucky to have you as an agent, but as every step passes I realize how extra, extra lucky I am. Explainer/fixer-of-problems/confidante/friend/sender of emails pre seven a.m. that should be post nine p.m. (you know the one) – you've done it all. Thank you.

Lauren – you came into our life and embraced Bella and me from day one – and made this book all the better because of it. Thank you for always making everything feel OK. I'm just sorry this wasn't cat-based instead #Stanley.

The whole Scholastic team. Thanks for being so supportive. Special shout-out to Pete's macaroni-cheese knowledge and spreadsheet patience, Jamie's second instalment of brilliant-cover-ness, Olivia's all-round genius and the Rights team who have taken Bella around the world.

Thanks, Pam, James and Tina Bean for always, ALWAYS being there, through the best times, the tough times, the big nights out, and the geeky nights in (and HIYER Aanand!).

Jess – still owning that Swiss-army-knife-friend title on a daily basis. Julie – remember me when you're on the front page of all the magazines I've never heard of. Rosanna – you have no idea how much your never-ending excitement has meant – I can't wait to do the exact same for you. Dan – you're one in a million.

And a massive thank you for my amazing friends who went above and beyond this last year. Matt, Mikey, Jono, Katie, Vivek, Lyndon, David, Becky, Sarah, Tom, Robyn, Holly, the Switch crew, my MTV buds – complete wonders, the lot of you. Lou – your services to Inappropriate Stories Via WhatsApp brightens my days.

Thank you to the amazingly talented writers, bloggers, librarians, booksellers and everyone I've met along the way who are nice enough to talk to strangers at parties and make imposters feel welcome. Special extra-big thanks and awkward waves to Team Cooper, Jen Bell, Jim, Chelley, the Charing Cross Foyles team, the Scholastic crew, and Mr Maxwell.

Lucy R. I'm basically Adam right now. So I'm just going to say it. Will you ... will you be my friend? Please?

Kev, Babs, Phil, thank you for your support – from books, hospitals and beyond. Best In-Laws Ever.

Thanks to anyone who read *Super Awkward* and got in touch. You guys rock. Awkward people are the best. This one's for you.

And to my wonderful family who are always there through the ups, downs and Walrus challenges. Daddles, Moomin, Becca, Ian, Rose. I lucked out. I love you.

And finally, to the person who I saved the emotional finish for. Who read it and told me to save it for just him. Chris, I did. So instead, thank you to the incredible staff of the NHS, especially the Royal London Hospital, for looking after you, and getting you back safe.